Garden of the Plagues

Garden of the Plagues

RUSSEL BROWNLEE

HUMAN & ROUSSEAU
Cape Town   Pretoria

To André Brink for his generous mentorship,
and to Christine Boyazis for her faith and encouragement.

We were mightily surprised to find one of the loveliest and most curious gardens that ever I saw, in a country that looks to be one of the most dismal and barren places in the world.

GUY DE TACHARD, A Voyage to Siam, 1688

I should explain that the islanders of Madagascar call them *rukhs* and know them by no other name and have no idea what a gryphon is. But I feel sure from the monstrous size they attribute to the birds that they cannot be anything but gryphons.

MARCO POLO, Divisament dou Monde, 1299

Cabo de Bona Esperança
1685

Landfall

IN THE MONTH before the outward fleet arrived there came into the bay a giant whale. There it lay, its dark bulk floating just off the shore, watching. The people watched it back. From the bastions of the Castle the soldiers trained their guns upon it. All were struck silent by the presence of this great beast; all felt the eye of the devil upon them. So many sins were recalled then, the prayers rose like smoke above the Valley Hamlet.

The captain of the garrison had a dream in which the brute lay upon him, its tiny eye pressed against his face. It was so like a human eye, it even blinked. When he awoke, it was two o'clock in the morning, he called the watch and they went down to the shore and set off petards to drive the creature away. Everybody heard the percussions, but were too afraid to go and look. If it was the English or the French who were landing, then there was nothing they could do. The devil's portent could not be avoided, and in this place, the furthest point in Africa, God's hand was weak. God did not venture here too often. He was not like the Mantis king who walked on his thin legs there beyond the flats, biding his time.

Then the beast came ashore. Nobody saw it happen. One morning there it was, no longer under the waves but out upon the sands, a black and stinking mass. "Who will cut up this Leviathan?" the Commander called. "Who will render it to its elements?" The townsfolk did not volunteer. The Commander, who was immune to the accusing eye, gave orders and the task was done. The devil's messenger was put into barrels. The barrels awaited the next ship out.

In such a way is the devil dealt with. There is a new spirit alive in the world and the Commander is its prophet. He is a

11

man of Reason; a man of Science. For the Commander of the settlement at the Cape of Good Hope there is no questioning the task at hand. He is a bearer of light in a dark and ignorant place. He is an agent of Civilisation.

When the fleet appears on the horizon the barrels on the jetty are almost forgotten. There has been so much to do, so much of a gathering of vegetables and fruits, so much of a slaughtering of beasts and a salting of flesh. The people of the hamlet have prepared every species of victual that their humble abilities permit, and now they stand in wait for the great, hungry ships of the Company. Inside the Castle, Commander Van der Stel is putting his name to the last of a pile of missives to be sent onward to Batavia. When the fleet, four months out from Amsterdam, casts anchor in the bay there will be no time for writing. He will have his hands full with whatever dignitaries are aboard. He will have to show them all the hardships of this far outpost, as well as some of its pleasures. The visitors will sail away full of wonder at what the people at the Cape have done and what a change they have wrought to this drab wilderness.

Commander Van der Stel stands up from his desk and goes over to the window. He is not a tall man, so he has to raise himself slightly on his toes. If someone in the Castle courtyard were to glance at that window now they would see two bright beads perched above the sill, observing them with unnatural calm, listing the things about their person that were wrong. The dull buckle, the unstarched collar, nothing went unobserved by those little bright beads. Nothing promoted a quicker smartening of the posture and a bending to a task than the calmly accusing eyes of the Commander. But now he relaxes his stretching and sinks below the window. He paces the room. What to do next? Perhaps, he thinks, there will be time to inspect the garden.

Of all the pleasures in Table Valley the garden is its first. It was created thirty years before by Commander Jan van Riebeeck, but in those days it was a mere cabbage patch, a mere plot for the cultivation of carrots and beans and other mean fruits. Now it is becoming something else entirely. The cabbages are moving out to the new plots at the Ronde Doornbosche, and in their place are coming trees and flowers and herbs from every corner of the world. The Commander heads out of the door, certain there will be time for a quick tour of his little Eden.

In the garden, the botanist Adam Wijk is hard at work attempting to save the lives of fifty new rose bushes recently received from China. To this end he has engaged the assistance of a dozen slaves armed with buckets. It will not do to have the rare blooms expire at such a moment. If the sun has its way then all will be laid waste, and that will not reflect positively on him at all. Thus it is that Mr Wijk himself lifts a bucket in the roses' defence, though not as many times as do the sweating slaves.

It is Adam Wijk's hope this morning that he will be left alone with his labours and not be subjected to any officiating by nervous worthies from the Castle. But a flash of scarlet glimpsed near the entrance to the garden informs him that it is not to be. The Commander – having completed his short walk across the parade ground, up the Heerengracht and past the Slave Lodge – has entered thankfully into the garden and paused a moment to catch his breath. Van der Stel has forgotten that March is not a time for gratuitous walking about in the outdoors. Though winter is not too far away the sun is still ruler of the southern worlds. All around the settlement now the earth is dry and the mountain has black scars from the fires that begin for no reason. But in the garden the trees have reached such a height that they give shade, and there is the sound of water from the modest stream in its cobbled furrow.

What kind of a creature is man? thinks Adam Wijk, observing the Commander from behind the safety of an empty bucket. Here he comes, on a summer's day, and he is drowning in a winter coat with all his reds and purples and his pretty lace, and truly he looks every bit a peacock in a stewpot. The evidence would suggest, thinks Mr Wijk, that on a day such as this a light summer coat, *sans* vest, would suffice. And definitely one could lose the periwig. Adam Wijk is fond of evidence, it is his religion. If a person says to him that he believes such and such, then he will say that such and such is unsupported by any measurable phenomenon in the real world and is thus not a thing that should be taken as true. It is sometimes a dangerous course to take, and it is said that this particular botanist has indeed paid the price for his insistence on rationality, that in the past he ran foul of some persons who disliked his disproving of their belief and exacted a revenge upon him. Quite possibly this man who busies himself the whole day with the peaceful contemplation and classification of flora is a man on the run. Perhaps he is here in this place because it is not permitted for him to return home. After all, nobody comes to live at the Cape, this *Cabo Tormentoso*, by choice. Everybody has a reason that has something to do with circumstance or with necessity. Except, of course, the Honourable Commander. This man, Simon van der Stel, is a man of destiny, everybody can see that. Like his predecessors, he will use this place as a stepping stone to greater things. At the very least, they believe, he will be promoted and he will go to Batavia and become Governor of all the Indies. He will leave his former subjects behind in Africa to be withered by droughts or blasted by winds or stuck full of darts by little brown men who want nothing more in life than a few old skins and a handful of cows.

The Commander advances upon Wijk, cutting a vivid swathe through the garden. His braided vest shows at just the right length beneath a coat of scarlet that fastens up from belly to chin with large gold buttons. The flare of the coat reveals breeches of royal purple tied in at the knees with ribbons, which, as Mr Wijk notices, are of the exact champagne hue as the vest and the floppy bows that adorn each gleaming shoe. As for the periwig, it is certainly a grander affair than the gardener has ever seen the Commander wear before. Mr Wijk smiles broadly at this approaching vision. Here he comes now, His Excellency the Commander of the Settlement at the Cape, his black *respondant* hat curled in a dashing wave, the sword poking out front and back, his moustache excellently twirled and his brow well-beaded with dew.

Mr Wijk holds on to his bucket as the Commander comes to a halt before him. The man looks pensive, answering the botanist's greeting with a mere nod of the head. He does not engage with Wijk but continues to look around him at the landscape, as if searching for something in the ordered geometry of the garden. He gazes down the straight avenues of young oak and citrus, he lets his eyes wander over the hedged squares of guava and quince, the experiments in cinnamon and vanilla, the fragrant bays of rosemary, lavender, and wormwood. Surrounded by clipped barriers of bitter almond lie rows of turnips, mounds of spiralling beans, great tumbles of gourds with their sweet, orange flesh. As far as the eye can see is a perfect flourishing of every example of beauty and of usefulness. And round about it all is a solid brick wall with a proper gate and its bold sign of the VOC and the date – 1679. The Commander counts these things he has caused to come to pass in the garden, and then he admits a sigh.

"Does the Honourable Commander have some instruction for me today?" asks Mr Wijk, still holding his bucket.

The Commander remains gazing at the distance for a moment then turns to his gardener. "I have been thinking," he says. "I have been thinking that there is something missing from this garden. Something . . . I cannot say what, but something not yet present." Van der Stel scans the garden, his eyes narrowed against the light. "Perhaps it is a thing that will arrive on a ship or be blown here, or perhaps it is a thing we will never find. Perhaps it is the thing that is always missing. There is always something missing, don't you think, Mr Wijk?"

"Generally, there is always something that is not present," says the gardener.

Van der Stel looks southwards towards the mountain. His vision scales its heights, as if this missing thing is perhaps sitting up there, smoking a pipe in a crevice where he cannot be seen. Van der Stel frowns. "I know it will come to me. Perhaps while I am sleeping I will awaken and know what it is. Then I will come and reveal it to you, my keeper of the garden. Even if it is in the dead of night I will come and share it."

"I will open some wine," says Wijk. "We will celebrate."

The Commander smiles, though his eyes are still drifting to the crevice where the missing thing lurks. Adam Wijk finds himself looking in the same direction. "In the meantime," says Van der Stel, "the roses we have brought from China are dead. Perhaps we should clear a space for something new. Perhaps it will be the thing that I am thinking about but which I cannot say."

"Perhaps, Honourable Commander, we should do the clearing tomorrow. There is still hope in these blooms. Quite possibly they will live."

"Quite possibly, Mr Wijk. We will save this decision for another day. And now you will excuse me. The fleet is almost at anchor."

There is a dirt road along the beach. Not surprisingly, it is called Zeestraat. It begins at the Castle and stretches westward along the beach until it peters out below Lion's Rump. Here, on the edge of the settlement, the poorer folk have their dwellings. Here is where the fishermen live and where the sailors come for their entertainments. Along Zeestraat are several dwellings from which homemade beer and smuggled arrack can be bought. Here also, one may find a slave girl for things other than polishing the cutlery. At the Cape of Good Hope the survival of the freemen is a thing that happens despite the Castle and the Honourable Company, and any manner of gathering an untaxed income is considered a necessity. The citizens of this far outpost, though free in name, are in practice no better than serfs to the almighty East India Company. It is the Company that tells them what they may buy and what they may sell and where and to whom. It is the Company that sanctions their marriages, that judges them on their misdemeanors and that sentences them. Not a lashing nor a hanging takes place that is not approved by the Honourable Company. In the world outside of the Fatherland, the *Vereenigde Oost-Indische Compagnie* is a country unto itself, a fluid state whose borders begin at the shores of the North Sea and extend as far as the Company's trading ships can safely venture.

It was, in fact, to extend the range of those ships that the VOC had deemed it necessary to set up this outpost at the Cape. They had in mind a little garden in the wilderness, a place to cultivate grains and vegetables and fruits. For the ships that limp into the bay four or five or six months out from Amsterdam and Texel, the place has begun to take on the significance of a paradise. For those who remain ashore the place is maybe less idyllic.

But on this particular afternoon there are few who think of their usual troubles, for now an outward-bound fleet is at anchor in the bay. Barring a few stragglers the ships lie safely at rest, their great sails furled and their passengers brought thankfully to solid ground. Between the shore and the anchored vessels the water is thick with small boats carrying out provisions and ferrying back goods and letters and sailors on furlough. Already the great exchange has begun, already money is changing hands.

In the Tavern of the Green Door the mad girl Hester sweeps the floor. She does so on her knees with a small broom made of a stick and a tuft of dry grass. Hester sweeps carefully, it is what she is good at. Sometimes there are coins left behind by the drinkers and these she sweeps along together with the dust. When she finishes sweeping a section of floor she picks up the pile of dirt between two hands and walks quickly to the window, then out goes the dust. The coins remain behind on the floor. Now she bends down to her pennies. "Lucky," she says.

Bart Meyer watches the girl with her coins. He opens his mouth to speak. As owner of the tavern the floor belongs to him, and likewise anything found upon it. But instead of speaking he turns his attention back to the new cask of sugar beer that has just arrived. There is no time for altercations now. It will only distract the girl, and soon the people will be here, very thirsty and full of stories. The place needs to look its best. It is a big day, after all, and it will be a long night too.

The Green Door, so conveniently located on the strand, is both a business and a residence. The public house occupies a large room facing the sea. The door that gives the *tapperij* its name opens northwards to give a view of the bay and to attract custom from that direction. Southwards, towards the mountain, is a kitchen – and further along into the house there is a bedroom and, further still, a second, larger room. This room was, until recently, the *voorkamer* – the place in which visitors were entertained – but it has now been transformed by the addition of several beds into what appears to be guest accommodation.

It should not be imagined that the layout of this dwelling follows any particular rule of architecture. One would imagine, for instance, that the rooms – being lined up one next the other as they are – would be neatly serviced by a connecting passageway. But such would be to assume too much of a freeman's dwelling in the Valley Hamlet. To achieve a more realistic perception of the situation, consider rather how such a dwelling would have been built. This one, like many others of its kind, began its life as a single rectangular room, built with mud bricks, floored with cow dung (polished to a high gloss), and topped with a thatched roof. It remained thus for several years, until new owners moved in and began to look about them with an eye to expansion. The Lady of the house, not being of the sort who would settle for life in a single room, wasted little time in convincing her husband to build on a further room in which to house the nuptial bed, and later yet another in which to house a proper kitchen, and then later still another in which to house the milk-cow and the horse and sundry other outdoor things. Imagine, if you can, that all these accruals to that first respectable rectangle happened in a single row, south to north, and you will have a true-enough picture of the Green Door tavern and residence. The last addition, the barn, is – of course – now doing time as the public house. One other thing that should be noted about this mélange is that the thatched roof, though dipping and rising quite abruptly at certain points, performs a dual function, serving not only to keep out the elements but also to create further living space – an attic, or as such are referred to here, a *zolder*.

When the first patron arrives at the Tavern of the Green Door the girl looks up from her sweeping and smiles. It is Dronke Piet. He stands in the doorway, looking unusually spruce and sober. Hester looks behind her to see if Bart Meyer has noticed their customer. She wonders what he will say about Dronke Piet's washed shirt and breeches and about his shaved face. "I think you have lost your way, Piet," calls Meyer when he sees the figure in the doorway. "This is not the *kerk*, it's the *tapperij*. The *kerk* is over that way."

Dronke Piet shrugs and steps into the room. He is a tall man who has a way of walking with his head bent forward and always looking left and right, so it seems he is constantly expecting trouble or is carrying something he shouldn't be. He had once been a Company soldier until fired for dissolute behaviour. Now he keeps himself together by collecting mussels and catching fish. Dronke Piet has a boat, but mostly it lies upturned on the beach where it serves as his house. Piet steps past the girl and sits down at one of the tables. Meyer has already poured a cup of wine and now he brings it over to his customer. The man hauls out a stuyver from his breeches and slaps it on the table.

"What have you done, Piet?" says Meyer. "Sold your boat?"

"Your mother!" curses Piet.

Meyer takes the stuyver and goes back to his work. "That money's for the whole evening," calls Piet. "You tell me when it's finished and I'll see if there's any more."

Hester stands up with her pennies but she can't take her eyes off Piet's shirt. It is the first time she has seen it white. "What you staring at?" demands Piet, hiding behind his wine cup. "Washed," says Hester, pointing at his baggy sleeve. "Isn't," says Piet.

"Leave him alone, Hester. Piet had to work today. He needs to regain his strength."

19

Hester moves away and Meyer makes a gesture with his hand towards the kitchen door. She has to help Mrs Meyer now. Dronke Piet watches her through narrowed eyes. "What you going to do about that girl, Bart? She's growing up now."

"Somebody will marry her."

Piet chuckles. "Ja, maybe it will be me. What do you say, Bart?"

"I say your mother also."

Dronke Piet lets out a guffaw and drains his wine. Then he begins to tell Meyer about the ships and about the fancy people he has seen. Piet is sometimes more pleasant drunk than sober, and there are those who have noticed this and said that in some cases, drink is a thing that improves character.

As the long summer afternoon wears on the Green Door begins to fill. Dronke Piet is still there, working away at his single stuyver. He sits with a short, crooked man in a soldier's jacket. This man is Jan Klou, so named because in the place where his left hand should have been there is a claw, a metal thing that makes a cold thump on the table when he sits down to wait for his tankard. Some people say that Jan Klou lost his hand in a battle, but others maintain he was never in the military and that the green coat he always wears was bought off a soldier who needed money for a gambling debt. There are several stories about the missing hand, all of them traceable – on their narrators' honest words – back to Jan Klou himself. If anything certain is known about this Jan Klou it is that despite the hook he is a first class horseman. Anybody can see it. What not everybody is supposed to know is that this Klou is also a smuggler and a procurer of native cattle. While bartering with the Hottentot is not an illegal activity in itself, it is not a field of commerce that is open to freelancers. All dealings with the natives are to be conducted by duly appointed representatives of the Honourable Company, this being so that the Company can extract maximum profit for itself, but also so that it can avoid the excesses so often perpetrated by those whose ambitions are untempered by considerations of politics and strategy. Further wars with the Hottentot are to be avoided, if not for love of peace then at least to ensure a steady supply of livestock to the Company's cattle posts.

When the farmer Dieter Krause enters through the green door he exchanges brief eye contact with Klou and sits down at a table by himself. He is soon joined by Captain Matthaus, a retired military man who has elected to stay on in the colony rather than return home to the Netherlands. A major factor influencing his decision to stay in Africa is his marriage to a slave woman from Malabar. Her name is Lina, and she has quite sensibly refused to spend her last days in a country that lies below the sea. "I notice we have an important visitor," says Matthaus after calling for a cup of wine. "Either that or we have a surplus of powder that requires blowing off."

Dieter Krause nods. "You weren't down on the shore? Everybody is talking about it."

"I am an old man. In the afternoon I sleep."

Dronke Piet overhears this from the other table and nudges Klou. "Old man was sleeping," he says with a wink.

"Only a demon from hell could have slept through that racket!" exclaims Jan Klou.

"Which is what I was saying," protests Matthaus. "I was disturbed in my rest; hence I knew that something was up."

"It's the High Commissioner," explains Krause. "He's come to answer our questions."

Jan Klou coughs theatrically. "You can be sure he has not come for your petty troubles, Sir. He has come to lay claim to your wife in the name of the Lords XVII."

"Then he must make his claim. She is capable of her own defence."

Matthaus looks thoughtful. "If they have sent out such a big-wig, then perhaps they have noticed us, perhaps it is a change. I declare it to be a good thing. We should drink a toast!"

Dronke Piet gives a wise smile. "I remember the last time something changed around here. It was a Sunday morning, about three years ago. This chap Piet was sitting in church and a prophet appeared to him and said, Piet, stop fouling the

21

Sabbath with your drunkenness. And Piet said Ja, I'll stop. And from that day he would not let wine pass his lips on the Sabbath."

"Ha! Good one," laughs Jan Klou, striking his claw on the table in appreciation of the joke. He raises his tankard and clinks it against Piet's wine cup.

Bart Meyer brings Matthaus his drink. "Well I don't mind talking to the Lord Commissioner about this," he says gesturing to the cup he has put down on the table. "In the end I make nothing." Meyer's patrons have heard this lament before, usually after complaining about the cost of his wines. Bart Meyer is the only taverner in the settlement authorised to sell imported wine – a privilege he has paid a tidy sum to secure. Like most things in the Cape, this particular market is run as a monopoly. If a person wants to supply the settlement with a product, for instance fresh meat, they have to buy a licence from the Company to do so. In return the Company ensures that nobody else sells the same thing. Poorer farmers like Dieter Krause, who cannot afford to bid for the concession, are prevented from selling directly to the townsfolk. They have to sell to the concession owner, who then sells to the Company, who then sells to the settlers. Everything ends up as profit in the Company coffers, and these coffers do not reside in Africa but safely abroad. With every ship that leaves the bay the freemen can stand and watch the fruits of their labours disappearing forever. It matters not that the money is going to the place called Home. Home is a country in a world of memory. It cannot bring you a new pair of shoes or a cow or a horse.

Dronke Piet raises his wine cup in solidarity with Meyer's complaint. "We should have been born Hottentots," he declares. "Then at least we wouldn't be done in by our own people."

Jan Klou bangs his hook on the table. "This is why I say we should leave!" he cries. "It's what I've been saying for years and nobody listens."

Captain Matthaus turns to Krause. "They accuse us of vain hopes, and then they come up with such a foolishness. Where will you leave to, Jan Klou?"

"East!" he growls, scratching an emphatic line in the table. "I will go East."

"The East sounds very far. Perhaps one should begin right away."

Jan Klou scowls and stands up abruptly, causing the bench to scrape loudly on the floor. Matthaus lowers his hand to his knife. Klou growls and makes a swiping movement with his hook, then he marches outside. Matthaus shrugs and looks at Dronke Piet. "Taking a leak," says Piet.

When Jan Klou comes back he is followed inside by a ruddy-faced gentleman wearing a grey periwig. He approaches Matthaus and Krause and sits down with them. This is Franz Rijkhof, accountant and burgher councillor. Like Matthaus, he was once a Company man but left its service when his contract expired. Now he does occasional work for the Castle and busies himself with municipal affairs. Rijkhof takes off his hat and fans himself with it. "Good God, is there nothing that can be done about the heat," he complains, unbuttoning his coat and removing it. "Impossible, it is impossible. A man cannot live like this. Where is my ale?"

Bart Meyer brings Rijkhof a tankard and sets it down without greeting him. He wonders who elected Franz Rijkhof mayor that he thinks he can order people about like this. Rijkhof takes a few deep draughts of the homemade brew and gives a rumbling burp. "Tastes like piss, but what can you do?"

"In Africa you take what you get," mutters Krause. "Nothing changes."

Rijkhof lifts his tankard in salute. "Unless they change for the worse."

Krause lifts his cup to touch Rijkhof's. "Speaking of which," says Rijkhof, leaning back so more of the room can hear, "I have been thinking about our recent visitor. I have been thinking about the whale." Jan Klou and Dronke Piet turn to listen. "Since it arrived I have felt somewhat ill at ease," continues Rijkhof. "I knew it could not be done away with by a melting and a barreling, and now it seems I am proven right." Rijkhof returns to his drink, pretending to study the tankard deeply. "When will they send us a brewer?" he complains. "This is something the Commander should tackle with utmost urgency."

"It is not clear to us what you mean," says the taverner, while pouring Piet another cup of wine. "The whale lives patiently in his little barrels and is no harm to any soul. I am not one for superstitions."

Rijkhof shrugs and takes another quaff. "I think we should hang that Widow Henckel for selling us her own piss. This is piss with frog fart bubbles, I will not drink it."

"Then don't," says Meyer and walks away.

"This beer will kill us if the Plague doesn't," calls Rijkhof in his wake.

Captain Matthaus looks up. "Now you are going too far," he says. "There is no Plague here. You should be careful of starting rumours."

"A rumour?" smirks Rijkhof, leaning backwards. "Why don't you go down to the Castle now and tell your Commander his agitation is based on rumour. I'm sure he will be grateful. But first perhaps you might cast an eye out into the bay to make quite certain there is not a ship there flying the colours of the pestilence. One should be certain of one's facts before petitioning the Honourable Commander."

Captain Matthaus stands up abruptly and strides out of the tavern. He is closely followed by Krause, Jan Klou, and Dronke Piet. Bart Meyer stands in the doorway but will not go outside. With only one patron in the tavern it is suddenly very quiet. The solitary drinker sits there glowing with satisfaction. "So," he calls eventually. "Is it true?"

"I cannot say," says Bart, returning to his tasks. "They have all fled."

The patrons of the Green Door have indeed fled, though not in any effort to escape a threat but rather to seek out news of what is undeniably a ship in distress. Captain Matthaus is first, striding out with the wide cuffs of his boots knocking one against the other. Then come Krause and Jan Klou, both feigning lack of interest as best they can. Dronke Piet follows

24

at some distance, abusing his compatriots all the while for their relative haste. He is only silenced when the taverner's wife passes him at full tilt, tossing him a curse for his barbarous tongue, and continuing up the strand in a manner that suggests more than just inquisitiveness is at play. And indeed there is. If the husband's mind was as quick as the wife's he would have been there too, but it will be some time still before Bart Meyer makes the connection between the Plague ship and their own fortunes. By then the truth of it will be confirmed, however, and he will have no time to prepare himself, no time to fortify his constitution with a tankard of Henckel's pisswater. It will come to him straight, on an empty stomach. Luckily for him, though, there will be little time for grief. Isabella Meyer will not allow him that luxury.

Quarantine

The Commander is not available for comment. His morning, which had started out so full of promise, has been irreparably soured. It does not matter to him now that the salute welcoming the fleet went off so perfectly, that the guests have showered him with their approvals and congratulations, that he is to be the honoured host of no less a worthy than a High Commissioner of the VOC. It is all spoiled by the one worm in his bright and shiny apple, that little barnacle farm that calls itself the *Tulp*. There she bobs out in the roadstead, lonely as a dog left out in the rain. Commander Van der Stel watches her from his position on the north-west bastion. He rests a hand on the muzzle of a 12 pounder cannon, unconsciously gauging its trajectory. Boom! he thinks. Then he sighs. If only things were so easy. And if only that would solve the problem. Commander Van der Stel has tried to persuade his doctors and surgeons to go out to the *Tulp* to see for themselves what manner of affliction this is and whether any of the cargo – human as well as material – can be salvaged, but all have declined. Whatever the name of the killer, it has dispatched four people already, and is thus not a thing to be courted *in situ*. Best let the poor *Tulp* be supplied and then sent on her way to Batavia, they say. If she reaches those shores then good for her; if not – well that will be confirmation of the wisdom of their decision to stay at arm's length. The Commander turns away, reminding himself that in fact there is no problem at all. Whatever material loss is to be incurred will not sink the outpost; there will be other ships. No, what bothers the Commander is that this *Tulp* has made a little hole in his dreams, it has frustrated his plans. But perhaps, he thinks, descending from the bastion to the courtyard, perhaps something can yet be done. He is an optimist, after all. Perhaps the girl's life can be saved.

On the Plague ship the cabin remains sealed. Four bodies have been brought out and thrown overboard. But there is still somebody in there, still somebody clinging to life. No-one will venture in to attend to her. It is enough that their captain has ordered them to haul out the corpses, that they have had to touch the diseased flesh. Who knows how many of them will succumb now, how many of them are seeing the sun set for the last time? It is perhaps thoughts like this that drive some of them to desperate measures. When it is dark, three men slip away from their companions, loosen the boat tied at the stern, and row for shore. They are aware of the risk to which they are putting themselves, but the promise of drink and happy company makes it seem worthwhile. It is a warm evening; the air still and the sea calm. A faint blue glow lingers in the sky above the embracing mountains. The sailors row silently, guided by the dull phosphorescence of the surf line and the lights of the dwellings along the strand.

When they reach the shore they haul the boat out of the water and set off towards habitation. They hear voices, the sounds of merriment. The men look at each other and slap each other on the back. What fools are those others to stay behind on that stinking ship. Let them all die; it is no loss. Now they take turns to smarten each other up – pulling right a crooked cap, tweaking a moustache – remarking how fine they all look and how clean and whole they are and not at all toothless from the scurvy. These three mutineers will tonight find a brace of lovely things to wean them off the pleasures of their own right hands, of this they are sure. And so to the taverns they go, and there do ply themselves with liquor in abundance, not caring if it be malt or spirit or vinegar.

It is not surprising then, that their secret gets out. They are men who have been too long without varied company, and soon the drink begins weaving its happy spell upon them and

27

dissolving like sugar the tight bands they have placed about their story. Enough of these silly tales of islands and pirates and great, wild storms – time for the thing that is burning us in our guts. And so they lower their voices, cast eyes about the room for spies and traitors, then bring their audience on board with them where on a night just like this, warm and breathless, Dirk the cabin boy is about to make a terrible, nay a gruesome, discovery.

It happens like this: young Dirk goes into the passengers' cabin to see what scraps he can beg from their evening meal. He does this often, see, and is a fat little bastard from all his mooning about with the ladies and feeding from their laps – but this time he is to get nothing. He gets nothing for they are dead. Four women and a man – lying there on the bunks or on the cabin floor, the unfinished meal still on the table. The boy finds one of them still alive, but she barely moves. The little blighter will not take of their scraps now. He wants to throw up. It is poison, says he to himself. They have been done away with – there is a murderer on board! But it cannot be so, thinks he, for the passengers are strangers and there is nobody on this poor ship who can profit from their death. There can be only one cause: It is the Plague, he cries, and flees the deathly place.

The sailors finish with their story and nod their heads somberly. Yes, if you are wanting to know of the Plague ship, then we are the ones to ask. We have seen it for ourselves: bodies lying in heaps, faces blue and frightened, bare legs of women exposed. And so are the raconteurs made heroes for a while, finding themselves doused in sponsored liquor, growing more bold and casting about them for those wenches they have promised themselves. They do not see one of their audience leave the smoky room and go out into the night. He does not join the other drunkards pissing against the wall of the tavern but carries on past them, joining Zeestraat and heading off down the moonlit road towards the Castle. This civic-minded gentleman is sure he will find persons there who will appreciate his tale.

By the time dawn breaks the soldiers are out in force, keeping people off the streets and patrolling the shore to prevent any further invasions of diseased sailors. The three escapees are back on board, adjusting to their new quarters in the stifling hold.

This is the last thing Commander Van der Stel needs: a crisis in the middle of an inspection by a high official of the Company. Commissioner Van Rheede sits in the Commander's office, paring his nails with a knife. The quarantine has made him irritated. He wants to begin immediately with a tour of the settlement, to interview the townsfolk and hear for himself whether there is anything amiss. But he cannot. So they have begun with the indoor things – the inspection of the books. Van der Stel is trying to find an entry in the records of the Council of Policy that the High Commissioner wishes to check. It is a large, heavy book, with entries going back years. What he is thinking about while he turns the pages is this: I am a fly stuck upon a pin. Here is the great man come to examine the affairs of my domain – as if there is something wrong, as if I have done something to warrant the displeasure of our masters. Of course, the accusations are not new to the Commander. He has been the recipient of several abrupt letters from the Lords XVII taking exception to any number of trivial matters. But clearly they do not know what it is to live out here; they do not know what expenses are involved in running a place like this. And what does it matter to them whether he employs his young sons at the Castle? Who else must do this work?

Commissioner Van Rheede gets up and begins to examine the contents of Van der Stel's office. There are a number of small paintings hanging from the walls, and a heavy carpet made in the East. "You paid for these yourself?" he enquires, then bends forward to squint at the detail on a scene of fishing boats on the River Maas. Van der Stel nods his head slowly. Van Rheede turns to him with a faint smile. He has decided already that he likes this short and swarthy man. He likes his energy and enthusiasms. But, of course, he will not let on to this just yet. There is much that he still needs to inspect here at the Cape. Quite possibly he will find things that will change how he feels.

Van der Stel pages through the book but his eyes do not take in what is written there. In Africa, he is thinking, when one dreams, one must do so on iron pillows. The idea surprises him. He cannot say where the formulation comes from, and he is not even certain what it means. In Africa, perhaps, one must guard one's dreams with iron-like resolve. This is more like it, and how true. He has told the Commissioner of his special reasons for being so disappointed with the loss of the women on board the *Tulp*. It is his plan, his dream, to build this neglected place into something more than just a dusty waystation. In this dream the bastions of the Castle preside over not merely one more possession of the Dutch East India Company but over a country in its own right. He is being audacious, granted, but the fates tend to favour the brave. He knows God is on his side. How can He not be when there is so much work still to be done on this poor continent? All this labour requires people, many of them, and it requires people creating more people – all of which can only happen if the surfeit of men in the settlement is balanced. There are plenty of young women in the Fatherland who will enjoy a life in the sun, of this Van der Stel is sure. It is thus with great hope that he has sent off requests to the Lords XVII to put out the word that such an immigration would be welcomed. Until now – and not counting the ill-fated *Tulp* party – only one small group has arrived. Five girls from the Rotterdam Orphans' Chamber, all now happily married off to grateful colonists. Five is good, but not nearly enough.

And now the hopes for a small increment to this figure are dashed. Only one remains of this latest group; though it seems almost certain she will join her sisters in the deep. Perhaps he should force the doctors out to the ship. It is within his power to do so. But then, could he trust what they said? Would their diagnostics not be laced with resentment? Van der Stel remains sitting thus for some while, brooding on the problem's complexities. Then suddenly he smacks his hand down loudly on the book. Van Rheede turns to him abruptly. "Found it?"

"Quite so," declares the Commander, shutting the book with a decisive thump. "I have found him – my doctor of the Plague!"

Adam Wijk sits at home nursing a bottle of Cape brandy. It is barely midday. He cannot work in the garden for the slaves are all being kept indoors. And he has tried to concentrate on his categorisation of botanical specimens but his mind refuses to stay focused on the task. It drifts always to that thing that lies out there in the bay, that ship with its cargo of bad news. Wijk takes another sip of the harsh liquor, then stands up. He wears the determined air of one who has made a decision, or of one who is merely looking about for a fault so that he may distract himself by putting it right. His house consists of a single room, part of which has been separated off with cloth hangings to form a sleeping compartment. In this is a single bed, much collapsed in the middle. Adam Wijk has thought of petitioning the Commander to have a proper wall built to divide the room, but he has never got round to it. And truthfully, what justification for the expense could he have given to those inquiring eyes? A man who lives alone has no need of hiding places. Opposite the sleeping compartment there is a raised fireplace. The black pot suspended by a metal hook over the coals does not always contain stews and soups. Today it is composed of a bitter green mixture that nobody – even an ageing bachelor – would be tempted to consume if they were not forced to do so. The remains of the ingredients, clearly some species of mountain heather, lie upon the large wooden table that is the major furnishing in the house. On the table also are a sheaf of papers, an inkwell, and quills. This is where Adam Wijk works at his grand task. He is preparing a compendium of the native flora. Already it has a name: the *Hortus Africanus*.

But there will be no work done on this project today. He has taken in too much of his favourite poison to make any fine

31

labour possible. Adam Wijk walks over to the cooking pot and stirs it with a look of distaste. He cannot say what properties are inherent in this substance he has cooked up, only that it should not be counted on for nourishment. Whatever botanical alchemy is under way in that iron belly it is certainly not one that will produce an experience that can be counted as victualling. If anything, the sensation after ingesting it will be more medicinal in nature, perhaps involving a gentle purging, or quite possibly something more dramatic – a fleeting moment of ecstasy, perhaps, followed by a brief choking, and then utter peace. He will have to find a way of testing this extraction at some time, but not now. The metal spoon scrapes dully against the iron vessel. It is too quiet in here, he thinks. Too still. And it is strange for him to find himself with this thought, for he is a man who values his solitude. If he were also a man who dealt in omens then he would have been able to etch this moment into his memory, saying this is when things changed – this is when I knew that something was coming. But he is not such a man, and he does not connect this stray thought with what immediately follows – a loud knocking on the door. Adam Wijk puts down the spoon. Perhaps, if he is quiet, they will go away. But when the knocking comes again he knows there will be no avoiding it. There is too much of an air of authority to those blows.

The question he will ask himself later is why? Why did he not just say no? Why did he not say that he no longer practised medicine, that it had been too long since last he dealt with plagues of any nature and that he had lost his art? But he says nothing as he stands blinking in the light of the open door, reading the paper handed to him by the sergeant. The military man keeps a respectful distance, though he cannot disguise a curious smile. He is waiting to see how the gardener will react. For while Mr Wijk has been known to attend to the ailments of his fellow settlers, it is only on request, and always with declarations of great unwillingness. Many times he has refused to answer the call, shouting through the door of his cottage that the fools should go away, that they will have more luck bothering the witch Halsenbach for a charm or a spell than trusting themselves to a man tainted by knowledge of physic.

So the gardener might well have refused this request – for it was phrased as such and not as an order. He might have said Yes, I have seen what the Plague can do and I am wise to her terrors, but I cannot help you. No man can do aught against the *Pestis*. Let that ship go, let it sail on into its darkness and find what mercy it can upon the open sea. But he does not say this. He curses the sergeant for the unnecessary vigour of his banging upon his door, and then he turns back into the house and packs his leather doctor's bag.

So it is that the gardener and part-time physician later finds himself aboard the *Tulp*, imbibing her noxious airs with what seems almost a relish. The kerchief clasped to his nose is aimed not at defeating the unseen killer but at separating out her more subtle traces from the everyday stenches of a ship too long at sea. He wishes he had something to shield his eyes from the bright sun and what it shows of the ragged crew formed up in the semblance of a row upon the deck. The captain, who looks no more than a regular beggar himself, is anxious to please. Like everybody, the first thing he wants to know is whether he is going to die. Secondly, he wants – in the event that he is not going to expire – to go ashore to eat fresh things and to fornicate.

Adam Wijk walks down the line of men, pausing before each one to deliver his diagnosis. He has a cane with a metal tip, and this he bangs on the deck in unconscious emphasis of his judgment.

"Scurvy," he says. "Scurvy . . . scurvy . . . syphilis."

But no Plague. The Captain, who should be pleased, shifts on his feet. "I think I have not seen everybody," says Mr Wijk. He is referring, of course, to the girl, the young woman. Van der Stel has informed him of her presence and given instruction that she be salvaged, if at all possible. Of her history Wijk knows very little, only that she is one of four parentless young women sent away by city authorities to find marriage in the new worlds. What is certain about her – and this he perceives as soon as he lays eyes upon her – is that she will need to delay, perhaps forever, any plans she has in this regard. The pale shape lying in the darkness appears to the good doctor to be more a corpse than anything that could ever warm the sheets of a colonist's bed, but the back of his hand applied to her cheek informs him that she has not entirely departed.

He looks around to ask something of the captain, but the man – having considered his duty done – has absented himself. Mr Wijk walks over to a window and forces it open, an action that brings not only clean air into the stultifying cabin but also more light. In the shadows now the personal effects of the other women and the man are to be observed lying on bunks around the sides of the cabin. Adam Wijk turns to the girl. He does not approach but remains standing at some distance. How much a creature of shadow she seems. He waits, as if expecting her at any moment to vanish back into the gloom from which she seems barely distinguished. Before the sickness she was a figure of beauty, this he can see. But the wasting has hollowed out her fine features and made them too easily reminiscent of what lies beneath, the uncompromising mortality of the skull. Wijk has seen such visions before. He is no stranger to them. When a person's death approaches like this it never comes for them alone. Death comes for all who see him, and it matters not that the observers remain breathing when he is gone, for they have felt him, and that is enough.

Adam Wijk looks towards the cabin door. A sliver of light shows beneath it, but when he moves it is not to respond to its invitation. Instead he walks over to a wooden crate he has spied lying against the far wall, and begins nudging it with his foot until it comes to rest at the bunk on which the girl is lying. Then he dusts the top of the crate and sits down carefully upon it, placing his leather bag on the boards next to him.

Now he will see. Now will be revealed to him the secret of this affliction. Adam Wijk closes his eyes and takes in a breath. His face is as stone. In that moment they are neither of them alive, the stone man and the alabaster girl. Then he opens his eyes and begins to search. She is clad only in a poor chemise, a thing that would once have been white but which now is soiled yellow with sweat and other effluences of the body. With arm outstretched he picks at the strings that hold the garment together at the breast. He lays the cotton aside and watches. And there it is, the slightest rise and fall, the faltering hint of life. The physician reaches across her to touch her in the pit of her left arm. He presses there against the skin, searching for the signs. And then on the other side, pressing in against her yielding flesh. Wijk turns his head away as he leans over her, as if listening to what his hands are telling him. Now he lets his fingers brush her neck, touching along the hairline, then edging down to the shoulders. Struck momentarily with the suspicion that he is being watched, he turns to look at her face. But the eyes are safely shut. Looking away again, and leaning very close over her body now, he moves his right hand down between her breasts, brushing over the cotton that hides her sunken stomach, until he comes up against the bony promontory between her thighs. With his fingers together he presses at either side, at first gently and then with more intensity. Once again he listens, and the frown upon his brow grows deeper.

Adam Wijk sits up straight and turns his attention to his leather bag. Searching in it he withdraws from it a serrated knife which he sets down on the mattress. Then he examines the bag again and brings from it a small glass bottle. The bottle has a waxed glass stopper, which he pulls free, setting bottle and stopper down on the bunk. Thus prepared, he picks up the knife and looks at the girl.

For a moment as he was being rowed out to the ship he had begun to hope that he might well encounter his old friend on board – old Black Dog, old *Pestis*. There he would be, rotten black hound with stinking breath, smiling up at him with that grimace smile of animals. Where have you run to, old adversary? Black Dog would say. I have come a long way to find you. See, I lay myself down at your feet now. I am yours. Take me. And he would be smiling at him with his coal black eyes

35

in the dark of the cabin, his tongue lolling over yellowed teeth, doing his best to feign submission. But Wijk would not be fooled. He knew that nothing would have changed, that the beast would merely be taunting him.

Now he sits in the darkness with his knife in his hand and he wonders if he is going too far. He knows Black Dog has not visited here. Whatever has caused this destruction is something else, some lesser cousin of the beast called *Pestis*. He does not know whether it is disappointment that he feels, or foolishness. In moments such as this his quest for the true cause of contagions seems like such a vain dream. He knows it is beyond him, that he will never find the truth, and that even if he does it will not bring back that which has been lost. So why does he now sit there with that knife in his hand if there is nothing more that he can do? He should carry the girl ashore now and let the doctors and surgeons of the hospital take care of her. But he does not get to his feet. He bends over her with his knife, his narrowed eyes scanning her form once again, then he reaches down to her calves and takes the hem of her chemise between two careful fingers. With a quick movement he passes the blade across the garment, ripping from it a small patch of fabric. This he deposits swiftly into the bottle, which he immediately seals. With knife and bottle safely back in the bag he stands up and walks over to the cabin door.

There is nobody outside; they are all hiding from him, fearing – no doubt – that he will ask them to enter the cabin and thus expose themselves to whatever affliction has so laid waste the passengers. Or maybe it is that they fear him, one who cares so little for the dangers of contagion. So he returns to the girl and, pausing a moment to gather strength, lifts her into his arms. His cane he has placed upon her body, the silver handgrip almost touching her chin. Then he limps out into the light. At the ship's rail he orders one of the two slaves who rowed him out to ascend the ladder and take her. It is not an easy operation, the girl limp as a doll and yet so much more fragile. Later she will remember opening her eyes, the ocean perilous below her, and then sinking back into dreams that are about drowning. When Wijk has satisfied himself that she is safely brought into the skiff he returns to the cabin and conducts a hasty search for any clues that might aid in a diagnosis, whether medicinal or criminal. Finding little of immediate value, however, he turns to go, pausing a while to gather up a selection of feminine attire before bidding the dismal place a thankful goodbye.

The journey back to shore is embarked upon with a growing sense of displeasure on the part of the rescuer. He knows what a picture they must present, the little boat with its strange human cargo and its mounds of vivid haberdashery. While he has salvaged from the cabin enough of what he reckons to be sensible feminine dress, he has also thought it wise to bring one of the more ornate affairs. No doubt the girls have been supplied with these for the purposes of courting, and the gardener is sensible enough to figure that if she recovers, the lone survivor will want to resume her intent in this regard. Now the vessel sprouts puffs of blue and gold, shots of iridescent green, and bowers of silk roses and taffeta bows. The poor gardener imagines they look every bit like some marine parrot, if such a creature could be said to exist. To counter this impression, he spends some moments attempting to perfect a visage of utmost indifference. He begins, in fact, to convince himself that the large group of people on the shore are there for reasons of mussel picking and other idle pursuits, and that he will be able to walk right past them and elicit no more than a casual glance. But, of course, it is not so at all. Those people are there for one purpose only – to watch his colourful progress towards land.

At first he takes the gestures of the soldiery upon the shore as signs of mere excitement, but when he spies a puff of smoke and moments later is splashed by a musket ball smacking into the sea a yard or two from him he realises he has done a foolish thing. They do not know what he knows – that the danger is not as great as first reckoned. The girl has some malady, that much is certain, but it is unlikely to be something that will kill them all. The high mortality amongst the group was surely the product of the victims' close confinement and their weakness after the long journey. Such conditions not being prevalent ashore, the populace should be quite safe, if they but stand back and let him handle the matter. Adam Wijk can see Commander Van der Stel and the High Commissioner standing on the beach amongst the curious citizens. The Commander is peering at him through a brass tube. Next to him a soldier takes aim with his musket. Wijk stands up in the boat and begins waving. He does not know how they will interpret this dumb gesturing, but he hopes they will be placated by it and reason that he would not be so foolish as to bring a real victim of the Plague to shore. He finds himself mouthing words of reassurance into the breeze: I-t's a-l-l r-i-g-h-t, he shouts voicelessly. Perhaps the eye of the Commander at the small end of that tube will perceive the movement of his lips and lead the mind to a correct interpretation of what is being said. And yes, it is so. The Commander lowers the instrument and makes a gesture towards the soldier. The danger is passed.

Now, of course, he must explain. The slaves have pulled the boat onto the sand and are on the point of lifting the girl out. Wijk motions to them to leave her where she is for the moment. He does not want to risk further warning shots. The spectators have formed a wide half-moon upon the beach, not quite sure what they should regard as a safe distance yet anxious to come as close as possible and examine the strange bloom their gardener has brought ashore. Van der Stel moves a step forward. "And?" he says.

"And, Sir, it is not Plague." A sigh goes through the crowd. Wijk glares at some of those bolder persons who have begun to edge closer. "It is not Plague, and yet it is no summer distemper either."

"Then was it wise to have brought her here, Mr Wijk?"

"She needs care, Honourable Commander. Food and water. Perhaps she will live."

Van der Stel turns to the sergeant standing near him. "Take her to the hospital. Have the doctors follow any direction Mr

Wijk should give." Wijk turns to his slaves and gestures towards the girl. They move forward and begin lifting her from the boat, when another voice calls out: "One moment, please." It is the Commissioner Van Rheede. The tall man steps forward, looking very fine in his maroon jacket and fashionable wig. He has an aristocratic face, finely carved, and the eyes of one who is used to being obeyed. "We should not forget," says he, "that this thing, this plague that is not Plague, has done some devilish work on board that ship. Four people in one cabin, all dead at the same time. What sort of a thing is this, mister gardener?"

Wijk looks straight at him, judging his words. He has been asking himself the same question and come to no definite answers. "It is one of two things, Your Grace. A fever of un-known origin, or something else." Van Rheede raises his brows. "By which I mean," continues Wijk, "that one should not rule out the possibility that they have succumbed to something non-contagious. A corruption of their food, for instance. It is not un-common aboard the ships. Perhaps one of them brought with them a dainty that over time corrupted and turned malign."

"What you suggest is quite possible, learned gardener. It sounds a likely explanation. And yet you cannot say for sure that this is what it is."

"No Sir."

"Then you cannot say whether you were truly justified in bringing her here, that this really is not a thing that will mur-der us all at one stroke." Adam Wijk is silent. "You cannot say, can you? Perhaps we should send both of you back to that ship and let it sail away. We have little to gain by entertaining this dangerous morsel amongst us." With these final words he ges-tures towards the comatose figure in the boat.

The situation has grown suddenly dire. Adam Wijk looks as crestfallen as does Commander Van der Stel. This will not do at all, this turn of the tide is something to be countered at once. And so the Commander steps forward. "Your Grace, perhaps – quite possibly – it will be enough if we keep her apart from us, if we find a place where we can observe her from a distance." Van Rheede looks at him tolerantly. "And where will we find such a place, Honourable Commander?"

The Commander turns to look at Adam Wijk. That look is at once hopeful and apologetic. With his eyes he is saying do not protest. Just listen, and begin to nod your head. "The only person, Your Grace, to have touched her so far is our gardener. Apart from him and these two slaves there is nobody else. And we are fortunate in this regard in that Mr Wijk is a man who lives alone, in a little cottage, in a place somewhat isolated."

Wijk is appalled. How has it come to this? Oh, that he had never answered that knock upon the door. He should have protested, should have told them he was drunk and incapable. The Commander watches him with pity. Poor Adam Wijk, alone in his house with a woman. What will he say to this? Adam Wijk looks down at the sand. He is counting the methods by which murder may be committed. There are many, enough for any number of days in a dark house with an unwanted guest. He looks up, lifting the corners of his lips in a smile. Commissioner Van Rheede nods his head. "Good," he says. "Let those slaves carry the girl to this little cottage, wherever it is. And then bring the slaves back here and let them row out to the *Tulp*. They will live there until we know they are free of contagion."

Proof and evidence

The hamlet rests in the lap of the mountains. At its back is the great wall of Table Mount, on the left Devil's Peak, and on the right the long ridge of Lion Mount. This latter feature is so named for its shape, which is like a lion resting with its head facing the Table and its rump extending out towards the bay.

On top of Lion's Head now a man sits propped up against a rock. He scans the sea, from the bay and the flat disc of Robben Island to the wide horizon. From the north, down the coast of Angola and the land of the Namaquas, will come the ships from *Patria*. And there from the West, to his left, will come the ships that have rounded Cape Point on their way from Batavia and the Indies. But he can see nothing approaching now. The heat makes the horizon shimmer. Dust blows from the dry northern coastline out over the sea, so there is a white haze that blurs the division between sky and water. Abram Moolman pulls his hat down lower on his brow. The light is like salt. It was never like this at home, never such a relentless clarity, such a burning insistence on exposure.

Before him the rocky pinnacle of the Head drops sharply to the part of the mountain they call the Lion's Rump. Down there he can see the signal cannon, and the signallers asleep in the shade of a tree. Moolman mutters a curse. What if he runs up his flag and they fail to see it for their sloth? There will be trouble, that much is certain, and he, Moolman, will not escape it. The flagman picks up a stone and hurls it down at the sleeping men, knowing it will fall a long way short.

To the right of the signal cannon and its delinquent attendants there is a path winding down the flanks of the hill and into the hamlet. Abram Moolman never uses this path, for he does not live down there with the others but in a cottage nestled behind him in the pass between the Lion Mount and Table Mount. The pass is called Vlaggemanskloof, after the profession of the one who dwells there. Abram rubs his eyes. He looks about him and then gets to his feet, searching the land below. It is clear he is no longer looking out for ships but something else. A person. Where is she, he thinks? She has been away too long. Moolman rests his hands on his hips and scans the flanks of Lion Mount, all the way from his cottage down into the hamlet. From up here the houses are so small and scattered. There are probably not more than eighty families living in the hamlet itself, not including the officials in the Castle. Moolman spits against a rock. These officials have a nice life, surrounded so comfortably as they are by the solidness of granite. There will come no hyenas or marauding natives into that squat fortress. The edifice stands there near the shore as a very symbol of permanence, its pentagonal shape with its diamond-shaped corners such a contrast against the wildness of the surrounds. Abram Moolman watches the ant-like figures at work in the Castle's inner plain. They are building a wall across it, dividing the space into two halves. He has been observing the progress of this defensive barrier for years now and he wonders if it will ever be finished. Money, he thinks to himself. It is always a problem of money. In front of the Castle is a rutted plain used as a meeting place by farmers. It also has a gallows and a scaffolding on which the corpses of dead miscreants are left to rot – a warning to any others who would attempt similar offences.

Abram Moolman lifts a spyglass to his eye and aims it at the streets below. It seems more than usually quiet. The only figures he can see walking freely in the town are soldiers. Not even the slaves in the Company Garden are at work today. And likewise in the cattle kraal and stables – not a soul. There in the wagonmaker's yard he spies a figure in a brown hat. Through the glass he can recognize the features of the wagonmaker, Jan Fredericks. A slave moves between the cart they are building and a stone shed. So they are not all dead, at least, thinks Moolman. Everybody is sitting at home, except the soldiers. He sees one of them looking about the house of Frederick's neighbour, Mrs Hasewinkel. She runs a guesthouse there and is often complaining about the sound of beating and hammering that comes from across the empty plot between them. Mrs Hasewinkel's house is one of the largest in the town, soundly built of brick and with a high stoep and little stairs leading down to the street. There are other houses like hers in the road, built by freeburghers who have managed to move beyond mere survival and have begun – in a moderate way – to flourish.

Up on the Head Abram Moolman grows more uneasy. He does not like his daughter to be away from him for any length of time while he is there. He is assured now, at least, that she has not been eaten by a leopard or some other predator on her way back up the hill. She has fallen foul of the great silence that has arrived in the town. Is that a fate better than the quick snap of a tiger's teeth? Abram Moolman cannot say.

The girl Greet Moolman is hiding in the garden. She had heard the rumours about the contagion before coming into town, but she had not known that the soldiers were keeping people off the streets. She looks up to the pinnacle of Lion's Head and sees the white speck that is her father. He is probably looking at her right now without seeing her. How strange that thought makes her feel. She decides to wait until the shadows grow longer before attempting to leave the garden.

In the *voorkamer*, amongst the beds, Isabella Meyer sits and weeps. Her husband stands before her, fidgeting with his hands. "Please don't cry, Isa," he pleads. "Hush now, hush." But she will not let up. She will not give him the chance to take the upper hand in this lamentation, though in truth it is he who has suffered the greater loss. If anybody deserves to weep it is the taverner, for the man who died aboard the *Tulp* was his brother. It was none other than his own sibling, Cornelis, who was guardian of the orphan girls.

So are the righteous taken before their time, say the people of the Valley Hamlet. It is one of the many truths they tell themselves as they hide from the *Tulp*'s mysterious killer. Within the dwellings on the Heerengracht and along Zeestraat and on all the streets in between there is talk of the scourge and of those who have already succumbed. What did they do, those innocent girls and that generous guardian? And what have we done that such a thing should come ashore? Again there is a supplicatory mist that rises heavenwards above the furthest point in Africa.

But Isa Meyer does not pray, and when she weeps her tears are not for the righteous. She has her own reasons for such grief. Like the Commander, she too has been frustrated in her plans.

There are four soldiers stationed around the gardener's cottage. They have not been at their new duty long, but already they are settling down in the shade and getting out their pipes for a comfortable smoke. Inside the cottage Adam Wijk surveys what is left of his solitary existence. It is not much. He has only the chair left to him, and the table. That whole corner behind the curtains has been annexed by the patient. Not that she is personally to blame, mind you. The gardener has placed her there himself. The slaves had carried the girl inside and stood there, looking about them and waiting for a sign from him. Wijk, in turn, had looked to them in a moment of helplessness. Where would he put her? The cottage, which might have been adequate for a married couple, was hardly a suitable habitation for two unattached members of the opposite gender. Perhaps she could sleep on the floor in front of the range, thought Wijk. It would be warm there. But no, she would be terribly underfoot. Perhaps in the front part of the room where his chair sat and where he retired of an evening to sip brandy and to think? No, that would be a distraction. In the end he carried her through to his little room, pushing the cotton hangings aside, and depositing her on his humble bed.

The Commander will be in his debt, this much is certain. Adam Wijk comforts himself with the notion that he will be able to exact some recompense from the man. He watches the girl from the curtained entrance to his room and shrugs. Best not to count on the Commander to do anything if it brings him no profit. He is saddled with this patient, and there is no arguing against it. Wijk resolves to move her from the bed as soon as he has prepared a more suitable space. In the meantime, he has to do something about that putrescent garment which, by all evidence, she has occupied since leaving the Fatherland.

And so it is that some few hours later the two soldiers positioned at the rear of the cottage are treated to a ritual of quite enigmatic import. For there stands Adam Wijk, sternly visaged, building a pyre of straw and sticks. Observing him in his labours – additional to the aforementioned guards – is his closest neighbour, a female goat. The goat lives at the end of a long piece of rope and is an occasional supplier of milk to the Wijk household. When the master of the house has finished with his architecturing he goes inside and emerges a short while later carrying an ember in a pair of tongs. He plunges the tongs into the straw and kneels down to blow. Soon the flames are licking at the wood and making a cheerful glow in the gathering dusk. The goat twitches its nose and retreats a step. Wijk disappears inside the house again and within a short while makes his reappearance. He still bears his tongs, but this time the instrument grasps not a burning coal but an item of feminine attire, one certainly that has seen better days. The doctor drops the garment onto the pyre and stands back as the flames turn to sullen smoke. Will he have to kneel down and blow upon it again? He prods the garment with the tongs, lifting it a little to allow the air in, and smiles as the flames return and begin to dispose of the ghastly article.

The gardener is about to go inside when he hears a whistle from the shrubbery. A third soldier appears, his iron hat perched lopsidedly on his head. "Round the front, Sir. Food." Ah, thinks Wijk, they have not forgotten us. He walks around the cottage and finds a wicker basket placed on the ground several paces away from the front door. A guardsman stands some distance away, watching him. Wijk approaches the basket and picks it up. He looks at the soldier. "And what of my bed?" he calls. "Where am I to sleep?" The man looks blankly and shrugs. Wijk realises he will get nowhere on this and returns to the cottage to examine the contents of the basket. It is a decent enough meal: roast chicken, bread, a pitcher of milk, two apples. On any other day Wijk's dinner would have been prepared by a slave. He does not possess his own, but by the generosity of the Commander is permitted the services of a woman from the lodge every day for the purposes of cooking and upkeep. The part-time slave of the gardener Adam Wijk is called Trijn, or Trijntje. She was brought to the Cape from Coromandel in the Indies. Like all her countrywomen, she is believed to be a poisoner. Beautiful to look at but not at all to be trusted. Mr Wijk keeps an eye on her while she cooks.

Now he sits in his shadowed cottage and finds a space on the table amongst the herbage. He knows the girl is in no state to eat. Perhaps she will drink some of the milk, and he will go to her later and see if she will take of it. But there is no sound from that corner, so he begins his meal in silence. Things are almost as they were before, reflects Wijk. If he does not think about his bed and what is on it then it is almost as if nothing has changed. The food could as well be a gift from a patient for some cure he has wrought. Wijk is often paid like this, in gifts of food or produce. Sometimes he will go outside to find a rough looking burgher holding a live chicken upside down by its feet. Here, take it in thanks. The lapsed physician always attempts a smile of acceptance. The chicken will have to live inside the house until Trijntje comes and does the necessary with it.

His meal finished, Adam Wijk reminds himself that he is not, in truth, alone, and that he should pay some attention to his visitor. It will not help to rail against her, for she is an innocent. He would like to have the guilty ones here with him now: the Commander and the High Commissioner. He would have words for those two. They should know, or at least the Commander should, that he no longer officially practices in physic, that he has given it up for a surer science. The field of botany is far more accessible to reason than medicine.

Wijk gets up and lights another candle from the one that burns on the table. Protecting the flame with his hand he carries it through to his sleeping space. There she lies, still barely alive, her breathing shallow and ragged. The gardener sits on the bed and looks at her face. It is slightly flushed as if with fever, but with no sweating. To most physicians the diagnosis will be fairly clear. They will say that the problem lies with a weighting of choleric humours, of a deadly buildup and putrefaction of the yellow bile. The treatment, too, is clear. Immersion in water to dissolve the heat and dryness of her condition, and, of course, a good bleeding. There is no better operation for the dispersing of foul humours than the puncturing of a vein. What causes such a humoral imbalance is not certain. It could be the action of the planets; it could be foul winds that blow from inauspicious directions; or it could be something that is conveyed from another person with a similar imbalance, in other words a contagion. If one were to ask most authorities what a contagion was, they would say it was the influence of one thing upon another. And if you were to ask them what was meant by influence – what were the mechanics of this influence – they would say, quite simply, that an influence was something inherent in the nature of infectious things. A contagion spreads because it is contagious. This is the sum of the wisdom relating to such things as plagues, poxes, and the various corruptions that the flesh is heir to. It is so because it is so.

The gardener touches the girl's forehead with the back of his hand. Beneath the lids her eyes move. Where is it that she goes? Does she imagine herself back home, or does she still sail the oceans on her fateful ship? Perhaps she is imagining her husband, the one she will find at this Cape of Good Hope. Wijk chides himself for such thoughts. It is no business of his at all. Moving upwards on the bed he pushes an arm beneath the girl's neck and shoulders, then lifts her into a semi-vertical position. With his other hand he reaches for a mug of water and brings it to her lips. "Drink," he whispers. And she does indeed take some of the moisture, as if her lips and throat know what this substance is, though her mind remains closed to it. When she will take no more he lets her sink back against the pillow. Wijk gets off the bed and goes through to the living space. He fetches his doctor's bag and a large bowl and brings them back to the room. The bowl he places on the bed near her hips. From the bag he takes a small knife, very sharp, and a leather strap. Now he reaches under the covers to bring forth the girl's right arm. How light it is in his hands, how pale and smooth. Adam Wijk takes the strap and binds it tightly about the upper part of it, then he runs his fingers down the underside, searching for the vessel. He knows it will not be easy to find. The young woman is so weak she makes hardly any blood at all. Then he sees it, such a fine blue stream beneath the almost translucent surface of her skin. Wijk positions the bowl below the spot and turns her arm so that the puncture will drain downwards into it. Then he picks up the knife.

The gardener remains sitting with that implement in his hands for some time. To an outward observer the scene might appear like one in an artist's studio, where the subjects must remain motionless for hours while the painter applies his colours to the canvas. An inner observer would see something quite different. There would be nothing frozen about this scene at all. For Adam Wijk is no longer in his little cottage in the Valley Hamlet, he is far away, in a city of vivid memory. He is hurrying along the narrow streets of this place, certain there is something following him. There it is, he can see it now, a shadowy creature loping down the cobbles, fixing him in its dead-eyed stare. The black dog has come to claim him; he has come to lick his master's hand and say, Take me home with you, I am yours. Old Black Dog works in secret; the mind of man cannot reach him. He follows no rules that man can discern; least of all people like him, the doctors. He has one gift he always brings them. Like a wormy femur dug up from a pit he brings them this thing without fail. It is a question: how can you trust your grand corpus of knowledge when there is something like me out there, striking left and right without pattern or reason? Think on it, dear friend, and tell me when you have the answer.

Thinking too much on this brings doubt and loneliness. Those whom Black Dog have visited will do anything, in the end, to restore their certainties. Even when they think they have given up trying they will still be working away at it.

Adam Wijk brings the knife to the girl's arm and presses it against the skin. All it requires now is a quick tap of the forefinger upon the blade to surprise the flesh and make it part. Such a simple operation. The gardener closes his eyes for a moment, then he sighs and lowers his hand. He undoes the confinement on the patient's arm and returns it to its place beneath the covers. When he has packed away his instruments he stands up and he blows out the candle. But he does not leave immediately. At the curtain he turns and watches her. Any observer, one who listens very closely now, will hear him whisper something into that space: "If I am wrong," he says, "forgive me."

And now, at the end of a long and most unusual day, the gardener sits on his chair, listening to the silence of the night. Outside there are men who guard the approaches to his house. Nobody can come in, and nobody can leave. If they only realised whom they had chosen to do their work they would not rest so easily. For Adam Wijk knows he cannot protect them. All his study has been brought to nought by this one question: what sort of thing is a contagion? He could shout this from the rooftops and no man would answer him. In all of Holland and Italy and England there will be not one man who will answer in any terms more helpful than to say that a contagion is a thing that spreads from one person to another, and that it does so because that is its nature, it is how God made it.

And what more is needed, most men will say? A plague descends upon a city because it is God's will that it do so. It is a meaningless question to ask about the mechanics of these phenomena. It is like asking why a stone falls to the ground the moment one releases it rather than flying upwards into the heavens. Quite obviously it is in the nature, the Form, of heavy things to require low places, and contrarily it is in the nature of light and fiery things to seek more elevated places. Everything has its nature, and everything its place. The world below the lunar sphere is a hierarchy of bodies and creatures moving towards the fulfillment of their potential, the heavy to the down, the light to the up, man to the Sublime. It is God who sustains this hierarchy, governing it through His laws and through his agents, amongst which are the angels and the planets. Such has been written in antiquity and is clearly indisputable.

And yet, of course, there are those who take issue with this consensus. It is the dawning of a new age of reason, after all. Let everything be doubted that cannot be shown to be true, say these dissidents. Be rigorous in this, even to the point of questioning one's own existence. How do I know that I exist? I exist because there is one thing that is indisputable – the intelligence that asks whether I exist or not. Start from that point, begin with the indisputable, and build upon that an edifice of knowledge based not on belief but on proof and evidence.

Such is the world inhabited by the Men of Science, that new breed of man going out so boldly with his rubble and his lime to seal up the dank trenches bequeathed him by Aristotle and by Galen and Aquinas. Amongst them one may count the likes of the Englishmen Harvey and Newton. Both have found answers to their questions and have been able to describe them and measure them and prove to their detractors that such and such is true. The task of the heart is to pump blood around the body. The reason why a stone falls is not because of God but because of Gravity. Such a blasphemy! And yet the eloquent Mr Newton escapes censure by laying down numbers and equations. He is able to say that the attraction between two bodies is a thing that is directly proportional to the masses of the two bodies and inversely proportional to the distance between them. Indisputable, if you but look at the figures.

And herein lies a warning. If one is going to be one of these new men, if one would challenge the wisdom of the ancients,

50

then one had best be sure one can find an answer to one's questions within a short period of time. One should not ask questions that could take a hundred years to solve. And such, unfortunately, is the category of question that fate has brought this poor physician. What is the name of the thing that travels between one person and another carrying illness? What is its name, how does it do its work, and how may it be stopped? At this time, in all the world, there is not one man who can truly say.

And no man shall. Adam Wijk reminds himself he is no longer trying to find his answer. He has given up on it. That scrap of cloth he took from the girl will not find its way into some ingenious experiment to prove a theory on contagion. It is taken merely as a memento, as evidence of things lost.

A faint music

The morning dawns bright and clear, yet there is a coolness to it that signifies a change. Perhaps the heat will subside. Perhaps it is the first breath of winter, when all things rest, when there is a refuge from the sun and all that it demands. Wijk opens his eyes but does not move. Slowly it comes back to him, the reason for his being on the floor and not in a bed, the reason for the numbness in his back. He knows today his limp will be bad. The silence from beyond the curtains gives no hint of any life there. Perhaps she is dead. Perhaps he has been released from this imposition.

The gardener wonders if it is too early for a shot of brandy. It will help for the pain that will almost certainly assail his body when he stands up. No, he thinks, it would be indecent to resort to such a measure. He has not yet sunk so low, although sleeping on the floor is certainly a step along that road. He lies on his back looking up at the rafters. Would the Commander be up to repairing the thatching, he wonders. It will certainly leak when the winter rains come. Perhaps he should get the brandy after all.

Now, with his thoughts adrift amongst the rafters, he hears her. He keeps still, thinking perhaps that in his flights of the mind he has imagined it. But then it comes again, a soft groan, a sigh. And there is no mistaking it, the sound comes from beyond the curtains, from the patient. So, he thinks, sitting up abruptly, she is not gone. She will not be done away with by a coffining, by a quiet burying. Then he stands up, wincing from the pain in his back and leg, and limps to the back door. There will be time to attend to the girl. First he needs to throw some cold water on his face and get a fire going. His day always begins so, with some brisk ablutions and a mug of herb tea.

Her long hair against the pillow is dark; her skin an almost translucent white now that the flush of illness has gone. Her eyes flicker and then open. Wijk looks at her and nods reassuringly. What does one say in such a circumstance? Does one say "Hello", does one say "Welcome"? All the options sound quite inappropriate, and so he adopts a concerned frown and occupies his attention with an examination of her pulse. Then he lays her hand back down on the bed, though he does not release it from his grasp. "Do not be afraid," he ventures, patting the hand. "You are safe. You will live."

Then he picks up the mug of water. "Now you must drink. Water comes recommended in circumstances such as yours." He helps her to a sitting position, she all the while watching him as if with suspicion, or possibly it is merely a surfeit of questions that cannot find expression. "Shh," he says. "Don't talk now. You must drink."

And so she drinks. She turns her eyes from him to the cool water, and with shaky hands she takes the vessel from him and lifts it to her lips. At first she merely tastes it, and then she is taking great gulps. "Slowly," says Wijk. "There is plenty more." She looks at him and hesitantly passes the bowl back. "More?" he asks, with a gesture of his arm. She nods. "In a moment. First we must look at you." Wijk reaches out to her face. She recoils slightly. "Do not be afraid. I need to see your eyes." He pulls down her lower lid and peers into each eye. "You were almost too far gone, do you know that? Almost you did not return. And perhaps still you are not quite here."

Dronke Piet sulks beneath his boat. All the taverns in the village have been closed because of the quarantine and he is without a bottle. It is an intolerable situation. He lies and gazes at the rotting innards of his vessel. Perhaps he could distract himself by launching it, perhaps he could catch some fish and use them to bribe someone to part with some drink. He could do that, certainly, if it were not for the wind, which on this particular day is blowing unfavourably for the catching of fish. In fact, it could be said that everything was blowing unfavourably for Piet. What was a man like him supposed to do with the fates so stacked against him? Perhaps one of his friends would have some brandy stashed away. Why were they leaving him out here under his boat and not fetching him for wherever it was that they were making merry? Typical. He was always sharing, but they never shared. It took a thing like this to let you know who your true friends were. In this case, he had none; that was quite clear. But not to worry, if they ever needed him, he would be magnanimous, he would pretend that this snub meant nothing, that he was above such pettiness. He would invite them back to his house and share with them what he had. Dronke Piet was always ready to share what he had, even if that something was very little. He had always known his friends would do the same, except that now his faith in mankind had been dealt a blow. Everybody thinks I am a nothing, he broods, but it is I who remember what it's all about. Here under my little boat, I am the one who knows.

Piet comforts himself with these thoughts for the greater part of the morning, but by eleven o'clock, or thereabouts, the heat radiating from the hull begins to make his eyeballs simmer uncomfortably in their sockets. It is clear to him that he has been abandoned, that he is the victim of events outside his control, or that some people know something and are, as usual, trying to get him. "Bastards!" he curses aloud. "I'll not stand for it." And so saying he rolls out from under his carapace and stretches himself to his full height. He knows exactly where the problem is. He knows the identity of the culprit. There he is, tucked away in his stupid garden, keeping quiet and letting the whole world go to hell. But Piet knows better. Piet knows that something isn't being said, and that this something is the something that is busy having its way with him there under his boat. All this must end now. He, Piet, will go to the source and set things right.

And thus it is that the wrathful prophet leaves his homeland and begins making his way through hostile territory to the den of his oppressor. It is not easy with the guards about, keeping people indoors, but neither is it impossible. When he finally reaches the brick wall that is the final obstacle to his purpose he looks about him once or twice, then he pulls himself up and topples over onto the other side. Piet stands up, dusting his hands on his trousers, then melts away into the maze of hedges and trees.

Adam Wijk sits at the edge of the bed and watches the girl. She has returned to the depths, her brief surfacing now erased by the waters of her sleep. He is not concerned about her, however, for her pulse is stable and her breathing even. She will recover. Perhaps, he thinks, he should go down to the Commander and tell him the good news. But, on second thoughts, he cannot be sure. Just because she has recovered does not mean the danger is over. Who knows, perhaps he himself will now be struck down. In fact, it is true that he feels a mite feverish. Wijk looks at the window and blinks. Yes, the light hurts his eyes, and there is an aching in his limbs. It will serve him right for being so cavalier in his handling of the girl. He has behaved as if she bears no more than a common cold, a minor sniffle. Had he really thought himself above the blind workings of nature, that merely because he had once made himself a student of the plagues that he would somehow be spared? What an irony.

But perhaps it is not this at all. Wijk comforts himself with the notion that he is merely feeling the strain of recent events and of his uncomfortable night on the floor. Such would be enough to make any man feel a little off colour, a little warm in the temples. Perhaps if he just rests a moment he will feel better. There will be time later to reassure the Commander. Right now he will just lay his head down on the bed and shut his eyes for a moment or two. The girl will not mind; she is swimming in her familiar oceans again; she is not interested in the greying head that lays itself down in the tranquil bay of her narrow waist.

Outside, from the shadow of a pomegranate tree, Dronke Piet observes the sleeping guardsmen. He, in turn, is being observed by the goat, which finds him sufficiently intriguing to warrant an ambling over and a sniffing. The goat stands there, wrinkling its pink nose and munching leaves with its funny, circular jaw movements. Piet glares at it. He picks up a little stone and throws it, striking the goat on the flanks. The goat stops chewing for a moment and looks at Piet. Then the circles start up again. "Go away!" hisses Piet. "Get away from me." But the beast looks unimpressed. So he picks up another stone, a larger one, and throws it. This time it stings sufficiently to alarm the goat and cause it to move off abruptly.

Piet waits a while to make sure the coast is clear, then he runs doubled over towards the cottage. He creeps along the back wall, past the door, to where a small window gives a view of the interior of the cottage. Piet rises slowly to the window and peers inside. At first he can see nothing. It is too dark. Then he makes out the table and the kitchen area. Nobody seems to be at home. Just to make sure, he reaches over and knocks on the door. If he sees any movement he will retreat at high speed. The gardener will put it down to mischievous children and think nothing more of it. But there is no movement.

Piet edges away from the window and moves to the door. Carefully he tries the handle. It turns easily, the door opening with only the slightest squeak. Piet moves in quickly, shutting the door carefully behind him. Now he will see what all this fuss is about. Piet looks around him. It is fairly dark with the door closed. The shutters on the window in front are closed, but there is a soft glow from behind the curtains where another window apparently stands open. That must be where the girl sleeps, thinks Piet. Silly of the botanist to leave her alone. Does he think the whole garden belongs to him, that he is safe from the prying eyes of the Truth? Piet shakes his head. He glances over the floral chaos piled on the table, pinching a sample between two fingers and raising it to his nose. Not something he immediately recognizes. Then he moves towards the range, his attraction captured by the iron pot. He remembers that it has been a while since last he ate. Hunger is not usually a thing that bothers him much, but now with the taverns closed his stomach is beginning to assert some claim on his attention. Piet lifts the lid and takes a sniff. "Ugh", he groans. It seems his stomach will go unsatisfied for now. But the experience is not a complete loss. He has at least ascertained that the man is up to something nefarious. Surely such a poison – if allowed to escape into the river, for instance – would be sufficient to dispatch the entire population of the settlement to its final reckoning. One did not require a plague for that, one required only an evil intent.

It is with this conclusion still resonant in his brain that Piet hears it. At first he does not know where to look, his attention captured by a faint music of tinkling glass. Does it come from behind him? No; turning around he sees nothing. He listens more intently, but now there is only silence. Piet shrugs his shoulders and resumes his contemplation of the evidence. Then it comes again, a delicate crystalline chiming, an eerie and yet quite beautiful sound. Piet doesn't know whether to be entranced or afraid. It is just such a noise as the angels are supposed to make. And then he looks upwards. First he blinks, then he swallows, then he speaks the Lord's name in tones of exclamation. For there, hanging from the rafters by wires or threads, is a forest of small glass jars, each of them, as far as Piet can see, containing some artefact of human origin. The light from the window catches the glass vessels in ghostly outline against the darkness of the roof, their strange contents floating above the world in a supernatural suspension. Buttons, scraps of cloth, a bone with withered flesh still clinging to it, all these things swing musically in the draughts above Piet's head. "Dear God in Heaven," he whispers. "Dear Heaven preserve us all."

The prophet has begun to regret having set out in search

of the Truth. It seems hardly worth it now. A feeling of coldness creeps up into his heart as he is seized by the facts of his poor existence. Friendless, alone, a poor lost soul helpless in the face of evil. Piet wants very much to disappear, to run from the cottage and find consolation beneath his wooden shell. But it is too late. Already he hears behind him the sound of a distinctly corporeal presence; already he knows the moment of reckoning is upon him.

Whirling around he finds himself standing face to face with the gardener. The man, in normal circumstances, is a somewhat fearsome character. He looks so much like a restless hawk, or worse, like some dangerous machine relentlessly running on a secret purpose. In these circumstances, however, the man is beyond description. And even more so now that he carries in his hand a long and murderous blade. The gardener fixes the intruder with his black eyes. Piet can hear him breathing. The man says not a word, he merely watches and breathes. Piet wishes he would speak; he feels he is going to faint. The gardener raises the sword to Piet's throat. "So," he says. "I have a visitor."

Piet nods.

"A visitor with strange manners, but a visitor nonetheless." Wijk lowers the blade. "It is a pity that we have such rules of hospitality, don't you think, Mr Piet? It's a pity sometimes that we can't be rude to our guests."

Piet doesn't know whether to shake his head or to nod. Instead, he looks upwards to the rafters. Does he expect his salvation to come from this quarter; is it that he once again mistakes the tinkling of glass for the rustle of angel's feathers? Quite possibly it is so, but if it is it does not matter one little bit. For he is wrong, and there is no salvation to be found there at all. "I see you have discovered my little secret," says Wijk. "You have walked about in my hanging garden, my little Babylon. Has it been a pleasant parade?"

Dronke Piet nods. He looks upwards again, his attention caught by the contents of the jars. "You are wondering about the nature of these strange blooms," says Wijk. "Some are quite obvious, as you can see, but some are less so. That one, and that one, for instance," he points with the sword, "are sadly corrupted and no longer recognizable. And yet I do believe they are organic in origin, most probably human. In fact, if I remember correctly, they are testicles. Yes, apart from what is obvious – buttons and bows and whatnot – these vessels contain the jewels of men. I collected them once; it was a hobby." Wijk swishes his blade to illustrate the action of harvesting.

"What are you going to do, Mr Wijk?" pleads Piet, suddenly finding his voice. "Please let me go. I am just a poor drunk who nobody ever listens to. I won't say a thing."

Wijk lowers his sword to Piet's crotch. "Can you keep a secret?"

"Yes, Mr Wijk."

"Those are not cods hanging up there. Those are all the plagues of Egypt. If I were to uncork one of those now, we would be dead within a day. Would you like to see?"

Piet shakes his head.

"Very well then. Now, it seems we have a problem. You have invaded my home. You have seen what is not yours to see."

"I will never tell a soul; honest."

"Perhaps you will, perhaps you won't. I require more certainties; I require something to keep here in surety."

"But I have nothing to give, Mr Wijk. I am a poor man."

"Not so," says the gardener. "I hear many things, Mr Piet. I keep to myself, but I know what is happening here. I know, for instance, that you spend more money in the taverns than you earn from selling fish."

"Not true, Sir."

"Oh, but it is, Mr Piet. Your boat hardly ever leaves the beach, does it? At least, not in the daytime."

"What are you saying, Mr Wijk?"

"I am saying that I know you are up to something. You and that one with the hook."

"Jan Klou?"

"That's the one. I know something about him and what he does at night with the ships." Piet shrugs and attempts a look

59

of bewilderment. "Come now, Mr Piet. Let us not play games. This Jan Klou is a smuggler, and the vessel he uses for his work is none other than the one you spend your slothful days hiding beneath. What an excellent ruse. The guards search the landing points for the miscreant vessel and never find it – and there it is all the time, right under their noses. They cannot imagine that Piet the drunkard would be capable of such a thing. They cannot see that his boat is anything but a wreck that should be dragged away and turned into floorboards for the houses of honest burghers."

"Please, Mr Wijk," cries Piet, dropping to his knees. "Don't tell anybody."

Wijk looks at him over his nose. Then he hooks the point of his sword into a moth hole on Piet's shirt and raises it, compelling the victim to stand. "Do we have an understanding, Mr Piet?" Piet nods his head. "Good, now I want you to do me one little favour."

"Anything, Mr Wijk, you just say it."

"I want you to go down to the Castle and tell the Honourable Commander that he is a pompous and arrogant little man who cannot fool everybody with his high-minded blustering. Tell him you see through his mask, and you are not alone in this."

Piet looks horrified. Wijk smiles. "On second thoughts, rather just tell him this. Say I require a bed; I will not sleep another night on the floor. Thank him for yesterday's victuals, but tell him we require a continuation of the supply, at his expense, and we require also brandy – for medicinal purposes, of course. Furthermore I require the services of my slave girl, Trijn."

"She is in the Lodge, Mr Wijk. They will let nobody in or out."

"Thank you, Mr Piet, I had forgotten. Perhaps it will help if you tell the Honourable Van der Stel that the danger is passed. He can send away these baboons skulking in the bushes round my house." Piet brightens at this news. He is picturing the tavern keepers swinging open their doors and looking

60

kindly upon him as he enters, knowing he was the one who got the quarantine lifted. "Can you remember all this?" asks Wijk. Piet nods. "And after that you will return and tell me what he says. Then, perhaps, we will have a little drink. What do you say to that? A deal?"

"Deal, Mr Wijk. A deal."

⌒

Still she will not cease her weeping. It is now the third day and still she languishes in the *voorkamer* amongst its useless beds. She refuses to partake in any activity other than a wailing and a sighing and an abusing of her husband. All the world is such a heap of uselessness and her husband lord sovereign of the whole catastrophe. Bart Meyer wanders in and out the house. He has no customers to distract him, and he has given up trying to comfort his wife. It has begun to occur to him that the situation is not quite fair. There is a heavy black feeling in his heart, something that makes him want to choke if he sits in one place too long. Is this grief? Is it anger? And what should be done with it? Meyer lies on the bed in the room next to the kitchen and tries to sleep, to forget. Truly it is not an easy thing to defy the fates as they have sought to do. How simple, how elegant, is the Lord's revenge. How has their grand intent been reduced to naught. The truth of the matter is that they are stuck in this wilderness. Always have been and always will be; nothing to be done about it.

When the black feeling gets too bad again Meyer gets up and walks through to the tavern. "Hester!" he calls. "Hester!" The girl comes down the ladder from the loft. This is where she sleeps. It is her nest, her eyrie. She looks up at Meyer. What has she done now? Meyer does not say. With no explanation he raises his hand above his head and then he strikes her. The girl drops to the floor. "Get up!" he yells. "Get up!" But she remains at his feet, covering her face against another blow. Meyer steps over her and strides out the door.

Left alone on the floor the girl does not weep. She watches the dust. The sun comes in like a tube through the air and all

61

the dust flies upward and glistens. She lies watching the dust. If she narrows her eyes the moisture makes colours in starry spikes.

Colours. When I am big I will have a dress like the one that came from the sea. I saw him bringing it with the whale girl. He carried her and the black men carried the blue robe and the shimmering green. Off they go and all following. I stay with them, they will not find me among the people. I follow through the garden. My peacock is scared and hides away. Then the door closes and she is gone and all the colours are gone. I must run back before I am found.

Good news

When the winter rains come sweeping in from the grey seas the Castle's inner court will be turned to an expanse of mud. But that time has not yet arrived, and instead of mud to torment the denizens of this stone refuge there is dust. It is a mist that rises from the ground, stirred up by the multitude of feet that cross the plain in a constant motion. From the walls of the Castle this never-ending movement gives the impression of a nest of insects, a hive of some industrious species whose members are never at rest but are always on the move, always heading off somewhere to achieve something small yet vital.

The captain of a foreign ship pauses on a step leading down from the wall to observe the strange life he finds in this distant place. Here comes a tinker carrying pots and hammers, a farrier bearing lengths of iron tied with wire, and here comes a laundry girl with a bundle of sheets. Over there a cook's apprentice carries turnips in a bunch and a slave bears a limp goat over his shoulder. Through the gates now comes a team of oxen pulling a covered wagon. The oxen are led by a brown man in canvas breeches and a red jerkin. The driver wears a coat of leather and a hat that is faded by sun and rain. Perhaps he has been away for a long time; he might be returning from a journey to the interior to find cattle and to bring back knowledge of faraway tribes. A group of soldiers watches him idly, pausing in their sharing of tobacco to speculate on the contents of the man's wagon. It is not a serious speculation, for they are easily distracted by a young woman who emerges from one of the buildings against the Castle wall carrying a basket of eggs and a pitcher of milk. One of the soldiers chuckles. Perhaps he has offered a wager that the contents of her skirts are more interesting than the contents of any number of covered wagons. Or maybe he is laughing at the man who crosses the plain now, dragging with him a slave at the end of a rope. Has he tried to escape, this wretch? Is he one of those ingrates who think life will be easier for them out in the wilds with the snakes and lions and the marauding Sonquas? Whatever the case he will have time to consider his sins in the *donkergat*, for that is where his master is taking him. Behind them follow two officials of the Castle, dressed in sober black. One of them carries a large set of keys, the other a book and writing implements. They glance disapprovingly at the wagon driver who has brought his vehicle to a stop in the middle of the court. A sergeant shouts and gestures to him to move his wagon to the side. Now comes the piercing whistle of the man in the red jerkin as he tries to get the sullen beasts to move. The driver swears and cracks his whip.

How will the foreign captain describe this scene in his log? Perhaps he will say something about the industriousness of the settlement's inhabitants and enthuse on the hospitality he has received. Perhaps he will be tempted to stay anchored in this little alcove of the seas as long as possible. For after all, he has not yet had a chance to try the Widow Frankel's famous jam made from quinces grown in the garden. It is quite possible, on the other hand, that the captain – who comes from a great city in a powerful nation – will be more interested in recording the dust and the general raggedness of the populace. Perhaps he will find small, sharp words to voice his irritation at having to buy overpriced goods from beggars with no teeth. And what words will he find to describe the endless stream of provincial bumpkins who engage him for hours in conversation, pressing him so earnestly for news of Home? Do they not see, these people, that Home has begun to forget about them, that year by year they have less in common with that place, that no matter how much they try to keep up the façade they will always be wearing their hair too long or their collars too wide or their wigs so inappropriately loose? It takes a foreigner to see what the locals cannot, that for all their earnestness and all their bravery they have begun to slip. Their lack of music has begun to thicken their ears; their lack of books has begun to cloud their eyes. They are slowly falling out of step with the onward march of progress, and there is nothing that can stop it.

But quite possibly our captain is a gracious man who will write no such thing. See there how he bows his head as two ladies walk by, sharing a parasol. At first he takes them for wives of local Dutch officials, but when he examines their dress and their bearing he sees that they too are from abroad. The women nod and carry on towards the Castle entrance, averting their eyes from the stares of the soldiers and other rough men. And what must they think of this place, these women? Most certainly they will feel a sense of gratitude that it is here to provide a respite from those ghastly seas, those months of illness and degradation, and yet quite possibly they have found themselves also uttering words of thankfulness that they are not here to stay, that they are destined for more graceful places. They can afford to look down at these rough men; they are the lucky ones who have been born with prospects, whose stars are leading them on to the East. Others have not been as fortunate. Some have arrived as orphans without a stuyver's worth of dowry; some have been girls so plain of countenance they have had to travel half the world to find a place where men are grateful for what they have to offer. And others, a rare few, have found their way here in the guise of men, having cropped their hair and bound up their chests and fled to the ships to escape their debts or their brutish husbands. When these are discovered they are hauled off at the nearest stop and married to farmers who cannot read and who beat their slaves and whip their cattle. Such are the people of the Cape. In the end, perhaps, it is best to sail on, if you can.

But if you cannot, or will not, then you will need to make the best of life in this place. You will attempt not to mind the sun that is so fierce or the winds that blow so hard, and you

will try to make some impression on this unappreciative landscape. You will, in some way, feel called upon to force it to do
your bidding. Whether it is keeping the dust out of the laundry or making a garden or building a farm, you will need to
draw deeply on your single, shared belief – that your God is a
lover of order and progress, that it somehow matters to this
deity that people can write their history and count beyond ten.
Without this you are lost. Without it, in fact, you would never
have come here, for it is this conviction that has launched
every ship your nation has ever sent out into the world in a
quest for knowledge or riches or a wilderness to tame.

Of course it is not to say that one's history is any guarantee
against failure. There have been some who have come out here
as conquistadors, only to fall prey to the great will of this place
to sloth and ignorance. Consider those shipwrecked sailors, and
at this time there are known to be several, who when found at
last by passing ships have not come running in joy at their salvation but have turned and fled. They have spurned their res-
cuers and returned to their mud huts and their several wives and
their endless days in the sun picking fleas. Consider these men
and see how deep into the pit one may fall.

But it is certain you are not like this at all. You are on the side
of order and of logic; in all likelihood you are a follower of
Science. It is clear that within you dwells an unshakable certainty that all things in creation are knowable if only you possess the
right tool of apprehension. And you know what that tool is. It is
Reason. It is the ability to name a thing and number it, it is the
ability to define the limits – the beginning and the end of a thing
– and to know that those classes of phenomena that resist such
process, that prove to have no beginning and end, no girth and
height, these things are the stuff of illusion and must be dis-
counted from serious regard. So it is clear you are not one of
those who believe something unnamable could ever wash up on
your shore. If ever somebody were to say to you: See over there,
see that black thing that lies upon the beach, that thing that fills
my dreams with its vastness, that wakens me with the echoes of
terrible depths in the waters of my brain, what is that thing? –

66

then you would say to them how simple it is and how clear – that thing is called a Whale. Observe how we dismember it, how we count the tons of its flesh and number its bones. In the end we have the whole of it there in our barrels. We have the sum of this whale, and there is nothing at all that can be said to be missing.

Behind a window looking out onto the Castle grounds an observer stands and counts. He is hardly noticeable amidst the clamour and the dust, and yet everybody knows he is there. The soldiers lining up in a marching order attempt to do so as smartly as possible; it is their hope that they will be left in peace, that no great bellow will suddenly erupt from that window and send them in a punitive charging up and down the square. Already they feel the eyes of the observer upon them, counting them one by one. In a moment the observer will arrive at a number that is one short of the full complement of thirty, and then the trouble will begin. But the window does not open and no command issues forth. The soldiers do not know it, but on this day those eyes are not focused on the world outside, and if they are it is only in a most abstract manner. In fact, the observer has been wondering why the idea of broken teeth has been turning in his mind, and he has suddenly realised that it is because the soldiers in their uneven ranks give every impression of a row of such deformities.

The Commander lifts his hand to the window fastening, but then another observation distracts him. He has only now noticed that all twenty-nine of those soldiers are wearing the same coat. Large or small, fat or thin, all seem to have on the same size leather buff-coat over their doublets. It is not something a person would notice right away; it is rather one of those things that come to you when you aren't looking for it, when you are looking at something out of the corner of your eye. But there it is – straining their garments like overstuffed sausages or drowning in them like urchins dressed in meal bags, the men are all wearing the same size coat. At least, thinks the Commander, there is some consistency in this, at least the effort at creating uniformity and order has not been all in vain. He finds himself praying that they will never have to defend themselves against an enemy from the sea, that the strength of these walls will never be tested by anything more than a spear or a copper-pointed arrow. At home, of course, this pile of granite with its five bastions would not be called a castle. It would be a mere fort. But here, well here in Africa one has the liberty to call a heap of stones on a beach anything one wants.

The Commander turns from the window and moves to his desk. He sits down behind it and reaches for a quill pen. There are many things that need attention, and he has been standing too long at that window. He could, for one, be attending to his guests. In the waning summer of the Year of our Lord 1685 the settlement at the Cape is quite aglow with a host of luminaries descended from abroad. There is the High Commissioner Van Rheede, Lord of Mijdrecht, whom we have already met. There is the Commissioner Rijklof Van Goens who has broken his journey to the East to enjoy a lengthy and meddlesome convalescence from an apparently undiagnosable malady. And then there are the French. At the head of this sparkling tribe, and sporting the very latest in Versailles couture, is the Chevalier de Chamont – Ambassador to the court of Siam. In addition to his lieutenants and assorted noblemen's sons, he has brought with him a contingent of Jesuit priests. These men, though of a more sober garb than the rest of the French group, are no less astonishing to the humble burghers of the waystation. It is whispered around the hamlet that the black-robes bring with them the evil eye, that they have come ashore for no other reason than to commit necromancy and other crimes against the Lord. Everybody has seen the strange boxes these creatures brought ashore, and some have even seen the contents and can confirm that they are devilish in nature and of no good at all to normal, God-fearing people.

The Commander knows it is not for this reason that the Pope's men have come ashore. It is for Science, and for this reason alone he has been prepared to tolerate them. These gentlemen are even now ensconced in the little guesthouse in the

Company Garden where, no doubt, they have made a start on their important observations. Perhaps, thinks the Commander, I should pay them a visit. Possibly they have found what it is that we have sought. They might have good news for us. The Commander sighs, feeling that on a day such as this a little good news will not be out of place. A little surprise, he thinks, a little something-unexpected-but-good, will be quite in order. But he does not get up and stride to the door. He remains seated, observing the quill upon which the ink has now dried. He dips it again into the ink and draws towards him a sheaf of paper. He will write a report to the Lords XVII. It has been days now and he has not written, and there is a ship about to leave. How much worse his case will be if no word arrives in the Fatherland from the wayward outpost in the South. So he bends to the page and begins the address: *To Patria*, he writes with a flourish at the top of the page. Then he leans back to examine it. What next, he thinks. Where to begin?

The Commander thinks of all the things that have happened since he last wrote to his masters. For one, there is the arrival of his various guests, already mentioned. And there is the matter of the burghers and their petitions to Commissioner Van Rheede. They had not waited a single day beyond the lifting of the curfew before they sought audience with him to make their various complaints. The Commander had tried to get Van Rheede to reveal to him the nature of the petitions, but to no avail. The man was keeping his thoughts to himself. Perhaps, thinks Van der Stel, my name was not mentioned too often at all. Perhaps it is all about trade concessions and cattle thieves. But these things, he comforts himself, are beyond my control. There is nothing I can do. Let the Commissioner resolve these issues and send word to the North that all is well here in the South, that all affronts to good order have been smoothed out, that all mischief-makers have received their just rewards.

Van der Stel turns his mind to other events, and finds himself thinking of the girl. Most certainly he will have to tell the Lords about her. He begins composing an explanation, but then he comes to a halt. He is imagining the silence that falls in the

Company boardroom as the clerk reads that word, as he briefly halts before it to savour the sweet and guilty pleasure that is felt by all who find themselves entrusted by God to be the bearers of bad tidings. He imagines that little man swelling with importance before he utters that horrible word: *Pestis*.

Of course, by now it is clear to the citizens of the way-station that no such plague exists, that it has all been an alarm. But in his telling of the tale, the Commander will have to mention it. Van der Stel tries to engineer the story so that all the pieces fit together without any reference to disease, but it is hardly possible. If he omits the threat of contagion, then he will have to consider the possibility that the passengers were murdered, and then he will have to try and explain why no investigation was launched into this outrage and why the *Tulp* was allowed to continue on her journey to the East with the evil-doer still at large.

No, thinks Van der Stel, none of this can be said. A letter filled with these details will be enough to end my career. They are the very worst words that could ever find their way into a missive headed north. Rather that the ship upon which it was borne was struck by a whale and sunk than that such words should find their way into the cauldron of power. Van der Stel reasons to himself that there is, in fact, no need at all to mention the girl, but he knows he is lying to himself. The Directors will want to know about the fate of the orphans they sent out, and it will be negligence not to tell them. Perhaps, he thinks, he can inveigle Commissioner Van Rheede into making the report. Then he shrugs, realizing that such artifice is below him, that it is dishonest, and that – in truth – whatever he says, or whoever says it, there is nothing that will stop the blame falling on his shoulders. So be it, he thinks, and lowers the quill to the page.

It is with regret that I am herewith compelled to inform the Honourable Directors, he begins. But Van der Stel does not finish the sentence. He leans back in his chair and examines it. Then he picks up the sheaf and crumples it into a ball. He pulls another towards him and wets the quill.

It is with pleasure, he writes, *that I bring news to the Honourable Directors of the safe arrival of a Winter fleet, and likewise too of your most Distinguished Envoy, the Baron Van Rheede, Lord of Mijdrecht, which gentleman has bade me send greetings to you and assurances of his safety and health, and best wishes for your health and fortunes likewise.*

Van der Stel reads what he has written. He takes in a breath and steels himself to continue. *And it is herewith on the subject of fortunes, both good and less good, that I am compelled to report to the Honorable Directors a great increase in the production of wheat this last season – the greater part of which we have placed in storage where there are now 3665 muid, no less, an amount sufficient to supply our needs for the fallow season when, it will please your Lordships to know, we will no longer need to lean so heavily on the goodwill of the Granaries at Batavia for our requirements in this regard.*

The Commander sighs and pushes the page away from him. This is not what he wants to say at all. What he wants to say is a thing that cannot be said in a letter like this. It cannot be committed to posterity in a letter that begins *To Patria.* It is more suited to a letter that begins *My Dearest X.* But, of course, there are no letters that go northwards on the waves with this address, at least not from the pen of Commander Van der Stel. If he had the chance to write a letter just to anybody, not anybody in high position, but just a friend, or perhaps even a woman, what he would like to do is to begin by saying something very simple. It is a silly little thing that is on his mind today – a thing that in the grand scheme of all things is not very important at all, especially if one looks at it in isolation, as a single instance of a something and not as a thing that stands for something else. And yet it is the Commander's job to see all things as symptomatic of everything else. Every single event is a harbinger of ten more of the same sort. Every harvest is a sign of bounty and assured success; every lost ship, every false accusation that comes from abroad, is a certain token of ultimate failure and decay. Thus the incident of the cooper is not just an innocent request for transfer, it is a mes-

71

sage from the underworld, a confirmation that all is not well above ground. If the Commander had someone to whom he could write a letter filled with trivia that perhaps meant something big and perhaps not, he would begin it something like this; he would say that today the cooper – a fine man, honest and true – has applied for leave to return to Batavia. There is not enough wood, you see, for him to make his barrels. This is what he would say. Van der Stel thinks of all the trees that are being cut down to provide fuel for the ships and to build houses. The trees will not last, he continues, and even if they do, they are not strong enough for the task of barrel making. In Africa the wood grows too fast, and this makes it weak. If the Commander were truly writing this letter he would end it by asking this question: How can a man make barrels from air? It is not possible, he would conclude. *It is not fair*.

And likewise, he would scrawl, how is a Commander to feed a multitude with a single rix dollar? This is the question that I ask.

Van der Stel has been leaning forward with both elbows on his desk, his brow furrowed. But now he leans back and admits the barest hint of a smile. He is imagining himself signing that letter. He has changed the recipient of the missive and it is now, once again, addressed to his masters in the Fatherland. Before the grand flourish of the signature he has written, in the neatest calligraphy, *Your obedient Servant*.

Van der Stel imagines them reading this and wondering amongst themselves, truly, how they could ever have questioned the miserliness of their humble servant in Africa, and how they could expect a victualling station to provide supplies and entertainments to every visiting ship without the expenditure of a stuyver or a doit. It is not possible, he hears them say. Let us apologise immediately.

But, of course, it is not to be so. The frown on the brow of the Commander returns. It is true, he thinks, that down here in Africa we are the doormat of the world. Everybody comes here to wipe his shoes, and it is we who sit with the dirt. Where is my good news?

A knocking at the door, though of a deferential volume, startles him. He barely has time to compose himself before the corporal of the guard appears, pushing open the door with a scrape of wood on stone. "Someone to see you, Honourable Commander."

Van der Stel sits up straight. Perhaps it is the Jesuits, come to tell him the results of their calculations concerning the moons of Jupiter. The learned men are trying to ascertain the precise longitude of the Cape of Good Hope, an operation that involves much observing of these planets through a very long telescope. Twelve feet, in fact, is the length of this instrument, one of the biggest in the world. Van der Stel is acutely aware of the importance of finally having an accurate number with which to pin the Cape in its proper position in space. To have this number will be good news indeed.

But the visitor is not Father Tachard or the Abbé de Choisy, or any of the other Frenchmen, it is a new face. A young, blonde face on a tall and bony frame.

"Joachim van Arckel," announces the corporal. "Teacher." Then he disappears, closing the door behind him.

The young man stands before the Commander, shifting slightly on his feet, clutching his hat tightly to his chest. He opens his mouth to speak, an action that causes a hunching of his already bowed shoulders. "I am Joachim van Arckel," he stammers. "I am a teacher."

The Commander nods tolerantly. "Good," he says, rising to his feet. "We need teachers. This is a most teacherless place, a very pit of ignorance. Do you bring with you letters?"

Van Arckel blinks. His mouth opens and he grows another inch shorter. "Letters, sir?"

"Of reference. Do you come of your own accord, or were you sent by the Honourable Company? Are you a privateer of knowledge, or are you a bonded man? Which one is it, Mr Van Arckel?"

"Oh, yes sir. Bonded. Three more years service in the Honourable Company. Letters from Batavia, Sir. From Mr Theulis." The Commander narrows his eyes. What has the

73

poor boy done to deserve this posting? Nobody comes from Batavia to the Cape of their own accord. The Indies are civilized, they have culture. This place, well – the best that can be said of it is that it has potential. The Commander, on most days, is a fervent believer in the potential of his little waystation. He has many hopes for the place, even grand ambitions. In short, the Commander is an optimist. With any luck, he thinks, this young man will be an optimist too. Perhaps he is not being sent here for some crime or some disgrace. Maybe he will bravely wield a sword of knowledge on this benighted plain; quite possibly he will attain greatness. Or perhaps some of his students will. And this, well this will be good news all round.

Joachim van Arckel finds himself hoping that the distance that has so suddenly appeared in the Commander's eyes is an indication of the impending termination of his interview. He shifts more pronouncedly on his feet now; any more and he will be in danger of toppling. Perhaps it is this very precariousness, the phenomenon of this lanky string vibrating so discordantly in that ordered space, that disrupts the tidy streams of the Commander's reverie and brings him back to the present. Where he went in that short space the teacher cannot say, but wherever it was it seems to him to be a place that is not quite in step with the familiar world. It is several sentences forward, or perhaps behind.

"In the beginning," proclaims the Commander, "there was a garden. It was a paradise." The teacher fights to suppress his dismay. "All the people," continues Van der Stel, "all two of them, lived in peace. It was rather like this place, this wilderness." Van Arckel gives a pale smile. He wonders if he should remind the Honourable Commander that he has come as a teacher and not as a minister. "From dawn till dusk," continues the Commander, "there was nothing but a sitting about and a chattering and a feasting. A great idleness; no industry. Nothing. Indeed, it was very much like this place, except for one thing. They were not separated from God. They were together, see."

Van Arckel frowns.

"But now, of course, it is no longer so. Now we have only the laws by which we may know God. The laws that are written, that are given to us, and the laws of Nature, that we discover for ourselves. All things follow the laws, and all laws lead back to God. This is the trail we follow, *Leermeester*. This is what people need to understand out here in the wilderness, it is what gives us hope. It is in this that we seek instruction."

Van Arckel smiles. At last he is getting an idea of how he fits into the Commander's world. "Perhaps, I can be of value there, Commander. I am a teacher, as you know."

"Yes, of course. And what are you going to teach?" Van Arckel is about to answer. He has practised just such a speech as the Commander seems to be inviting. But he is not given the chance. "What is it," Van der Stel continues, "that you are going to teach, the thing that lies at the basis of every law?" Van Arckel clutches his hat more tightly, but no words come. "It's easy," says the Commander, leaning towards Van Arckel and tapping him on the breast. "The answer is Numbers."

There is a moment of silence before Van Arckel responds. "Numbers," he says cautiously, "are very important. I agree." The Commander crosses his arms and looks at the teacher with narrowed eyes. "Numbers are used for counting," volunteers the teacher. "And for adding, of course. And subtracting. Adding and subtracting are some of the important things we use numbers for. I agree, Lord Commander." Van der Stel nods slowly. The teacher imagines he should feel encouraged by that nod, but he feels instead that he has somehow disappointed the man. "Numbers," he continues hesitantly, "are the things that we need in order to know what the laws are by which we are to find what we don't have, which is, as you have said, salvation and, I think, God. I understand, Lord Commander." Van Arckel wonders whether the Commander heard the last part of what he said, for by the time he ends the man's gaze is no longer focused on his face but has drifted over his right shoulder. Van Arckel does not need to turn around to see what object has so distracted him; he knows already there will be none. The Lord Commander, thinks Van Arckel, is 1,225 miles off the starboard bow. And then he remembers how far away he is from home, and about how that distance is quite immeasurable.

Then the Commander is back, one-point-five yards eye to eye in an instant. He has come back so quickly Van Arckel has not had time to compose a suitably optimistic countenance. But now the Commander wears a faint smile. He walks over to his desk and sits down. "In the end," he relents, "numbers are not so grand at all. In the end, what we have come here to do is to make money. We can employ numbers very plainly and very usefully in the making of money, firstly by adding, and then by subtracting, and then also by multiplying and dividing. Not so, Meester?"

"It is indeed so," agrees the teacher. "I can give instruction in these useful and civilised things, Lord Commander. I am quite a good teacher of these things, even if I have to say so myself."

"I'm sure you are," says Van der Stel. "We will have you begin as soon possible."

Van Arckel leaves the room and the Commander remains seated. For some reason he is feeling better. Perhaps it has been the presence of an educated man that has lifted his spirits. Quite possibly it is the teacher's promise of pedagogical enlightenment that has given him the strength to face his own uncertainties. The Commander leans back in his chair and gazes upwards at the ceiling. The distance from the ceiling to Jupiter is fifty thousand miles, he thinks. Between these humble boards and the heavens – if the mathematicians are to be believed – are fifty thousand measures, fifty thousand steps. That is a lot of steps, but far from infinite. It is a mighty distance for a man to walk, but not so much for God. Between man and God is a great distance, but not so great that it is without end. The Commander sighs, and then he closes his eyes.

A single word

Dusk falls on the valley. Men return from their labours, children cease with their play and run indoors out of sight of the shadows. Behind the Lion Mount the sun is still up, but here in the hollow the coolness of night has begun to settle. In the darkened doorways of the cottages now are flickering lights from oil lamps and wood fires. Smoke curls from chimneys in tenuous columns or sifts upward from broken roofs and crooked lintels like slowly absconding spirits. From the edge of the settlement the jackals watch. They smell the boiled offal and the soup that is made of bones. They watch the dark shapes in their doorways.

In the garden, a place lost deep within the shadows, a light bronzes the pane of an open window. Within the dwelling the gardener sits in silence. There is a single candle burning on a wooden table near his chair. On the table is an earthen flagon, its cork lying on the table next to it. In his hands he holds a glass half-filled with a golden liquor. When he moves it to his lips he does not immediately drink, but swirls the liquid in the glass, observing its rich colour, noting its aroma. It is not often that one can take such a pleasure from a local wine. This particular example comes from the Company farm at Rustenburg, where Commander Van der Stel is experimenting with winemaking. It is only he who is making anything that is at all palatable, the other farmers not having the patience to wait for the grapes to ripen before they press them. The gardener has received this as a gift, for his work with the girl.

The candle burns high and is in need of a trimming. A draught from under the door causes it to gutter, casting agile shadows upon the walls. On the other side of the curtain the young woman is asleep; the sound of her breathing occasionally discernable. Wijk lifts the glass to his lips and drains the contents. He does not place the glass back on the table but holds it absently in both hands on his lap.

What is he to do with her now that she is almost well? Send her back? He knows already that within a day or two she will be ready to be moved. He has given her enough, and there is nothing she can give him in return. He had hoped, for a brief time, that he would be able to get something from her, that she would help him unravel the question that has so obsessed him. But it was a mindless, unexamined hope. Mere proximity to one who suffers under a contagion will not be enough to reveal its secret to him. What he needs, if he is to reopen his investigation into the true nature of plagues, is contact with fellow investigators and access to the minutes of the Royal Society. He needs to be able to rely on correspondence that does not take four or five months to reach its destination and the same to return. There is no denying it, he is in the wrong place entirely for such an endeavour. It is one thing for a group of visitors, like the Jesuits, to come and take a series of measurements and then move on – it is quite another to have to do all one's work in this remote place. All he hears are rumours, fragments gleaned from passengers on the outward fleets. There is a man, they say, who has made an optic glass in which one may spy tiny animals upon the skin of one's hand. How preposterous! Yet quite possibly it is true. What he could do if he had just such a glass, if he too could examine these animalcules. Perhaps they would furnish him with a clue. But he is not back home, he is here in this cottage with its guttering candle and all that it reveals of the humble contents of his life – the single chair, the table piled high with fragrant herbage, the pot on the range (now filled with edibles, the part-time slave having returned), and the curtain of Indian cotton. Behind this flimsy barrier stands a wooden sea chest and a narrow bed with its single, quite unexplained occupant. This is about the sum of it, not counting the goat outside and one or two chickens nesting beneath the kitchen table.

Wijk leans forward to splash himself another helping of the wine. He sits back, imbibing a generous sample. The thought occurs to him that he should write to his one ally abroad – the man he calls his benefactor – for confirmation of this discovery of the animalcules. But why does the man not write of his own accord and tell him? He knows of the gardener's interests, his obsessions. But no, the benefactor only ever writes to request further objects for his collection of curiosities. Wijk sighs and lets his eyes wander to the pitched roof and its dancing shadows. The source of these shadows is, of course, the other defining characteristic of this abode – the hanging garden.

There is a new addition to this feature. It is a square of soiled grey cloth neatly caged in one of those tinkling glass jars. The receptacle bears a label affixed to its neck on which is inscribed the legend *Tulp*, followed – as if as an afterthought – by a question mark. This enigmatic bloom was cultivated aboard that unfortunate vessel; it is that very scrap of cloth harvested by the doctor during his first examination of the girl. The parent article – the chemise – is now returned to its elements. Wijk smiles over his wine. Of course he had not foreseen that his burning of the garment would precipitate a catastrophe of any kind. After all, he had taken sufficient haberdashery from the ship to clothe at least two women, a fact upon which he had later congratulated himself and imagined himself quite the gallant. In effect he was not far off the mark, and indeed he could have equipped more than one woman from his salvages, if it were not for one small point. As soon became apparent, it was not enough to present to one's rescuee an outfit of modest daywear, plus silk and satin courting gown, if – in one's haste – one had neglected to procure a garment of underwear to replace the item one was intent upon incinerating.

So it was that when his seagirl awoke – when he heard her footsteps beyond the curtain, and he made no attempt to help for he knew she would blush at his presence, and he knew that she would find the clothes that he had brought for her – it took a while for him to realize that the evidence emerging from beyond the veil was not such as to indicate appreciation. He became alarmed at the sound of silk and cotton being cast about; in fact the curtain billowed with the violence of this throwing about of clothes. Wijk wondered briefly if he should go and look, whether perhaps some help was required, but of course he was a man of gentle sensitivities, he would not burst in upon a woman engaged in her dressing.

So he waited, sitting on the very edge of the chair as if about to spring up and run. Eventually there was silence on the other side of the curtain, yet this did not make him feel any much the better. So he stood up and approached the sanctum. He paused before the entrance and cleared his throat then called out tentatively, "Do you need any help?" When there was no answer he brushed aside the cotton hanging and he looked inside.

How will you always remember that moment, honest gardener, for what you saw was not something you would at all have imagined. The girl – or woman, as you fully perceived – was indeed beautiful. Yes, there was no denying it. And yet it was not because of how charming she looked in her country-woman's skirt and embroidered red apron, or how fine she appeared in her robe of cerulean silk, her dark hair falling upon her bare shoulders and her ivory bosom so gently elevated by the tight-fitting bodice. It was none of these things that you noticed, gentle doctor; what you noticed was the fact that she was standing there facing you and she had not an item of clothing on her body.

When you had composed yourself sufficiently you apprehended that her face was cast not in soft tones of appreciation for this marvellous wardrobe but was set, rather, in an expression more akin to that of anger. Of course, you did not know whether to enquire as to the reason for her state or whether to make a hasty retreat from the sanctum, all the while uttering apologies for indiscretions you could not even think to name. As it happened, your indecision was ended by a cry from the woman. It was not a sharp command or a word of complaint that issued from her lips, but rather a cry as a wounded bird would make, a large and vengeful bird with ready beak and claw. She had picked up her beautiful gown and thrown it at you with such vehemence that it propelled you from your vantage point in the entrance and sent you backwards into the room, clutching that wonderful blue thing of which you were so proud. There followed a scene in which you stood and caught all the other items of clothing you had so thoughtfully brought, until you were standing there with such a mound of haberdashery in your arms that you were in danger of toppling. Thankfully now you could not see that naked demon and could take respite behind your barrier of cloth. You turned and began to search the room for a place to put those wretched linens, and the only place that would keep them from the floor was your single chair. Oh, what an indignity for that artefact to play now a clotheshorse for items of feminine attire. There followed a banging of wood as the creature beyond the veil threw open your old sea chest and began to hurl out your own collection of clothes. It was not an operation that took any great length of time, and soon there was a moment of quiet as she stood, no doubt, and surveyed her spoils. You feared that perhaps she had found the Diary, that book of secrets you kept hidden at the bottom of the chest, but then you heard the rustle of cloth and you surmised that some garment was being donned. You did not know whether to be thankful or horrified.

When silence returned you approached the curtain, you cleared your throat again, and gently brushed aside the hanging. The woman was no longer standing; she had cast herself down upon the bed – quite clearly overwhelmed by her exertions. As you approached the bed you saw that she had clothed herself in one of your long cotton shirts, the hem of which reached down below her knees. You leaned forward cautiously, and saw that she had returned to sleep. So you took up the bedclothes and gently covered her. Then you quietly picked up your own clothes and laid them back in the chest, and silently made your exit.

It would be a while before it occurred to you that amongst all the unusual things that had happened during that encounter, perhaps the most unusual was that no words were exchanged at all. And now, as you cork the flagon of wine and prepare to retire to your mattress in the corner, you ponder this matter once again. It has been several days that the woman has been under your roof, perceptive physician, and though she has been much of the time in sleep, yet has she still to utter a single word.

A dream

In the Tavern of the Green Door there is a new attraction. It is a feature that has caused a considerable amount of comment in the town. At first the regulars could not figure out what Bart Meyer was up to with his long willow poles and his nails and leather thongs. He was building something, that was beyond dispute – but what sort of a thing he was building, that was a matter of much debate and of equally much silence from the only man who knew. "Patience," was all Meyer would say. "All good things come to those who wait."

He is going mad from grief, said some. Not so, declared others. He is building a cage to imprison men who complain of the wine or fail to pay their bills. In the end these latter commentators were proven at least partly right – for it soon became apparent that the taverner was indeed constructing a place of confinement. There it stood, an elongated dome of vertical poles lashed to a tubular framework of willow branches bent round into circles. It was of a size that could quite easily have lent itself to the task of confining a defaulting drunkard, though this was a theory the regulars preferred no longer to entertain, settling rather for the notion that it was intended for the housing of some manner of beast – a baboon, perhaps, or a rather large bird. The construction sported a door, a rudimentary thing with leather hinges, and was furnished inside with a small bucket and sturdy crossbar on which, no doubt, the future inhabitant would sit or perch. Bart Meyer, of course, having satisfied his customers' initial curiosities as to the nature of his handiwork, had been quite content to remain silent on the new mystery that troubled their minds. "Wait and see," was all he would say. "All good things come to those who wait."

83

Now Isa Meyer lies upon the bed and counts the previous night's takings. Her husband watches her. He knows what she is thinking, that what he has brought her is an insult. It is not a bad sum, but it will never come anywhere close to matching what they could have reaped from their great Plan, the one that disappeared over the horizon along with the unfortunate *Tulp*.

Isa divides the coins into two unequal piles. "This," she says, pushing the larger pile to one side, "is for debt." Then she scoops up the smaller pile, letting the coins fall through her fingers. "And this great wealth here," she muses, "is for us to be extravagant with. Now what shall I buy, do you think? I know – I will buy me a new cap. I will stand with the other wives in the dust and wait for storeman Krige to lay out his wares, and then I will haggle for a good price like a common woman. This is what I will do, husband of mine." She looks up at Meyer. "Or perhaps I will not do that at all. Perhaps I will rather save up and buy a new parasol for the summer. I have all of winter ahead of me in which to do this; how fortunate."

The husband remains silent. He knows what will come next, the reminder of just which one of them it was who had married beneath their level and which of them it was who had had to stand by and watch her dowry being frittered away on so many useless enterprises. Yes, there was no mistaking which one of the pair had had to be forcibly dragged away from lovely Delft for a life in the swarming tropics. Likewise, there was no mistaking which one of them it was who had such an eye for a sinking ship, such a talent for spotting worthy holes in which to throw buckets of money, and so forth. The recitation will end where it always ends, on that wonderful summer day in Batavia (it is always summer in that place) when the Company troops came to escort them to the ships and to their life in exile, far away from honest people who pay their debts and do not get caught smuggling liquor. So now it has come to this, dear husband, Mr Chief Merchant Admiral Meyer, it has come to this.

The taverner feels his gall rising. There are so many things that he wants to say, but as always in this oft-repeated trial he has very little evidence to bring forth in his defence. Ultimately it is all true; every word of it. Their grand ambition has indeed come to this. Of course, he could launch a trial of his own – the wife being less than innocent herself. In fact, if the husband were quicker and more courageous he could have had her sent straight down in chains. He would only have had to mention the Plan. But this is a thing that is not talked about in the Meyer household at this time. It is far too dangerous, not only because of the choleric humours of the wife, but mostly because of how things have taken such an unforeseen turn with the Commander. Neither of them had imagined that the man would take the girls – what was left of them – for himself.

Isa Meyer sighs and gets up from the bed. "Come, husband," she commands as she brushes past him in the doorway. "I have a new idea." She leads the way to the *voorkamer* with its four beds, still unoccupied. "We have two options," she says, surveying the room. "We can forget that this ever happened, or we can try and salvage what remains."

"He will never let her go," says Meyer. "He has his own plans for her."

"And they are bound for disappointment. He has only to enquire from his beloved masters and they will tell him the truth. They will tell him not to waste their time with imaginary orphans."

"It will take him a year to hear the answer."

"And we shall not wait that long, shall we?"

Meyer looks at his wife. He has just thought of something he should have said earlier. Always, when there is a Plan, it is she who dreams it, not he. Meyer smiles weakly. "No dearest; we shall not wait."

She has worked it all out. First, the room needs to be cleared. One of the beds can stay, the rest must be sold. These are Meyer's tasks. For herself she has reserved the more skilled labour. Meyer looks at her with raised brows when he hears what she intends. "It is not at all impossible," she says. "I have justice on my side." Isa knows it will take more than justice to

85

get her own way in this. While she will be able to point out to the Commander that the dead man shares a name with her husband, it will not be proof enough to secure her possession of the girl. Mere coincidence, the Commander will say. He is convinced the passengers were travelling at his instigation. Nevertheless, she is certain she can convince him at least to let her play chaperone until the girl can be married. The Honourable Commander cannot be entirely immune to the wiles of an attractive and determined woman.

Isa turns and is about to leave when there comes a sound from within the room. It is a scratching, rustling sound – and it comes from under one of the beds. She turns back. "A rat," she declares. "Get the broom." Meyer pays no attention to the command, going down on hands and knees instead and peering under the beds. There are two eyes looking back at him in the dark. "Little mousie," he says.

"Kill it!" demands his wife.

Meyer looks at the creature with its blinking eyes. He moves back on his haunches and then stands up, making a gesture with his hand over his mouth. "That girl!" cries Isa, turning and marching out of the room. "She had better stay out of sight. I have another idea for her."

The girl emerges from under the bed clutching what she has found. A coin, old and tarnished. She licks it and rubs it on her sleeve until the metal begins to glow. Hester walks out of the house holding her new coin. She will go and show it to the lady in the garden, the peacock lady. She will know what to do with it; she will help her buy a new dress for herself, one made of silk that shines blue and gold like the sea before it goes dark.

In the garden stands a tower. This is the name that is sometimes applied to it, though in truth it is not really a tower, it is an old toolshed made up into a guesthouse, and it has an upstairs room with a balcony from which one may gaze at the heavens. Here the members of the Society of Jesus have set up their telescope, their single eye that peers at God.

Below their rooftop observatory the garden spreads out in its rows and squares and all its unexpected wonder. It does not quite match the glory of their Versailles, in fact it is a long way from it, but here in this wilderness it is quite enough of a pleasing surprise. Father Tachard, from his vantage point upon the balcony, finds himself wondering what could be done with the place if the Dutch were to be a little more forthcoming with their monies. He wonders whether the little stream that flows so clear and bold could become a fountain, whether this flat plain could be transformed into a water garden. I should imagine it is quite possible, he thinks. But I have no doubt also that it will remain a mere dream. These Protestants would not be able to squeeze a penny from their fountain, and lack of pennies is a crime to them.

But then the good Father reminds himself not to be so ungracious. They have been given all they require for their purposes, for their observations. It could not be better. In fact, he considers, perhaps it is somewhat too good. The luxuriousness of this little paradise has had a corrupting influence on his fellow brothers. Since their arrival in the garden they have taken to parading along its walkways like common laity. He has tried to encourage a little more sobriety of demeanour on their part, but they have explained that they are passing along those paths merely to whisper the True words of God to all they meet. The wise Father knows what is really in their hearts, that they are more concerned with a converting of peaches and pears into items of their own possession than with a winning of more souls for the Faith.

Father Tachard moves behind his telescope and tilts the eyepiece upward, so that instead of looking at the heavens, the long brass tube points into the garden. He is going in pursuit of his wayward colleagues, gliding like a spirit through the silent world that looms through the dark tunnel of the instrument. A jewelled ring upon a hand, a shining bead of sweat on the eyelid of a slave, and there upon the ground – a scarab pursued by a sparrow. Sparrow, sparrow how bold you are, how like a towering Phoenix, oh sparrow do not devour me! Now I run and hide, I am lost in the water of the little stream. It is a rushing ocean, a great flashing sea; I must look away before I swoon.

The priest stands back from his telescope and blinks as his eyes accommodate again to the vistas. And now what is this he sees? On the lawn before a spreading loquat tree a group of people begins to gather. Along the paths now they can be seen approaching: ladies in their silks, ladies with parasols, (common kitchen wives are absent), boys with willow hoops, girls with straw dolls, gentlemen in coats and wigs. A soft breeze carries the susurrant bubblings of these creatures down the walkways and through the sighing hedges, so that to the man in the tower it is quite as if a flock of excitable yet delicate birds has begun to descend on the place to celebrate the appearance of some rare and irresistible morsel. With a start, the observer remembers that he himself is expected down below at this feast. The occasion is a little spectacle of music and dance to be performed by members of the French delegation – a gift from the Ambassador in honour of his hosts. From the left side now approaches Admiral de Vaudricourt, Commander of the fleet, together with the Chevalier and his lieutenants. Colours, colours, will the brightness of this place never dim? And here come the masters themselves, Commander Van der Stel and the High Commissioner Van Rheede. How much of a likeness are those two, he thinks. They are two peas in a pod: 'Your Grace,' it goes, 'My Son,' it goes – all the day and all the night, the same little song. It makes the priest glad of his lonely tower. He will stay there safely and observe.

Mr Cardamom – Famous Traveller, Chancer Extraordinaire – has appointed himself master of ceremonies. He stands up tall, clasps his hands together, and proclaims thus: "Hendrick Adriaan Van Rheede – Keeper of Destinies, Creator of Laws, Dispenser of Wisdoms, High Mandarin of the East – Welcome!

We have for you today a small surprise, a little show presented by our new friends and former enemies, or that is to say the sons of Charlemagne and nephews of Gallus the illustrious fowl. It is a dance invented specially for us by *Le Roi Soleil* himself, a comment on the greater glories of our enlightenment and on our common brotherhood as agents of elevation in the nether regions."

Van Rheede turns a quizzical eye on Van der Stel, who shrugs. "He is a former Englishman, Your Grace, and there is nothing we can do about him. He is an expert at conjuring, though he himself refuses to vanish. Let us enjoy the show."

"And so, without any further ado," continues the mystagogue, "let our guests begin with their sawing and their blowing and let us applaud them for their artistry, their high taste, their nimbleness of foot."

The musicians step forward. A drum, a flute, a violoncello and three fiddles. The dancing boy awaits them, standing still as a creature cast from metal, as if not meaning to be human at all. He is dressed only in a pair of white breeches, fastened around the waist with a sash of crimson. His smooth chest, flawless in every way, they have painted gold. Also his arms are gold, and so also his hands and feet. On his face he wears a half-mask, and this too is a thing that glitters. A spray of green and orange feathers outlines the shape of the eyes. In the darkness of those sockets one can see the dancer blink.

The musicians watch the drummer, who begins a count to three. The boy stands on pointed feet, he bows, and the music begins. The name of the dance is not explained, but it is clear that the protagonist, this animate sculpture, is some embodiment of the sun. He is Lord of Measure, of Timing, of Grace. Perhaps it is the sun's incarnation as *Sol Invictus* – the godman. Pure, perfect, unblemished, he is the one who has overthrown the shadow worlds, the one who has proven such a torment to their unclean huntresses and smouldering, inarticulate Titans.

Van Rheede watches the dancing boy and smiles. Out of the corner of his eye he watches also the Ambassador and his silken coterie. De Chamont stands with folded arms and nods his head in time to the music. For a short while the garden belongs to him; he has annexed it in the name of the Sun King. Behind the Ambassador stands his deputy, the Abbé de Choisy. His head also moves, but he is not following the music, he is following the golden boy and his pirouettes. Van Rheede bends to Van der Stel's ear. "To foil a conjurer," he whispers, "it is only necessary to look where one should not." Van der Stel frowns, and then he nods. His right foot, which all the while has been counting the beat, continues with its tapping, but his eyes now scan the crowd.

Under the laurel branches a little brown mouse spies upon the world. Feet in boots and shoes with ribbons, legs in pink hose, knees with blue bows, pretty parasols and swords on sashes. This is what she sees, and the golden man who is trying to fly, his feet grassgreen beneath.

The little brown mouse, in reality more a dirty-kneed girl, is hiding. There is nobody who knows the garden quite like her, nobody who sees quite what she sees. The big people will not find her, and that is all that matters. As long as the children do not tell. The children are the most dangerous, they see things from the same angle. They can spot a mouse in the hedge by the blinking of its eyes, and they are quick with their stones.

There is one now, a little boy. He has grown bored with the spectacle and he hides his face in his mother's skirts. Soon he will look away and he will see her. The creature in the hedge prepares a face. When the boy emerges from the skirts and his gaze chances upon the hedge his attention is arrested by something that is not quite a natural arrangement of twigs and leaves. It is, as becomes clear to him, a gargoyle of quite horrific countenance. The boy cries out and runs to stand in front of his mother. The dryad of the hedge giggles. She wonders whether the boy has been at all scarred by his experience, whether there is any chance that perhaps his vision will not stay politely beneath the hedge but will follow him home and take up residence beneath his bed. That would be perfect.

Now here comes the man who speaks so strangely and with so many words. He has a dirty beard on his face and around his shoulders he has a blue cloak with golden stars on it. It is not like anybody else's cloak at all. The man walks with a bouncy movement that flows with the music, he walks behind the people and touches the ladies on their dresses. Now he is talking to a gentleman and he touches the man's coat. There he finds something, he pulls something from the pocket. It is a leather bag. He puts the bag into his own pocket and stays talking to the gentleman a while, then he moves off in his musical, wavy motion, in his strange dancing step that is like walking through water.

When the man with the blue cloak sails on his way he has a little something following him, a little invisible thing that has seen what it should not have seen. The garden is like a maze; it is very easy to follow someone without being detected. She can see his heels flashing beneath the hedge where the leaves are not so thick. When he gets to the gate and open road she has to leave her refuge and follow openly. The man walks quickly, turning away from the Slave Lodge and going upwards towards Lion mountain. Past the burghers' cottages they go, past the smithy, through the parked wagons, past the pigs with their babies, past the granary to the stables. The stables are big and dark; the cows in the corral next to it watch her blankly. They have long horns that can murder you with one swipe, and big hooves. Now he is gone. Hester enters the stables on tiptoe. She can hear the horses behind their wooden doors. All along the one side of the building are doors where big animals breathe loudly. They look over the doors at her, their necks shiny like stream water. Ruiter, Mercurius, Swartjan, Kaptein. She knows all of their names. But here's a door without a name. Hester puts her ear to it. No breathing inside, no heavy body that you can sense with your skin. Nothing at all. Perhaps she should go home; she cannot remember why she has followed the man here in the first place.

Yes, she will go home and they will be cross with her and

beat her. Hester sighs. She looks upwards to say goodbye to her horses, yet what she sees is not the softly brutish heads of her animal friends but something that makes her scream. It is a man, looking down at her from inside the stable. His eyes are wide and fierce and his hair stands out from his head like a devil. Hester stands frozen. Then the face disappears and the stable door opens. No more hiding for Hester.

"So," says the devil, looking down at her. "So it appears I have been found out. Well, only one thing to be done about it – I surrender."

Hester stays frozen on the spot.

"Come now little girl, little orphan of the tavern. Do not be afraid of Mr Cardamom. Would you like to see a trick?"

Hester shakes her head, but Mr Cardamom pulls some bales of hay to the centre of the stable floor and jumps up onto them. "Sometimes a little trick is all one needs in order to feel better. I have been around the world, little tavern girl, I have many wisdoms and many skills of magic to display. Sometimes a little magic is all one needs, yes indeed. How do you think I escaped from the Barbary hordes in Egypt, from the Mongols of China? Not by these thin legs, my child, not by the speed of these poor feet, oh no. I escaped with wings, that I did, and none of it due to newfanglement, oh no – pure magicianry it was. Undiluted, plain as daylight, something-out-of-nothing magic. Now as for the trick – here it is!" And so saying, Mr Cardamom whips the cloak with the stars from around his neck, flourishes it in the air, and disappears.

Hester starts to cry. "Hush now, hush child," comes the voice of Mr Cardamom, "I speak from beyond the bales. Come closer and take a squint. It is a mere trick of attention. I have done no harm to myself." Hester comes hesitantly into the stable and peeks over the wall of straw. The robberman is indeed there, lying comfortably under his cloak with his one leg crossed over the other and his hands beneath his head.

"See, no damage done, no creature harmed." Mr Cardamom springs to his feet, causing Hester to jump back a step. "Now," he continues, swirling the cloak back around his shoulders, "what is it that we are going to magic for you today? Will you tell me?" Hester shakes her head. "Ah yes, I remember now, you are a lady of few words. And I agree with that philosophy. There are over many people in this world with over many words, it is all a great babble. Ugh, sometimes it is a triumph just to hear oneself think! Well, be that as it may, and be it that you are a proponent of the single-worded exegesis, I will attempt to magic for you today a thing without words, a thing that cannot be spoken of, a thing that defies all verbs, nouns, adjectives and confabulatives. In short, what I shall perform to you, my eager audience, is a transformation of a sort not mechanical but entirely alchemical, a water-into-wine experience, a complete something-into-another type of thing. Do you understand?"

Hester stands staring. "Good, my child, good. Now what we want for you to do is to likewise climb upon the bales from where I of late disappeared myself, and for you to stand there in expectation while I perform the miracle. That's right, up you go – now, let us see, what will the nature of this amazement be?" Mr Cardamom scratches his forehead and taps his foot. It is a pose of deep meditation.

"Yes, yes, now I have it!" declares the magician. "In honour of our recent frolickings in the garden, in honour of our French boy and his wicked leaps – you liked him, did you not? – we will transform you into a fitting mate, we will make you into a bird, a golden bird that charms all men with a simple melody. Yes, that's it, the matter is quite said and done – it is a bird you shall become. Now just hold still a moment and close your eyes." Hester holds still as she is told, but she peeps through her lashes. The magician steps back and tears off his cloak, which he proceeds to flourish vigorously in the manner of a housewife with a burning tablecloth. Hester begins to giggle.

"Hush, hush girl, a little solemnity please. Do you not believe that it can be done, that in a moment you will be feathered and beaked and ready to fly up into the heavens?"

Hester shakes her head.

"And how would you know, dear heart, that my conjuring

had not worked, had not transformed you into a parrot? You would not, quite simply. You would say to me 'but sir, I am a girl'; and I would say to you 'but that is because you are dreaming. In truth you are a parrot having a girl dream'."

That is the moment at which Hester leaps from the straw stage and flees. She runs out the stable, past the smithy and past the granary; she runs all the way down the road. When she gets around the corner, out of sight of the funnyscary man, she slows her running and glances behind her once – just to make sure – and then she picks up speed again. But now she runs with her arms out straight beside her. And once or twice, or perhaps more, she waves them up and down, she begins to flap.

Joachim van Arckel watches the girl run past him in the road below. Ah, he thinks, a student. The teacher follows her until she disappears from sight, and then he turns away from the window and looks at the bare room. Well, as far as circumstances go, it is not exactly disastrous as a venue for a classroom. The fact that no space could be found other than an attic above the granary had been a source of much apologising on the Commander's part, and much insincerity on his. Of course it would be just fine, he had said, picturing already how he was going to spend his time crying with hayfever from all the wheat dust.

Van Arckel moves to the middle of the floor, deep in thought, and sighs. Then he looks around him, trying to remember what it was that he had been about to do when he was distracted by the girl. But he can't think of it, so in the end he merely continues standing there, furrowing his brows in an attitude of thought. There is a gentle light from the windows at either end of the room, one of which serves as a door from which things can be hoisted up from below and through which one enters and exits. To get to Meester van Arckel's schoolroom, you have to climb a ladder, you have to be very careful. The teacher finds himself praying that no child will ever fall from the rickety ladder, and then he prays to the Lord to forgive him for being angry with the Commander and for forgetting that not everything can be absolutely perfect all at once.

The teacher observes that it really is quite a pleasing light that comes in through his two windows. Perhaps he will be happy here after all. And then he begins to think about his children and about what he should teach them. We will teach reading and writing, he affirms, and we will teach numbers. Numbers, of course, will receive special attention. And what else? Yes, of course – we will teach manners. Manners are important if one would make it forward in life. One cannot survive in society without a measure of decorum, without a knowledge of the rules by which a civilised people governs itself. Manners are indispensable, and especially, most especially, they are in dire need in this strange place that is quite – he fights against thinking it – quite absolutely in the exact middle of nowhere.

Joachim van Arckel, now armed with lesson plan, begins to wonder what the next step in his plan of action should be. He drifts again towards the window, pinching his nose to stifle a sneeze. Then he remembers what it was that he had been about to do before being distracted. "Ah yes," he says aloud, "a broom. What I need most in all the world is a broom."

The teacher does not know yet who he will find to fill his classroom. He has not had the pleasure of meeting more than a handful of the waystation's inhabitants. The Commander he has met, and some of the officials, and he has been to the Lodge to visit the woman who has been appointed to teach the slaves. He is glad he does not have to work in that cramped and pungent building. Joachim van Arckel does not yet know of the hidden people of this isolated waystation. He will yet encounter one of the whores of Table Mount when out walking, and he will try to help her, thinking she is lost there on the barren slopes. If he gave her a stuyver she would be happy and would allow him any pleasure he asked for; but of course he will flee from her.

He has yet to find out about the white men who visit the Lodge and sire children who will become slaves. One can watch them approaching in the evening shadows, their hats down low to cover their faces. The supervisor will let them in for a price. Once inside they will have their choice of girls of any shade and temperament. They will do it quickly, up against a damp wall, or they will take their time, lying on the straw afterwards and listening to the never-ending sounds of the place: an exotic flute melody echoing down the passage; the sound of a hammer on metal coming muted through the walls – a tinker perhaps, repairing a pot or a kettle. Babies cry, a man laughs, somewhere a woman scolds her children or her husband. For such visitors it must seem, for just a moment, like Paradise. As for the women, they do not complain – and if they do it is but once.

Outside in the street an old man walks alone. His hair is thin and grey. He should wear a wig, but such a thing would be foreign to him. Along the wall of the darkened garden he comes, past the dulled fires of the smithy, past the swaying smudges of cattle in their rank corral. He walks this way most evenings, coming down from the mountain at the time when the smoke begins to twine in the air and the dogs go hunting door to door in their ragged packs. Past the Lodge and down the Heerengracht he goes, looking not left nor right, but fixing his gaze on the pool of blue mercury ahead, the dusk-swept sea. He will stand by the jetty and watch. He will count the ships and wonder if his beloved is there.

To his right, beyond the Castle and the mouth of the Salt River, lies the camp of the lime maker with its smoky kiln and piles of seashells. In the dusty yard his dogs whine for dinner scraps. Their ribs show beneath their mangy hides. The lime maker's apprentice crouches outside the shack, licking gravy from a tin plate. The dogs snarl and yelp, weaving about him, waiting for him to finish. When night falls they will all of them, boy and dogs, huddle together in an old wooden packing case in the yard. The dogs will come and go in the night, but the boy will stay where he is, for his ankle will be chained to a post in the ground. In the shack the lime maker drinks palm wine and swears at the shadows cast upon the walls by a tallow candle. "Back! back!" he cries. The boy does not know who assails the man so, and does not care. He grabs one of the dogs and rests his cheek on the oily flank, hearing its stomach groan. Fleas dance upon his nose and his eyelids but he will not move. He is far away, in a place where fleas and lice cannot go, where food grows plentifully on trees and where his father and mother live like kings and queens.

On that side of the river you can hear, in the distance, the singing of the Hottentots. They are a defeated nation but they cling to their old beliefs. They have no love for the Christian god, the god of power and might. Their god is the moon and the empty sky. And their cousins the Sonquas – their god is an insect, so it is said, a liar and a thief. What do they do there in their kraals out beyond the Salt River? Their priests dance and whirl and their eyes roll back in their heads, the people clapping and singing their songs about men who become animals. And there he is now, a crow or a jackal hurrying across the plains, coming to the settlement of the Christians to spy on them, to eat from their pots, to shit in their water barrels. You can see him there against the bald face of the mountain when the sun drops over Vlaggemanskloof and the last golden rays sweep across the granite. There he flies, that shadow, that thing that you see only from the corner of your eye – and now he is gone, taking something with him. There will be a child dead in the morning, you will see.

Amongst the inhabitants of this place, then, one must count not only the living but also the phantoms and the dead. The beach at night is full of wandering spirits. The bay is a treacherous place – it is not for reasons of poetry that the Portuguese called it the *Cabo Tormentoso*. Here are the ghosts of dead sailors and those of the men hanged for stealing bread. That sound at the water's edge, high pitched like wind in a ship's rigging, that is the sound of the broken women who pine for their husbands banished to Robben Island or to Mauritius. Today they burned a slave down on the Parade, tying him with chains to a post and lighting a great fire next to him. What did he do, this unfortunate? He has killed his master, and now he is free. There he flies now, across the sea, back to his Palm grove in Morondava or Macassar or the coast of Coromandel.

One needs to be careful here about who one counts among the real and the unreal. See that old man who watches at the jetty; take a closer look. Why does he wear that old-fashioned Portuguese doublet? Such a style has not been seen on these shores for a hundred years or more. Now look again. Are you sure you see him? Is he not perhaps a mere swirl of smoke, a gathering of mist? The people tell a story about him. They say that once, back home, he was in love with the daughter of a nobleman. It was an impossible love for a common man, but he would not let this stop him. One day he asked for her hand in marriage. The beautiful people of the court laughed at him and spat upon him and told him to leave their city. And he did, fleeing to this place so far away, hoping that here he would be able to forget. But, of course, he could not. Now he waits every day in the hope that she will find him, that she will come to him and bring an end to his exile. In this place, where all have come with secrets and with losses, the old man is a guardian spirit, a sign of luck to those who see him.

Such are the people of this *Cabo de Bona Esperança*. The slaves, the shell burner, the Hottentots, the jackals who are men, the phantoms and exiles. And up there on his pinnacle, watching over them all, is the flagman. Sometimes he has a visitor with him – an old man with wispy hair and ancient doublet. They sit in silence and wait for the ships. Perhaps it will be this one that brings her. There is my salvation coming now; out there on the horizon, see – a forest of sails!

Curious things

Once we shared our world with dragons and monsters. We lived in fear of reaching the end of the world and tipping over the edge. Back then we saw meteors and thought of giant birds with wings made of fire and with great talons that could snatch a man up and bear him into the heavens. We knew to be afraid of Leviathan and the Kraken. In those days the cartographers would draw upon their maps in places nobody had yet explored the image of a winged serpent or some other fantastical invention. They would write a statement of what they believed might be possible in that place: *Hic sunt dracones*, they might write, or even *In his locis cenocephali nascuntur*. And even if those places later proved to hold no dragons or dog-headed beings, it was enough that people believed it possible that such creatures could exist somewhere on their God-given earth.

But now things have changed. There is a new species of man abroad in the world – there he goes with his telescopes and his microscopes and his sundry instruments of polished wood and brass. He has come to take the measure of the world, to name and describe hitherto nameless things, to push back the blank spaces where the *dracones* skulk and make their mischief. Everywhere these men go they send back artefacts and curiosities for the wonderment of those at home. They raid the natural treasure troves of Africa and the East, collecting pressed flowers, grasses, the leaves of giant trees. They export boxes of dried insects, cases of arrowheads, wooden masks and ancient lizards caught in stone. All these things form the basis of a small yet brisk and profitable trade. Suddenly the world has become a curiosity, a thing separate from ourselves that can be subjected to experiment, named, described, and claimed as a possession.

And what if one were to try to find a symbol for this new spirit? If one did, one could not go far wrong by choosing that imposing piece of furniture that is finding its way into so many parlours and studies of the well-to-do at this time – the curiosity cabinet. There these objects stand, their doors heavy with lead and glass, giving access to a world that is strange and wonderful and, perhaps also, a little menacing. For who knows what spirits have followed these specimens across the waters. At night, when the sobering rays of the sun are gone, it is less easy to maintain one's certainties about the names one has written so carefully on those little white cards.

So, in the end, the curiosity cabinet is an artefact of contradictions. On one hand it stands for things extracted, divided, denatured. On the other it affords to those with sufficient imagination a sense of the magical, it provides a portal to a world of dreams. It should be clear that only a culture already divorced from this world would find such a contrivance necessary. We have abstracted ourselves from the world of the nameless gargantua and the holy terrors, and now we yearn to find a way back in. Something is there, something missing whose name we cannot say. Most people will not put it in so many words. They will hardly realise the truth of it. They will boast about how many objects they have in their cabinets and how strange they are and how dangerous it was to retrieve them. Some, however, will dream, and they will long for the world where dragons lived and fiery birds singed the air with their terrible wings. Such a man is the benefactor. It is not necessary to describe how he came to Adam Wijk's acquaintance, only to say that it happened in the days when the gardener still earned his keep from the practice of physic. The benefactor is a kindred spirit; he is a man who understands doubt. He has built for himself a fortune based on the certainties of profit and loss, and yet he is aware of the price he has paid in his own soul. He himself has sent out squadrons of ships to tame the world and convert it to the god of capital. He is one of the guilty, if destroying the ways of the weak and silent can be counted a crime. So now he is anxious to make amends. Or perhaps that is too strong a phrase – he is a Realist after all, and he knows that what has been set in motion cannot be stopped. Let us say, rather, that he is anxious to preserve evidence of those things that once were true, but which now have lost their places on our maps and our taxonomies.

So it is that the painter Hendrick Claudius comes to the Tavern of the Green Door to find those who will undertake a quest for the impossible. It is not a quest in a true sense that he has in mind, more a polite inquiry, a casual sifting of the natural phenomena encountered until that which is sought is turned to light. He comes at the gardener's behest, the older man never deigning to venture into the drinking holes and the other less salubrious quarters of the hamlet. These two are friends, both finding their delight in the intricacies of botany and the recording of the phenomena of the natural world.

In the tavern a fire burns in the grate; candles gutter and cast looming shapes in the smoke-filled air. In the front of the shop, close to the ladder going up into the loft, is the cage, still empty. It is thought that perhaps now the tavern keeper will reveal his mystery. A sailor of the *Amersfoort* has already this evening tried to climb inside, urged on by his drunken comrades, but the jealous taverner has threatened to call the watch. They will have to be patient.

Hendrick Claudius is a welcome figure at any gathering, having many stories to tell of his adventures in the East. He was sent to the Cape from Batavia some years previously to make a compendium of medicinal plants, and was retained by Van der Stel after the completion of this task to collaborate on a more ambitious project, this being the *Hortus Africanus*. Now the young man fetches himself a beaker of a reprehensible red and draws up an empty crate near the table annexed by Captain Matthaus and a few of the local regulars. He has lost heart for talking with the sailors. The men of the *Amersfoort* and the *Helderland* are already too far gone; he will return the next day at an earlier hour and spread amongst them his promise of reward.

The locals know already on whose business he has come,

that distant and limping Jeremiah in his walled paradise, he who never deigns to enjoy a companionable soak in friendly liquors, he who has – of all things! – taken for himself a wench, when all had thought him too pinched and parsimonious for such a humid venture. He comes on this man's behest, and doubtless there is reward in it, so they say (man doing naught without profit), though who could guess what could be had from the man excepting dry talk and a listing of the names of things herbal, medicinal, toxical, and scientifical. What profit is in it they cannot know, and yet it is quite simple: mutual respect, even friendship, and certainly money. The locals are ignorant of the precise history of these requests; they are not aware – as is Claudius – of the personage whom the gardener has taken to calling his benefactor. Claudius knows it is a man abroad, most likely in Holland, and one most certainly with the means to finance, and quite generously so, the procurement of such items of interest for his cabinet of curious things.

"It is a thing not to be found on these shores," explains Claudius when prompted to reveal more. "So if you would profit from this you would needs have stomach for a voyage, though not of too lengthy a duration. I speak of Madagascar, a mere four weeks away, and more particularly of the giant bird that dwells there. It is called a Rukh, so he says."

"Ah, the Rukh," sighs Mr Cardamom. "It is a bird, my friends, that eats no common food but sups on frankincense and myrrh. It is close cousin to the Phoenix."

"A nonexistent creature," reminds Matthaus.

"A rare one, perhaps, but quite extant," answers Cardamom. "I, myself, have seen the feather of one of these giants; it was at the court of Sultan Amid Bey, in Persia." The lapsed Englishman, of course, is quite familiar with that place, having served there for several years as translator of European texts into Arabic. It is a tongue, he assures his listeners, that he speaks with some difficulty yet understands with great clarity. "It is uttered at the back of the throat, like so," he asserts, gurgling dryly in demonstration. "There are no vowels, as you can hear, and all is done with intonation."

"It sounds like the draining of a well," snorts Franz Rijkhof. "But I wonder if it is possible for any person to speak like this, even though he be a heathen."

Cardamom frowns. "Do you question me, Sir?"

"I think it is quite possible," intervenes Krause, the farmer. "You have only to experience the jabbering of a Hottentot to know how far a language can sink. Hearing a band of them gossip is like walking into a tinker's yard in a hailstorm. It is an offence to ear and soul."

"Quite an offence," agrees Rijkhof.

And so is the firebird, so briefly introduced, for a while forgotten. The creature folds its wings and slips back between the lines in the pages of the Benefactor's letter from abroad.

But I have seen you, firebird, I have heard your name.

Hester stands watching the men; turning that new word over in her mind. Then Krause grows uncomfortable with her silent presence and shouts at her: "Go scamp, stand not and stare like the idiot you are, fetch more wine!" And so she runs, fetching more wine and more of whatever the men should want. The sailors watch her come and go. They have an eye for such things as she. It is only a matter of time.

Vrou Halsenbach bangs her tankard on the rough table at which she is sitting. She does not look up, she keeps her eyes always hidden, and she bangs again. It is not a common thing to see a woman in a place like this, but then Vrou Halsenbach is hardly a common woman, she is a witch. There she sits, a mound of rotten flesh, a toothless old hag who drinks with men, who spits against the corner of the room, who spreads her arse wide upon the bench and hangs her lips upon the tankard while she breathes. It is a breathing that could wake the dead; it is the breathing of an animal, of a creature that has held its air too long in the deeps. Vrou Halsenbach – this honorary man (for she can drink more than any man and match curses with the worst of them) – has the evil eye. She carries a collar of bandoliers round her neck filled not with black powder but with unguents and draughts. This is how she earns her living; she makes things of roots and herbs, chewing them with her own spittle, mixing them with arrack, brewing things that give people dreams or calm fevers or mend broken hearts or break them. It is said that Vrou Halsenbach has about her enough venom in those little pouches to kill an army. You would not leave your drink unattended in the presence of the witch Halsenbach. Perhaps she would be the bringer of your fate, the one God had chosen to do His black work, His reaping.

This Halsenbach bangs upon the table and the girl approaches. "More?" she asks. The woman does not answer. She points with her tankard, and there is no mistaking the object of her blunt gesture. It is the dome, the cage. She bangs with the tankard on the bench and points again. Round her now the lads of the *Helderland* stop with their sniggering, their lewd sniffing of the air. Something is up. Some sport is at hand. Bart Meyer, lord of this rebellious domain, notes the fall of silence and apprehends that the time has come. And it could not be better. "Gentlemen," he cries, attempting a speechifying voice. "And Lady." The sailors snort in anticipation, stealing a glance at the broad back of the witch.

"I have, um, a little something new, as you may have guessed. It is an entertainment, of a sort." The taverner, not used to so holding forth, glows red and falters. He feels he should say more, even if it is to counter the whoops from the back corner where the lads are imagining an entertainment comprising some plump Venus, but instead he advances upon the wooden ladder that leads upwards to the loft. "Excuse me, clear the way," he says. "This won't take long."

"Please be patient," calls a mischievous wag, happy to recall for everybody's benefit the late refrain of the taverner on this subject.

"Patience, patience," agrees Meyer, carefully climbing the ladder.

"Somebody bring his wife," calls one of the sailors at his disappearing backside, "he needs his britches sown." The joke earns a few chuckles, and then silence falls in the tavern – the gathered clientele finding themselves caught up in a nervous expectation. Then from a position not directly above the tavern but further along, above the kitchen perhaps, or the *voorkamer*, comes a scuffling sound, as if some struggle is underway. One of the lads takes hold of the ladder and is about to ascend. But the scuffling comes closer and he backs off. Now there appears in the square, dark hole above their heads the figure of Bart Meyer. He is standing, so his face has the impression of being very far away, as a ruddy moon in a summer sky. It is clear the man is dragging something. He crouches and turns around so he can descend the ladder. Down he comes, but he does so holding on with only his left hand – his right grips a rope that stretches upward into the loft. Whatever thing he has on the end of the rope it is not a bag of meal or a slab of beef; it is a thing that moves of its own accord. Meyer reaches the bottom and looks upwards. "Come on!" he commands, and gives the rope a yank.

So now in the dark square cut in the ceiling boards there appears this dragged thing. There it is – a face. Another moon face, though one not ruddy like Meyer's but yellow. The wide cheekbones of this face hide small, dark eyes that look fearfully below. Now they can see – a man, yes, but not quite a man; it is one of those Pygmies of the bush – a Sonqua, a *bosjesman*!

Meyer gives the rope a hefty pull and the owner of the face falls to his hands and knees before the loft entrance. There follow several strong words from Meyer, to the effect that if this person does not immediately descend he will be dragged down without benefit of the ladder. To this the assembled patrons laugh rowdily, some of them with relief. There was a moment when that face appeared above that they had not known what response was required. No man dared be the first to laugh or the first to cry out in alarm for fear of attack – how many of these creatures were still up there was not known, and all of them expert murderers. It is, afterwards, to some of them still a matter of concern that all the while they were drinking in apparent safety, a Sonqua was hiding in the roof above them, listening to all they said and pouring scorn upon their honest, Christian ways.

The young man climbs the tower. He is on his guard; the men in their black robes unnerve him; but also he is excited for what he is about to see. The clocks, the telescopes, those sharp-eyed men who dare to take such liberties with nature, with God. He is not certain whether these men are devils, and yet he cannot stay away. There is something important happening in this tower, and he would be a part of it. Father Tachard had met the young man in the garden that very morning and was charmed by his enthusiasm, and also by his mention that he had travelled in the East. The priest was anxious to gain what intelligence he could of the oriental lands to which they were going, and also to glean as much information as possible about this little Dutch possession situated so comfortably at the gateway to the East. Guy de Tachard is a man of several loyalties, foremost amongst them, of course, being to God, and secondly – though it is almost synonymous with the first – to the King of France. And then there is his dedication to Science, for which reason he has been accorded such courtesies by his Protestant hosts. It is clear that the territory being carved out by the men of Science is becoming a nation of its own, populated by all who share its principles. Though wars may rage between kings and emperors, their subjects are free to engage each other peaceably in debates on such elevated subjects as Optics, Gravity, and Astronomy. The country of Knowledge is a free land that cares not for the common rivalries of mankind. The only enemies of this state are those nations not built upon the same rational and reasonable constitution. And it is not considered war to destroy their adherents, merely progress.

So now the priest welcomes the physician and artist into his scientifical outpost and introduces him to the instruments that are indispensable to their tasks. He shows him the thermometers and the air pumps, which are to be used to conduct certain experiments dreamt up by the Society in Paris. And he shows him the microscopes. With these, he explains, one may observe the intimate parts of a flower, or the head of a louse, the sting of a bee. Claudius asks him if he may see the animalcules that he has heard talk of, and Tachard laughs. "We will have to grow some for you. Mix some cut grass with water and bring it here in a few days, and I will show you what you wish to see."

Claudius examines the pendulum clocks, and then walks over to the telescope. This is for him the most interesting of all the pieces of apparatus the Jesuits have assembled. "Does it work with the new method?" asks Claudius. "With mirrors."

"No, it is with lenses," answers the priest. "But they are sufficient."

The artist is about to ask whether he may look, when he hears footsteps on the stairs and turns to see an elderly priest stepping into the observatory.

"The Abbé de Choisy," declares Tachard, by way of introduction. "Dear Abbé, I am glad you are here. We have a visitor who is being most helpful on matters close to our hearts."

"Ah, so you have asked him where we may find a bottle or three of wine, not so?"

Claudius looks at him with surprise. It is not what he expects from a priest, but then there is something about him that is not quite priest-like. The man has too cheerful a smile. And despite his drab costume, he has the manner of a dandy.

"I was thinking more on other things," says Tachard, pointedly. "Like China and Japan. And also he has been on journeys to the interior of this continent. Perhaps you would like to ask him more on these things."

"Later, later," cries the abbé, waving his hand. "Right now we should be showing you our beautiful instruments. Have you seen the clocks?"

"Yes, and the microscope, the air pump, and the telescope. I am hoping to be able to look through it."

"And what is it you would see, young man?"

107

"Jupiter, of course, and our moon. I have heard it said that the marks upon it are mountains and seas."

Tachard looks at the abbé with raised brows. The older man smiles and winks. "Do you know, young man, that to find mountains on the moon would constitute a heresy?"

Claudius looks puzzled.

"Don't get drawn into this one," cautions Tachard. "It is an old argument that has seen better days."

"Oh, but it is not old at all, it is very topical. If the moon has mountains and seas, why then it is a flawed body and not a perfect sphere at all. And if it is true that the moon is no perfect heavenly body, then what of the other planets – may they too be mere lumps of stone with seas and mountains and men? And if this is true, then there is no reason for these bodies to move around the earth at all, as is required of perfect bodies – and they might as well revolve about the sun! This is why I say one should be careful of what one spies through our cunning glass. It could lead to mischief."

The artist is at a loss as to how to reply. He wonders if the abbé believes the argument he has just delivered, or if he is playing a game. There is a definite twinkle in the man's eyes, and Claudius finds himself smiling in response. "Perhaps, then, I should look at something else."

"Indeed," responds Tachard. "Let us show you Jupiter."

"And her several moons," interjects de Choisy.

"And her moons, though you will spy on them no mountains or little men."

Father Tachard explains how they are to measure the longitude of the Cape by observation of the moons of Jupiter. The heavens work like a giant clock, visible from all the corners of the world. In this instance, the hands are formed by the moons of Jupiter – Callisto, Io, Ganymede, and Europa. When one of them disappears behind the body of Jupiter the event can be witnessed by observers anywhere in the world. Though each of the observers will experience the event at once, they will each record a different time, depending on their degree of longitude. If these differences are compared to a table of the moons, calibrated from a fixed point on earth – in this case Paris – then it is a simple matter to calculate the degree westward or eastward from this point that the observation was made.

Tachard points the telescope heavenward and spends a short while aiming it at his target. Tonight they will merely test and calibrate the instruments, the observation itself being scheduled for the next evening. Claudius looks out over the darkened garden, feeling privileged to be in this rarefied company. He spies a light coming from the gardener's cottage, and he wishes his friend could be there to share the moment. He will know just how to answer the strange priest with his dangerous questions.

"Do you know who discovered the moons of Jupiter?" asks the abbé of Claudius. The artist shakes his head. "It was an Italian – of Pisa, I think," answers De Choisy casually. "Sadly though, he is no longer with us." Claudius is about to ask who he was and what happened to him when Tachard clears his throat loudly. "That's right," answers the abbé. "Galileo."

Tachard stands up from the telescope. "Galileo was an arrogant man. He imagined that the bounds prescribed by Holy Mother Church did not apply to him."

"Ah yes. As the Church teaches, it is one thing to observe the planets moving around the sun – it is another to believe that they actually do."

Tachard gives the abbé a silencing look and glances at Claudius. "I am sure our guest is not interested in Church philosophy. He is more interested in taking a look at the Heavens." Claudius gladly moves towards the telescope.

"I was merely making an historical point," chides the abbé. "Nothing to do with religion at all."

"In the end it is all religion," counters Tachard. "Everything one may observe is evidence of God. It does not matter, in the end, whether the Earth goes around the Sun or the Sun around the Earth. It does not matter whether perfection is to be found in the movement of the planets in their crystalline spheres or whether it is to be found in the mathematics of the true orbits of these same planets. Perfection is perfection."

"Ah, now the confession."

"It is no confession. God is still at the centre of the world."

"I know a confession when I hear one," insists the abbé, enjoying himself now. "But let us hear what our guest has to say. What do you think, young man? Are we engaged in sin to question the works of nature so?"

"I have never thought much upon this matter," answers Claudius, turning reluctantly away from the telescope. "But my friend, the gardener, has oftentimes spoken of this. He is of the opinion that the order we observe with our instruments is no sign of God but merely proof that the world is a machine, that it runs by itself."

"Now that," interjects Tachard, "is the true blasphemy. A philosophy that seeks to elevate Man above God. The universe is indeed a machine, but who is at the centre, who is the impelling and perfect force? That is the question you must ask."

"I think, Father, that he would reply that order – whether in mathematics or in botanical taxonomy or in any science – is enough in itself. It will not permit a deeper questioning. He is against asking *why* a thing works; he is content with discovering *how* it works."

"By way of illustration," suggests the abbé, "he will take this clock and he will dismantle it to see how it is constructed. Then he will put it together and announce that he has discovered the whole of this thing called 'Clock'."

"Quite so, I think."

"And he will be right," affirms Tachard. "One can describe all the forces that go into making this instrument what it is. You can never argue with such logic, for in its own world it holds absolute truth. But this is not to say that other worlds do not exist. We can see quite plainly that beyond the world of gears and springs within this instrument there is another world – that of the creator, the one who made the clock, who *dreamed* it and made it real. Let me hear you deny that, dear Abbé."

"It is a point not worth denying. But even so – if we can prove that the world of First Cause must exist, we are still at a loss to prove exactly what it is and how it works. Dreams,

Scripture, holy visions – all can be doubted. Thus I agree with Mr Claudius's friend – the only world that can be taken seriously is the world of measurement and force. Anything else is a mere fancy. Now prove me wrong."

"Proof, dearest Abbé, is a thing invented by the clockmakers of this world. It is a requirement for certain categories of endeavour and was never meant to be applied universally. It was never meant to deny the worlds that weren't accessible to its methods. This is why I say, let not the world of measurement deny a world in which there is no length and breadth and time. Let not the articulate deny the inarticulate."

"Observe, young Claudius, the manifesto of the new man – Priest and Mathematician all in one. It is quite moving, don't you think, though somewhat ambitious?"

Claudius has grown used to the older man's ways and knows this is not a criticism, it is a fond mocking. "I am a botanist, a physician, an apothecar, and an artist," says Claudius. "Perhaps I qualify for this new Society."

"I am sure you do," nods De Choisy.

The next day Claudius relates all this to the gardener, and watches his nostrils flaring in indignation. "Did you think to ask them, young Claudius, what they are doing on this journey if not to deny worlds that are unfamiliar to their own? The people of Siam – they will be robbed of their religion soon enough, and their treasures too. Their world is already lost."

Claudius bows his head, once again unable to answer.

"Who are these men in their skirts, anyway?" continues Wijk. "They speak like a bunch of timid women. Why don't they just admit they have come to plunder the East, as we have done? We do it because we can. Those who have words for how things work must always win; it is the way of this world, it is the future." Wijk is silent a moment, his face red. "I do not like them in my garden. I do not wish them here."

"They have requested your presence tonight, at the observation."

"Well, they shall not see me there."

But, of course, he is lying. There is nothing on this earth that will keep Adam Wijk from climbing that tower and seeing for himself how the Frenchmen extract their numbers from the compliant heavens.

Adam Wijk is delaying the inevitable. Within a short while – today perhaps, or tomorrow – he will have to go to the Commander and break the news to him. But now he walks in the garden with the young woman clasping his arm. She is unsteady on her feet, yet her face shows a pale determination to succeed at this exercise. Adam Wijk, on the other hand, wears a look of stern detachment, hardly glancing at the person on his side at all. This is for the benefit of any passers-by, lest they get the wrong impression. It is inevitable that they will; the sight would be unusual enough if this were just an ordinary woman – but she is not, she is something of a *cause célèbre*, a dangerous creature who not so long ago inspired fear in everybody's hearts. And here she is now, visibly recovered, and hanging on the arm of the irascible gardener. Such a sight – it is worth breaking away from one's labours just to come and look!

Wijk has wanted to show her the peacock, and there it is now, coming towards them like a king with its tail trailing gloriously behind it. He knows she will be surprised, for she has likely never seen such a thing or imagined that such a creature was at all possible. "Ah," she cries as she sees it, bringing her hand to her mouth in astonishment. She let's go of Wijk's arm and crouches down, trying to tempt the bird to approach. "It does not care for people," remarks the gardener. "We are too plain for it."

The woman stands, but has to grasp onto Wijk's arm to steady herself against a faintness. "Not so fast," he cautions. "Perhaps you should sit." She looks at him questioningly. He gestures with his hand towards the grass. The woman spreads her brown skirt and sits down in the shade of a pine tree. Wijk remains standing, preferring to maintain a strict decorum. The gardener also wants to assure that he is in a position to ward off any curious townsfolk who should come fishing for a story. He can see over the trimmed hedges how people slow as they walk past, trying not to meet his gaze but craning their necks in an effort to spy his patient. They will have to come closer if they wish to catch a glimpse of her.

And it is not long before one of them does. A generously proportioned man approaches, his florid face shining with sweat. It is Franz Rijkhof. He stops in front of Wijk, mopping his brow with a white kerchief. "Ah, good doctor, I see our patient is doing well." Rijkhof looks at the young woman expectantly, but Wijk makes no attempt to introduce her. "As beautiful as our peacock, no doubting it. Though one presumes, quite sadly I am sure, that she will soon be flying off." Wijk raises an eyebrow. "She will be married, is what I meant," says Rijkhof. The gardener merely nods his head. "It is a pity, Mr Wijk, that I am bound myself, otherwise I would offer to relieve you of your burden." Rijkhof laughs with a crackling of phlegm in the throat.

Wijk gives his half-smile that is no smile at all. "Indeed, a pity Mr Rijkhof. Though being unmarried is merely one of the requirements for this position. The other being capability."

The woman observes them warily, knowing they talk of her. She sees the stout man turn and walk agitatedly away. Wijk looks ahead of him, but she can see he is pleased with whatever it is that he has said. The peacock sweeps in its stately fashion past her and disappears through a gap in one of the border hedges. Wijk watches his charge from the corner of his eye. He sees her smile at something ahead of her, cocking her head in an attitude of curiosity. She is amused by a face that watches from a hedge. The owner of the face, a girl, appears intensely interested in them – and yet she keeps her distance, as if she, too, were a shy bird that knew to be wary of humans. Adam Wijk sees the object of his patient's attention and frowns. "Shoo! Shoo!" he scolds, making a driving motion with his arm. "Move away there." The girl in the hedge looks at him unafraid. Now the woman watches him too. It is clear whose side she is on. Wijk coughs and pulls his hat down lower on his head. Sometimes it is possible to argue against a female. Against two – that is something a man should always avoid. The wise gardener steps closer and offers the young woman his hand. "I think we've had enough for one day," he says. "We can come out again tomorrow."

But he does not take her walking the next day. He sets out, instead, for the Commander, knowing that what he has to say cannot wait an hour longer. As he walks he wonders how he will broach the subject. Van der Stel will be expecting good news, and indeed Wijk had thought that by now such would be possible. He had not counted on something as unexpected as this. So, will he announce her condition straight out, or will he relate its discovery in every detail, allowing the listener to be carried along with it so that he will find himself beguiled by a certain pathos in the telling?

He thinks of that moment when it became clear. It was the morning after the episode with the dress. He had been out in the garden and had returned at ten o'clock to check on his patient and to refresh himself with a late breakfast. When he came in through the door he saw her sitting at the table with her back to him. She did not move as his footsteps approached. Coming closer he saw that the object of her rapt attention was the pile of greenery on the table. Her face lay seemingly buried in the stems and leaves and the tiny inflorescences of the mountain herbs. Her right hand hovered above the cuttings, lightly touching, almost caressing. The gardener watched. Still she made no movement towards him, no sign of recognition, lying as if in a waking sleep with her face against the green and fragrant pillow. He was afraid to speak, lest he wake her with a start from whatever reverie she was lost within. So he walked slowly back to the door, which he opened and closed again, making sure to produce a noise that was not too startling, and not too soft. Then he approached her once again, making sure to be very definite with his footfalls. But still, nothing. "Pardon me," he said gently. "I do not wish to startle." The girl lifted her head and sat up straight. Wijk prepared a reassuring smile, certain she would turn around now and acknowledge him. But her attention had been captured by something else. In her right hand now she held the stem of a flower, an orchid. It was one of those astonishing blooms that Wijk was attempting to name and categorise, and which, in fact, the artist Hendrick Claudius was due to come and sketch later that very day. The girl held the delicate white petals to her throat and cocked her head. It was a mere moment that she sat thus before suddenly replacing the cutting on the table. The quickness with which she did so suggested, perhaps, a certain embarrassment at catching herself in an act of vanity. Imagining an observer now, one who had witnessed her conceit, she turned and looked behind her. How great was her surprise then to find an actual person standing there. She rose to her feet with alacrity, her right hand touching at her throat. Adam Wijk stepped backwards and made a gesture of reassurance. "I did not mean to alarm," he said gently, though he knew his words were spoken in vain. "I merely came to get us some food. I am sure you are hungry."

What, indeed, is he to tell the Commander? That his hopes have been in vain; that what is left to them from that forlorn expedition is something unusable, something broken? For who will marry her now? Wijk scowls as he walks. Of course there will be found someone to marry her. What was he thinking? She is no idiot, not necessarily so. It will all work out right in the end, he tells himself.

But no, in the end it is not to be a thing that works out right. This much he realizes as soon as he stands before the Commander and hears himself utter those words: "Deaf and mute, Sir."

Van der Stel nods slowly and looks down at his desk. He picks up a quill and twirls it absently between his fingers, then he puts it down and looks the gardener in the eye. "I want you to marry her, Mr Wijk," he says. "There is none other as worthy."

"I am afraid I must decline, Sir."

"And why is that?"

"I am not of the marrying type. I have need of only two things: my work and my freedom. She deserves better."

115

Van der Stel gets up from his desk. "And then she shall have it. You are familiar with the tavern on the strand known as the Green Door? I have received a petition from the wife, offering her refuge with them until a suitor can be found."

"That cannot be, Sir. It is a place of low reputation."

Van der Stel has moved over to his window and now stands gazing out onto the court. "It appears we may have made assumptions that were not ours to make," he says.

"Excuse me, Sir?"

But the Commander does not answer. He is thinking of something else entirely now. He is thinking of a journey he is planning, a journey that will take him away from this colony and all its petty concerns. He is going north to the copper mountain and onwards, God willing, to that place no white man has been to in a thousand years. There it is, he can see it now, he can hear it – that name, the one that sounds like the breath of wind in the grass, or like a soft beating of a drum: Monomotapa! How like a song is that word, thinks the Commander. Onward, onward, it sings, onward with boots that march, with oars that dip into a holy river, onward until there is light that glints from ivoried towers in the long lost kingdom of Solomon and of Sheba. The Commander's eyes grow distant now. He is not here in this fortress, he is out there on the plains, marching onward through the dark body of Africa to its golden, Christian heart. Mo-no-mo-ta-pa . . . Mo-no-mo-ta-pa . . .

Ah yes, there are words that sing, and there are words that are short and very much to the point. He does not want to think of Isabella Meyer and her sharp demands. For he has nothing with which to answer her. No, he cannot prove that the girls were sent out by the Company. Yes, he has paused to wonder why the man who escorted them bears the same name as her husband. And yes, there is something that does not add up, that much is quite clear. But what is he to do? Until word comes from the Company to prove the thing either way the young woman is his responsibility. It is up to him to decide where her best interests lie. "Mr Wijk," he says, turning his

116

attention back to the room. "Are you sure? Will you not take this girl and make her yours?"

Adam Wijk hesitates. Of course he is sure. The question of marriage is not a question at all. So why does he not say it, why does he stand so like a fool with his mouth open yet not saying a word? For after all, she is no use to him now, having failed to deliver on the subject of plagues. On the other hand, perhaps a profitable study could be had on the subject of deafness. The doctor has thought upon this and emerged from the exercise dejected. Of what possible use was a study on the subject of deaf-mutes out here, where even if one made an advance in deciphering the language of silence one would find oneself locked in the stillness of this great isolation. One could be the Galileo of Africa and still there would be none to listen to one's holy rantings. Such was enough to make any civilized man a little melancholic.

Commander Van der Stel raises his eyebrows. "Well?" he prompts.

And the gardener decides. "Quite possibly, Sir, I will repent of my last conviction. One should not rule out the possibility that with the passage of a certain short time I shall discover a need for marriage."

Van der Stel eyes him narrowly. This answer is neither a yes nor a no. He turns back to his window. "You have a certain short time of one month, Mr Wijk. In thirty days I will expect to hear from you concerning a date for the happy occasion. If that is not forthcoming, then you will say goodbye to your protégé and you will deliver her to her fate in the Tavern of the Green Door. It is agreed, Mr Wijk?"

The gardener agrees, then leaves and walks home along his familiar paths. He stops to correct a slave in his digging; he pauses to test the ripeness of a peach. He wonders why there is a great open space in his mind that he cannot touch. Why does he not just go back to the Castle and stand before the Commander and say a definite no? Let the girl move out, let her discover her fortunes on her own, whatever they may be. Or better still, why does he not say yes? Why does he not take this gift that is washed up from the sea for him and treasure it?

But that would be too much to ask of our gardener at this time. Let us rather pause a moment and spare a thought for him as he drifts towards the cottage that once was his alone. That heaviness in his gait, it is nothing less than the certainty that his nicely ordered life has been pushed yet another step away from him, yet one step closer to dissolution.

It had been Jan Klou who brought the *bosjesman* in. "A gift from my master," he had said to Bart Meyer, using his hook to swing the trussed-up creature off the back of his horse.

"What must I do with this?"

"Kill it, sell it, I don't care."

The taverner looked with disdain at the groaning figure lying in the dust. "Why me?" he asked.

"Lord knows," said Klou. "Now, let me have some beer."

Klou tied his horse and went inside. Meyer bent down to look at the *bosjesman*, keeping a careful distance as if it were not a man lying there but a puffader or some other untrustworthy beast. He straightened up as he heard the quick footsteps of his wife approaching. "Ah," she said. "He did not forget." Meyer fixed her with a quizzical look. She flushed slightly and eyed him back. "A business arrangement," she said.

Meyer nodded slowly.

"Well, get it upstairs," ordered Isabella. "And do something to stop that whimpering."

Meyer thought a moment. "I will give it some arrack," he said.

"And you will write down its value. It is going to pay for its lodgings."

Now Jan Klou's master sits at a table in the Green Door. He sits alone, as he always does. Herman Bolck is a farmer, though one would not easily guess it from his appearance. He wears a clean burgundy coat, breeches tied in at the knees, riding boots turned down into wide cuffs. And as one would expect from a man who rides in the wilds, he often carries a flintlock, and always a sword. Those who come to speak to him at his table in the Green Door do so not for pleasure but for reasons of commerce. There are not many who care to swap trivialities with him or share a glass of wine. The only one, perhaps, is the one who watches him from the door to the kitchen. Now, why could I not have found me a man like that, she thinks, appreciating his strong features, his arched black brows. He does not look much like a farmer at all, and in truth it is not from agriculture that he earns his wealth. If one wants to know the secret of his success, then one must ask those who come to see him at the Green Door. Or one must ask those he visits at the Castle; but of course none of these will speak. The only one who knows the greater part of it is the man who works for him, Jan Klou. And if he speaks, it will only be to curse you and tell you not to ask what is not yours to know.

Bolck finishes his mug of wine and looks to Isa Meyer, who approaches with a flagon. "No," he says, covering the mug with his hand. "I am on my way out."

"I'll write it up," she says.

Bolck gives her a cold smile. Before she leaves, he gestures towards the cage at the front of the tavern. "I see you take good care of your purchase. But you have not told me what name you have given it."

"Name?" echoes Isa, with some surprise. "I had not thought of it." She turns to her husband who has entered the tavern, carrying a keg of ale. "Come, Bart, let us think of a name for our pet."

Meyer puts down the keg and thinks deeply. "Ah, well, he is such a popular little fellow, perhaps we should call him Simon."

Bolck chuckles deeply. "That is a good name, Bart."

Isa claps her hands in agreement and marches over to the cage. "Simon, Simon," she sings. The man in the cage turns his head to hear the sound. "Little Simon in his little castle." She eyes him critically for a moment, then gets an idea. Turning around she picks up a peacock feather that Hester has left lying on the floor and brings it back to the cage. "Turn around," she commands, making a turning gesture with her finger. The *bosjesman* hesitantly turns to face away from her. "Good boy, Simon," says Isa, then reaches through the bars of the cage and thrusts the feather into the back of his loincloth where the buttocks are so shamelessly exposed. Isa stands back and laughs at the transformation she has wrought. "I knew it all along," she cries. "You are not a man. You are not a Simon at all. You are a bird. Look Bart, we will have to call him Vogelmannetje."

"Come and see the birdman at the Green Door Tavern," proclaims Bolck. "Come and give us your pennies to hear him sing."

"How like a man, he is, and yet how unlike a man at all," enthuses Isa. Then she giggles. "And just observe his hefty cock. What does a man that size need with such a tool?"

"It is because they spend so much time in fornication," explains Bart. "Just think of how their women must look."

Isa laughs and hides her mouth behind her hand.

Bolck gets up to leave and Isa follows him outside. There is a favour she wants to ask of him. Alone in the tavern, Bart stands before the cage. Vogelmannetje shifts uncomfortably in the confined space that he shares with a bucket and a wooden bar. Meyer watches him closely. Vogelmannetje, Vogelmannetje, he muses. No, the name is too long. It is not as satisfying as being able to say Hendrick! or Simon! He will have to become Vogeltje, or just Voog. Yes, that name is far better. Voog! How like a curse it sounds. The man christened Voog sits cowering on the wooden bar. Meyer looks intently at him and shakes his head. "No, that is not good enough," he scolds. "Up on the bar, with your feet like so," and he demonstrates the act of perching. Voog clambers onto the bar and crouches there, using one hand to hold onto the side of the cage. "Good," says Meyer. "You will have to practice your balance. From tomorrow, no more holding the sides."

The gardener is engaged in a task of manual labour. He has procured for himself the services of a Company slave, who he is directing in the construction of a wattle livestock pen outside his back door. It is not because he is turning to farming, it is because he can no longer live with the chickens so under foot in his cottage. Once it was possible, but now – with the additional burden of the patient – the place is just too crowded.

Is one to read from this that Adam Wijk has decided on allowing the young woman to stay? In the end one cannot, for such building operations might well have been conducted for their own merits and owe nothing to the instigation of his charge. The gardener, if truth be told, is himself still undecided. He watches the slave, and he watches also the woman as she kneels in the dirt outside the back wall of the cottage. She is planting a small garden of herbs. Rosemary, she has found, and thyme – both purloined (though quite innocently) from the Company Gardens. There are also some other herbs of more indigenous origin, taken boldly from amongst the specimens on his table and thrust into the earth of her little garden. It must still be seen whether these cuttings will take, and though the gardener is somewhat sceptical in this regard, he makes no attempt to stop her. Part of him is glad to see her so recovered, but another part is heavy to think that perhaps she assumes too much. He has not told her of the Commander's plans for her. Even if he wanted to he would find it a near impossible task to convey the specifics without the use of a spoken or written word.

How much easier it would be if they shared a common language. He has been thinking on the problem these past few days. It all begins, he assumes, with sounds. There is an alphabet that stands for sounds, and sounds stand for things in the real world. If a thing has a name, then everybody has to agree on what that thing is, or what is encompassed by that name. Luckily some things are easy, for instance a tree. There can be little dispute about the beginning and ending of such a thing.

There it is: roots, stem, and branches. If you stumble over a root you will know the cause of the pain in your toe and you will curse the tree. Or will you? Maybe you will curse God as well, or fate. But does this make the tree more than a thing of wood and shade; does it make the tree an agent of the fates, and thus a thing about which you cannot say with certainty that it begins at the tips of its roots and ends at the leaves of its crown. Wijk thinks not. That is a dangerous line of inquiry. A tree is a tree, and that is that.

Adam Wijk turns his attention back to the woman and the slave. If he is not careful he will begin to find the scene mildly idyllic. But he catches himself, remembering some urgent task he had committed himself to doing earlier. He goes inside the house and enters his sleeping compartment. The bed is neatly made; the woman's unused clothes folded carefully on top of his sea chest. Wijk looks about him, then bends to lift up the clothes and deposit them on the bed. Now he opens the chest and reaches into it, searching beneath his own clothes. When he finds the book – the Diary – he removes it from its hiding place and puts it on the bed, then he closes the chest and restores his guest's clothes to their resting place. The cautious gardener smooths the bed covers so she will not know he has been there, and then he picks up the book and goes through into the kitchen area.

There is a cabinet there with a lock that he uses to store spare coins, documents, and poisons or dangerous medicines. It contains, also, a little pouch filled with a heady green tobacco procured from the East. He calls it his Malay smoke, a perfect antidote against bodily pain and restlessness. Adam Wijk removes a key from his vest pocket and opens the cabinet, placing the book inside. Then he locks the door, pockets the key, and walks nonchalantly outside.

Four names and none

The mist comes down off the mountain. The gardener can see that it is not only mist but also rain, and it is moving towards the village. The cold makes his leg ache. He wonders if he should send for Claudius, but realises it would be unfair to drag the young man out in such conditions. Instead, he will work alone, continuing his description of *Sisyrinchium Aethyopicum*, of which there appear to be at least two varieties – branched and unbranched. He is about to turn from his contemplation of the mute scenery when, from deep within the garden, comes a sound that makes him halt. It is the peacock. He knows it is the mist that makes that mournful cry so loud, so chilling. He stands on the threshold, waiting for it to come again.

Wijk remembers what Claudius had said once when he heard that sound: "How can a thing of such beauty make so lonely a cry? Is it an agony to bear such glory?"

"Quite possibly," he had answered. "For how are we who are ugly to know?"

Adam Wijk could see his friend was not thinking only about the peacock. There was something else, something equally beautiful and tortured that had captured him. When he talked of the peacock, he was talking of the young woman, the patient.

"In Siam, I am told, the women are as beautiful as these birds. They wear crowns of iridescent feathers; they are birds of pure desire. I have heard it said they do not speak above whispers, and when they whisper it is more like singing. I will never return to my land of rain and mud," he declared. "I am altogether more at home in the sun."

Now the sun is gone and the rain begins to fall. It is a soft drizzle that makes all the world seem hushed. He can hear the drops upon the leaves, upon the thatch of his cottage. The mountain hulks sleek and black, its vertical buttresses disappearing into the cloud. When the clouds cover the top of the mountain like this it is easy to imagine the great edifice towers upwards forever. There is no end to it; the mountain goes upwards to God. He had thought once he would like to climb to the top, but now the bleakness of it repels him. On a clear day, he has been told, you can look northwards all the way up Africa, you can see the world curve out of sight across the great North, across the Commander's copper mountain, across the river Camissa to the kingdom of Monomotapa and beyond. Yet he knows it is not an infinite horizon, no matter that one might see it disappear into the white heavens, the horizon ends somewhere. It ends in the place from which it all began, a place that now shuns him, that has turned its back on him. And more than that, he thinks with a trace of a bitter smile, it is a place where he will no longer be recognized. For how would one recognize somebody who has been in exile so long? Surely they will have changed; they will have sought to erase their past and become something different, something quite unfamiliar.

He shakes his head and goes inside. He sits down at his table with the heaps of plants, both known and unknown. In the end the problem is names. What are the names of these herbs? What are they good for? Are people who they say they are? And what is the name of this creature that has come into his life, this woman who cannot speak, who comes to him with no history at all? He had searched their cabin aboard the *Tulp* for papers but had found nothing. All he knows is what he gleaned from the Captain, that the man's name was Cornelis Meyer and the women were Elsje, Katryn, Magriet, and Klara. This is all that is known. Now only one of those women remains. Which one of them is she? Elsje, Katryn, Magriet, or Klara? The woman has four names and none. Is this a lucky thing or not?

Adam Wijk picks up the fibrous bulb of the *Sisyrinchium*. In the end, these last questions do not matter greatly. For she is gone. Adam Wijk has not been able to let go of his history after all. He has let this chance pass him by.

For a while they live all three of them up in the attic – Hester, the mute woman, and the little brown man. The *bosjesman* sleeps curled up on a piece of cowhide in a corner; the other two sleep together on Hester's old mattress. At night the woman of four names and none puts her arms around Hester and rests her face in her hair. Hester breathes in the cool smell of this woman and strokes her arm where she holds her. For this brief time the world is not quite so strange. Even the man in the corner who watches them with his sad eyes is not strange. Like them, he too cannot speak. He makes a sound like birds make. Hester decides she will learn how to speak his language. Perhaps this is the language she was meant to speak all along, the one that makes people sound as though they are birds.

Silken threads

There is a woman in Amsterdam who sits at a window and looks out at the rain. She is wearing black; her face is pale. It is not clear whether this is from the cold or from some deep sorrow. To comfort herself she sips from a glass containing a clear liquor. Why are we looking at this woman alone in her house? What is she to anybody? She is Johanna Jacoba Six, daughter of a former mayor of Amsterdam and the wife of Simon Van der Stel.

When Van der Stel came out to the Cape to take up his commission he brought with him his four young sons, his daughter Caterina, and his sister-in-law Cornelia. He left behind his wife, whom he accused of being a drunkard and unfit mother. The move did not earn him many friends in Amsterdam, and he sometimes wonders now whether his current troubles with the Directors owe anything to his desertion. Still, there are some who understand and would have done the same. A woman should not be an embarrassment to her husband, and her body should not be cold and bitter. If the Commander has found anybody here at the Cape to warm his bed then he has done so in secret. Nothing is ever recorded of his taking a mistress, and nobody will claim later that she was the one who provided for his manly needs. For all we know, he is sufficient unto himself. We can imagine he has no need of women; he is wedded to this new land of his. In his heart he imagines himself the father of a nation – a new Holland that rises from the wilderness of Africa. And already his first child is born. It is a town a day's ride to the north-east. He has called this place Stellenbosch, in honour of himself. Van der Stel takes any opportunity he can get to escape the Castle and head out over the flats to the mountains where this new settlement lies. The first crops are in and they are promising indeed. Within a short while the output will rival what is produced at the Cape.

And when the Commander is not escaping to the north-east, he is fleeing to the south where he has found a piece of land for himself and where he has begun a new dream. This place on the lush slopes behind the face of Table Mount will be his monument, a great farm that will lay the standards for agriculture, and most especially, for the making of wine. He has called the place Constantia – this in honour of his muse, whose other names are Faith, Hope, and Discipline.

It is High Commissioner Van Rheede who has granted him title to the land, this being a reward for his good work here at the Cape. One assumes thus that Van Rheede is pleased with what he has found, and in this one will not be far wrong. Not everything is perfect, but much of what has been lacking has not taken too much effort to put right. Amongst other things, this is what he has found:

The slaves: thin and hungry, underdressed and ignorant. As remedy the High Commissioner has ordered the following: A second set of clothes; a blanket. A freedwoman by the name of Margaret has been appointed to teach the slave children Bible stories and the Dutch language. The Lodge itself is a shame. Odious, filthy, damp – with men and women living together in a pagan tangle. From now the Lodge will be segregated. Furthermore it has been necessary to speak sternly to the Commander about his treatment of Company property. Slaves cost money and need to be cared for. They are not to be allowed to fall ill at the first rain of winter.

The half-breeds: thirty-two yellow-skinned boys and twenty-six yellow-skinned girls – that's how many products of the illegal union between white men and slaves the High Commissioner counts when he visits the Lodge. As remedy, he orders the following: No European man shall sleep with a slave or Hottentot. It is not, in fact, a new law. It is a restate-ment of a dictate that has been in existence for some time;

everybody knows it and everybody feels at liberty to ignore it. The High Commissioner, realising it is a hopeless piece of legislation, sets down the following rider: All children born of slaves and Europeans will be freed by the age of twenty-five, or twenty-two for girls, provided they profess Christianity and speak Dutch. And any European wishing to find a wife amongst the slaves may do so, provided she is not of full colour. There are many burghers who avail themselves of this opportunity.

The exiles: Van Rheede listens to the Commander's complaints in this regard: "The Cape, Sir, has become a dumping ground for every troublemaker and rebel on earth. It is not fair." The High Commissioner admits it is a problem. The Company is expanding in the East and is all the time encountering forces of resistance. What must be done with the leaders of these malcontents? It would not be fair to execute them all, so let them rather be sent far away to a place where they can't cause too much mischief. The Commander now sits with a growing population of these *woelgeeste*. In truth, he is not unsympathetic towards their plight. He finds many of them to be highly civilised and to offer pleasant company. Van der Stel is at present host to the King of Macassar's brother, Dain Mangale, as well as the Prince of Macassar, Crain Lambungu, with his wife and two slaves. This group was previously incarcerated in the Castle in Batavia, where they cost the Company twenty rix dollars a month, plus rice, salt, and pepper. Van der Stel, of course, is instructed to keep them for less. What can be done, he asks? The High Commissioner has no answer. Instead, he orders Van der Stel to pay the king's brother six rix dollars a month so that he might buy himself luxuries.

The Hottentots: the High Commissioner orders that nothing should be done to disrupt the peaceful and profitable co-existence of Hottentots and colonists. The wars of supremacy are now a thing of the past, the issue of who is boss having been established in no uncertain terms. It is of some concern to the High Commissioner that the Hottentots insist on living a nomadic life and wandering where they please. The solution: Hottentot tribes shall be tempted by means of gifts to settle down and accept the boundaries defined by their masters.

When Van Rheede continues on to Batavia he will send a glowing report back to his masters in the Netherlands. The Lords need not worry about their fledgling colony in the South – it is in good hands. But in his private instructions to the Commander he will offer some advice: Be courteous with your officials, he will write, do not speak to them like common labourers. A Commander must be polite and humble; he must listen to his subordinates, he must not love himself above the people he serves. Words like this could be seen as a mere formality, a mere stating of the obvious. But in this case the High Commissioner intends them to be taken to heart and acted upon, for they are motivated by troublesome reports. People have come to him and told him of things they have seen but have been too afraid to speak aloud. One is compelled to believe, they have said, that the Commander is a god of light and industry. One must look at all the work he is initiating, all the cattle he is bringing in, all the farmers he is settling happily on fertile land. One must not see the unjust bannings and the freeburghers starving on their plots with no market for their goods. One must not question the allocation of trade concessions and the whereabouts of goods from ships that are wrecked along the coast. No, one must not see that this Commander is a Janus god, with one face turned always to hidden things.

The stern words of the Commissioner sting the master of the Cape. This is why he rides now to Constantia, to escape to the solitude of his distant domain. There he will dream his dreams, and he will brood also on his failures. He will sink into a glowering silence. Commander Van der Stel knows in his strongest moments that he can drive away the darkness from himself and from the land – he knows that his fondest ambition is possible, that this far-off place in Africa can be made to resemble in every way a province of the Netherlands. Nothing less is good enough. And he will do what it takes –

regardless of who finds themselves displeased by his actions – to make it so. In his weakest moments, however, he realizes what is plain for all the world to see: that some day he will have to admit defeat.

The rider, strong of arm and loose of limb, drives his horse through the drift. He has come a fair distance, that much is apparent from his clothing – the linen shirt now browned with dust and sweat, the leggings flying loose of their garters. The man's name is Anton Visser. He is twenty-one years old and he is riding this way because he can, because he is young and strong. When he comes into the town he will let the horse kick up dust, he will set up a great clamour so that people will look. The rider will cause old women to curse, but they will not stop themselves looking him up and down and wondering what they would have made of him had they not lost the requisite litheness of frame. Perhaps he will be for their daughters or their granddaughters, but all the same may God strike him from his horse for his arrogance! Pride comes before a fall, you'll see.

Anton is the oldest of five. Apart from him there are three brothers – Barend, Arent, and Lukas, and a sister, Anneke. They live on their farm near the Tijgerberg, half way to Stellenbosch. It is time for them all to be married off, especially that Anneke – already sixteen and walking about like the eternal Virgin. There is a highway beaten to the farm Allemanskloof by the suitors for this beauty, but none have been found suitable. Old man Zacharias Visser will have none of these ragged merchants and retired sailors. He wants somebody finer, somebody educated. He has learned to read, but he has not been able to pass on the desire for it to his sons. Their only interests are hunting, fishing, and looking for women. The third oldest, Arent, has sometimes picked up a book, but the patriarch has not had the patience to teach him. And his daughter, well she has taught herself the alphabet, but he has not had the inclination to instruct her further. She is a girl, after all. Zacharias Visser wants now to bring somebody into the fold who will broaden the family's horizons. Until such a one can be found, the girl must learn to contain herself.

Not so for the boys. They may ride to town like the horsemen of the Apocalypse and find what pleasure they can. It is only boyish vigour and can cause no harm. One day they too will be married, and then they will have to act like respectable gentlemen.

Up on Lion's Head now the flagman's daughter lowers her spyglass. Nobody can mistake that rider down there on his black horse. She hides her smile from her father. "Nothing happening," she says. "I feel ill. I'm going home." Abram Moolman nods his head. "If you have to." Greet Moolman waits till she is round the back of the pinnacle and then she begins to run.

Anton Visser has several items of business he needs to attend to before seeking more pleasurable pursuits. He needs to see the blacksmith and the Company grocer, but first he needs to visit the granary to collect on an outstanding debt. Before he enters the airy building he realises he is being watched from a window of the upper room. He assumes it is a Company official and pays it no attention.

The observer is, in fact, the new teacher. He stands often thus, watching the world below. All day long the farmers and their sons come bringing the produce of their fields, their horses damp and lathered from long rides. He watches the strong young men, and sometimes they glance up at him. The teacher moves away from the window now. The children look at him expectantly. One plus one is two, one plus two is three. How much further does this go? they wonder. But Meester Van Arckel is not thinking about numbers. For some reason he is thinking about love. It came to him as he turned back to the room – a single line, a question, like something a poet might receive from his muse; and the question went thus: Who shall say whence love comes? The teacher stands before his pupils, trying to remember where the lesson had been left off. He chides himself for neglecting his charges, for wasting time on frivolous thoughts. There can be no love for him. This has been made quite clear.

Greet Moolman waits in the Garden for the man with the black horse. When he has finished whatever business he has in the town he will come to her there. She will show him the hidden place she has prepared. There, under the cover of a loquat tree, she will lie back and let him take her.

Isa Meyer sits the young woman down before the mirror in her room. She runs her hands through the girl's dark hair. "Why have they kept you from me, why? And just look at these tangles. Lord knows what they have done to you in that place." She takes her comb and begins running it through her tresses. "We will have you looking like new," she croons. The girl watches back from the mirror. "Now, let us think of what we shall call you. Such lovely hair, such lovely eyes. I think we must call you Maria. It is the name of the sea." The girl smiles as if she has heard. "Do you like that name, then? Good. Now let us see about your clothes. This peasant costume will not work at all; we need that lovely silk thing they carried off the ship for you. We are going to make you look as beautiful as we can, my dear. There are people who want to meet you."

There arrives for Adam Wijk a small parcel. It is not delivered while he is at home but is left before his door for him to find on his return. The gardener picks up the cloth-wrapped bundle and opens it, discovering a small earthen pot of the type used to contain jams or preserves. He smiles and carries the gift inside. It is not unusual for him to receive such donations; it is often, in fact, in such humble things as these that he is paid for his occasional doctorings of the poor folk. He tries to imagine what recent patient it could be, but there are several that spring to mind. In the kitchen he tears off a hunk of bread from the loaf he bought the day before and opens the pot. It is jam of some sort, and judging from the colour most probably quince. Adam Wijk is pleased, for this is his favourite. Whoever it is who brought the gift, they know him well. He dips the bread into the red jelly and takes a generous bite. Ah, very pleasing, he thinks. It is rather more tart than other examples of quince jam he has tasted, but he finds this quite to his liking. The gardener allows himself another generous helping before closing the lid and telling himself he would be wiser to ration the stuff and not act so like a sensuous heathen.

But it is too late. He has already taken enough of the poison into him to do its work. The first thing he feels is a heaviness in the stomach, a numbness. He is about to go out and resume his work in the garden but he pauses before the door as the first wave of sickness hits him. His head begins to whirl. There are little spots of light before his eyes. Wijk moves carefully to his chair, thinking he will rest there a while longer until this spell of discomfort is passed. Perhaps it is his heart, he thinks. He presses against his chest and is alarmed at the rate of its beating. Adam Wijk tries to rise from his chair, thinking he should call for help, that this could be more than a mere fainting spell and that death could be close at hand. But he cannot move. The room sways, black shapes run along the rafters, shadows grow into creatures that breathe, swelling and pulsing in the gloom. "Oh God, oh God," moans the gardener. It is all he can think to say. "Oh God, oh God." But, of course, it is not a prayer, and there is no answer. Only the shadows come nearer, breathing there in the corner, there behind the curtain. In the darkness of the pitched roof now the forest of suspended bottles begins to swing wildly as if some wind were driving it. He is afraid that the lids of the bottles will fly open and all the demons imprisoned there will swarm out in a great buzzing cloud, that they will come to him and force themselves upon him and he will be overcome by their filth, by their putridness. And it will be his just deserts. Who was he to imagine he could redeem himself? All his grand designs, all his working at salvation, all is as nothing before this living, breathing, hell. Adam Wijk tries to call out, but his mouth is dry and all that emerges is a dull, pathetic, croak. He closes his eyes, hoping to shut out the swaying of the world, but inside it is far worse. He cannot escape, he is locked into his torment – Oh, will it never cease?

When he awakens it is late afternoon. The cottage is darker, though it is no longer swaying and breathing. Adam Wijk is lying on the floor. He has thrown up, and his face rests in a sickly pink gruel of quince pips and half digested bread. "Oh God," he groans as he rises to a sitting position. He looks about him. There is nothing behind the curtain, no great beast lies breathing on his bed, of this he is sure. He looks at the rafters – it is absolutely quiet there, no running shapes, no unstoppered bottles, no putrid artefacts swarming there like flies. So, he thinks, touching his chest. So it is not a matter of the heart, this visitation of ill, it is a matter of evil intent. He does not want to think now about who it could be or why. He wants to clean himself up; he wants to sit outside in the air and let the numbness leach from him and life return. Suddenly he feels very lonely there in his cottage. It is too quiet, too easy to slip again into nothingness and to disappear without anybody knowing or caring. He finds himself wishing the girl were with him, just for now. She would bring him a bowl of water and light a fire to make some tea. She would look concerned, and she would try to ask him what had happened. But, of course, the girl is otherwise engaged at this time.

Johanna Jacoba Six dresses in black and sits childless in a room in Amsterdam. She is drinking gin. She ties knots in embroidery silks and whispers the name of her husband while she does it. May his hearth be cold, may his bed be of ice, and may he die in winter with no-one to watch over him. Let him suffer, O Lord, the same fate as I.

A dark tide

In the far outposts of the world the people walk always with one eye to the land and one eye to the sea's horizon. For this is the direction from where all new things come. People come, letters come, strange creatures wash up from the deep. For those sent far away from home, all new things come from across the waters. And so also do the missing parts of their stories, the missing parts of their hearts. It is their hope that one day, on some unexpected morning, the missing thing will arrive and that they will recognize it and say, Ah, this is that of which I could never speak but which I have sought my whole life. Here it is; I have felt its shape within my heart since the time I was born, though I have been blind to it and deaf and could never take the measure of it or hear its name. This is their hope, and there are indeed those who have found their saviour this way. Yet those who walk the shores with empty and restless hearts are never sure that they will be like them. Perhaps they will be like those others who have found upon the strand a thing that appears not familiar and beautiful to them but wild and monstrous, a thing that cannot be tamed and made to speak in manners pleasing to their ears. Yes, quite possibly they will be like these. For what else should one expect to come from across this dark and pitiless sea? One should not expect one's familiar words and measures. Those who live in the far outposts at the edge of the known should not expect this at all, and secretly they do not.

They have gone down to the beach to look across the water, the man of many words and the girl of but one. "Magic," she says to him holding out a shell. Mr Cardamom looks at the shell with disdain. "A bigger one," he says. The girl scratches in the debris at the water's edge and finds, as instructed, a bigger shell. Cardamom takes it in his hand, displays it to the crowd, makes a sudden gesture with both hands, and displays his palms once more – this time empty. Hester claps and then casts about her for another shell. But her friend looks out over the sea, his eyes are distant. When the girl holds out her hand to him for another trick he does not see. She lets the shell fall and looks out to the ocean. The sea is heavy with winter, the colours all dissolving into shades of grey. A little way to their left is Piet's upside-down boat. Hester has already been to check if he is home but has found him not to be. They are alone on the beach, but for the gulls and the thin-legged birds that chase the surf up and down the sand.

"Can you keep a secret?" asks Mr Cardamom. The girl nods. "The world is round," he says. "It is round on the outside and round on the inside, if you follow." Hester nods. "So even if one has come to the ends of the earth, then is one barely at the beginning. It is a roundybout world, my girl, and you should know this, for it's a lesson few men or girls are eager to learn, but that the roundness makes it not possible to be going anywhere, least of all if, in one's going, one is going away from a something you hope never to see again. You follow?"

Hester thinks of the place she came from and wonders if this means she will see it again. She wonders if she will recognize it when she gets there, because she can't remember anything of the place, it being too long ago and she too young at the time of leaving. This thinking bothers her, so she stands up and runs after a gull that has been stalking them, eyeing them for tidbits. Then she finds a driftwood stick and swishes it in the air like a sword. All above them now the gulls circle in lazy alarm. Hester begins looking for shells again. She finds three that are nice and shapely and not damaged at all. There's a white one with a pink blush, a brown one spotted with black, and a strange green thing with horns. She puts them in her apron, holding the end up with her left hand to form a basket. Her searches take her in the direction of Piet's house, where

136

she stops and checks underneath again, just to make sure. Then she takes out one of the nicest shells – the white one – and leaves it just inside. She straightens and moves quickly away, carrying on further up the strand. When she has gone far enough she lets the hem of her apron fall and sets the remaining shells free. She watches the surf come up and wash over them, then she turns and runs back down the beach, her arms outstretched like a bird.

"Are you a parrot now?" calls Mr Cardamom. "See, my trick worked. My powers are not to be doubted."

Hester comes to a landing, breathless. No, she shakes her head. No parrot I. She calls up the word, that strange word heard only once before. "R-o-o-k," she tries. "Rukh."

"Aaah," cries Cardamom, shielding his eyes. "A terrifying creature, a gargoyle upon the wing. God spare us all!"

Hester puts forefinger to lips. Hush. She cups hand to ear. Cardamom closes his eyes and listens. Presently he begins to nod his head. "Ah yes, I hear it. The roar of her fiery wings. Her passage through the air – a hissing, burning arrow!"

Hester sits down and looks out over the sea. Her lips move as if she is whispering, as if trying out a word but not speaking it. Cardamom tries to apprehend what word it is. "Malady, malaprop, Mohammetan. I give up." He leans back on the sand. "It is a long word; too long for me."

Hester looks at him. "Madagascar," she says.

"Ah, now I have you!" cries Cardamom. "Madagascar, your home, your fiery nest! It be over yonder, child. If we had a ship we could go there tomorrow." Hester points down the beach to Piet's house. "And we will be drownded before the sun goes down," he says, shaking his head. "It is a big ship we'll be needing. With sails and rigging and men to climb them."

Hester looks away. She gets up and goes down the strand, kicking at the shells and driftwood. Out in the bay there is a ship about to leave. They have been loading it all day, barrels and wooden boxes, and men passing bundles up the sides. They are going that way, over the horizon. Is it onwards, or is it backwards to the beginning? If you carry on going, as Mr Cardamom says, will you return to where you started, and will you then know where you are, or will you know only that you really are lost, and by your travels you have merely proven this as fact? Hester sits down, twisting absently at the hem of her apron. On the ships you sail and sail and never reach the end of the world. The ships are always sailing and never resting, always finding some new land and making it old. Where does it all begin, and where does it end? How strange is this world and beyond reason. Hester stabs with a piece of driftwood in the sand. Other people know how the world works, but she does not. She is the tavern girl, the halfwit who knows nothing, not even where she comes from or who her mother and father are. She knows not even how to speak. Hester looks out to the ship that is about to leave. They are pulling up the anchor now. The shouts of the sailors carry across the water. I have come ashore, she thinks, not even knowing my own name. Hester, Hester. Whose name is this? It is not mine. Mr Cardamom came off a boat, just like me, and he changed his name. His father did not own that name. I can see he dreamed it himself.

Hester looks up to see a figure coming towards her along the beach – a man, walking as if the sand were heavy mud and were sticking to his feet. It is Piet, coming home from the tavern. She can hear Mr Cardamom call a greeting, but Piet does not respond. He goes straight to his house and dives under it like some lanky crab. Hester gets up and goes back to her friend. Together they watch the upside-down boat, from which are presently heard loud snores. "It is very much like a guitar or a drum," says Mr Cardamom. "The hollowness of it magnifies the sound by principles mysterious."

They listen to Piet's troubled sleep, with Mr Cardamom offering speculations about the possible contents of the poor man's dreams. Hester shakes her head or nods to indicate which scenes she judges possible and which just invention. Eventually the snores grow less resonant and they are both agreed that he is now sailing his house across a giant lake made all of wine.

They are silent a while and then Mr Cardamom speaks: "Do you want to hear another secret?" he asks.

Hester doesn't know if she wants to, for the last one has made her sad. But then she sees that her friend is himself looking grave, so she nods her head.

"A man has to tell his secrets to somebody in the end, otherwise they eat at him, like worms and serpents, you understand?" Hester nods. "Good. And I know you will not speak it, for you are not like those who speak when they should not. You are one of those who hold their peace and keep a-lookout – for what I cannot say, but one day perhaps you will know, and then you will be counted amongst the lucky of this world."

Hester shifts uncomfortably. "Secret," she says, prodding his leg with the driftwood stick.

"Indeed, well, it is no short secret this, it is a story type of secret. It begins – as all stories do – with a once-upon-a-time, and this once upon a time was some twenty years ago or thereabouts, where there lived a young man."

Hester smiles and points at him.

"No, not me, child, another man. And don't ask me to say what man it was, for that is the part of my secret you need not know, suffice to say it was a man. It was in a place far away from here, in a great city upon a river. You have not been there, I should think, though I know you came here from a ship. It is the place where I was born, my far and distant and never-to-be-seen-again home."

Hester holds up her hands in question.

"Why never to be going home? It is plain before your eyes, girl. Look at this Cardamom and see what he has become in his years away. He is now quite otherwise, would you not say? Quite upside-down in a roundybout world, that's what he is become. He is no longer a comfortable Englishman, he is a something in-between, a something that is a vexation to himself and to his new companions likewise."

Hester shakes her head vigorously and strikes him on the leg with her stick.

"All right, I'll not be continuing in that vein, and besides –

139

we have lost the plot. We were talking of something else, were we not? A man, as I said, a man that lived in London town, though he was a foreigner and but newly come to that place."

When they leave the beach it is almost dark. Mr Cardamom bows to her at the Green Door and then enters alone. Hester goes round to the kitchen to see if she can sneak in unseen. She does not want to be called to work now. She does not want to see the men who drink and the poor creature in his cage. She wants to be in the darkness of her room. Hester slips into the house and goes into the *voorkamer* with its single bed. She wishes she was still sleeping up in the loft with her sister, for tonight will come nightmares, this she knows. Mr Cardamom should not have told her of those things that happened in that once-upon-a-time that was not so long ago at all.

And yes, she does dream. She walks in the city with its palace where a king and queen live and where a river flows so wide you can sail upon it with ships. She watches the ships from a bridge that is like no other bridge in the world. There are houses upon it and towers and mills and the heads of dead men upon spikes. Underneath it there is a dark tide that shakes the pillars day and night. All is a-tremor with it, the water flowing like a silent army making all the world shake with its ceaseless marching. She watches through the stone railings, seeing heads and faces pale below the surface. Men and women go by, children go by cold and blue. Every one of them looks like her, though their eyes are plucked by ravens, their ears and noses torn by rats. Now they are singing to her. They sing softly, singing We in the river we have no names, we in the churchyards we have no names. We leave our bones for the future but they will have on them no names. Ten thousand bones of the leg, five thousand bones of the jaw, innumerable teeth, wads of matted substance that once was hair, dark or fair you will not tell; so many of us undone. So she weeps into the river and the words of the nameless multitudes flow and flow against the pillars and all is set a-tremble, all trembles without cease.

~

Mr Cardamom takes her with him through the city. His beard is gone, his hair has lost its grey. He lives in a dark alley where the wooden houses crowd upwards, jutting out over the mud and cobbles, blocking out the sun. It smells of burnt porridge in those warrens, of smouldering seacoal, human waste. There are shadows that dart along windowsills and lintels, that drop from clapboard eaves and fall to the ground and vanish. They are rats. Rats. Not like any she has ever seen. They eat through the walls of the jammed tenements, making of the whole city one big house for themselves. There is nothing that lives as comfortably as they, except perhaps the king and queen.

He works in the tanner's yard down by the Fleet River. A terrible stench it is, the hides swimming in piss and dogshit for days until they are cured. Perhaps it is a good thing to work there all the day, for when he comes home he cannot smell the sickness that rises from the churchyards. He watches the carrion crows pulling morsels from the generous earth and smells not a thing. St Martin's, St Michael's, St Paul's – how many are buried there he cannot say and does not care. They are not people now, they are mere numbers on the weekly bills. When he comes home he finds there will be an increment to this figure. His mother lies in a cold fever; his father puts his hand across his mouth to muffle him. Let not the neighbours hear. Let not the men with their boards and their locks come to seal us in our tomb.

But I could not stay, he tells her. I turned and ran. There was a physician I knew of, one of the last still in the city. I begged him and so he came. I do not know why he followed me, for he could see I was poor and had no payment for him. So he came to our house and before entering he set a bunch of wormwood to a pot of coals he carried and made a smoke, waving it about to fill the air with its fumes. Then he came to where my mother was and he said, Sure enough, it is the tokens. Are you to lance them? asked my father, but he said no. The people die of the lancing quicker than of the Plague, so he said. My mother was cold and she was growing mad. We had tied her to her cot where she cried out curses and spoke prophecies of ghastly things. The physician asked what moneys we had to pay and my father said there was nothing, he not being able to work these past months with everybody fled. So the physician nodded and we thought he was to leave, for in truth there was hardly any person ever cured of the Plague and it would be a waste, anyways, to spend good money on it. But he did not leave. He took from his bag a dried, black thing, which was the carcass of a toad, and he laid it on her belly, tying it there with cloth. Then he gave her also of a Mixture whose composition he would not reveal, only to say it was recommended by Hippocrates, or some such, and that it had cured whole cities likewise afflicted in ancient times. And then he was gone, and soon after came the men with their boards to shut us in our tomb. Oh Lord, oh Lord, I shiver just to think on it. Pray you will never live like that, all closed as in a great familial tomb. Pray the pestilence does not return, as even now it was almost upon us once more. And do not fret now, child, for we lived not long in that pit. On the third day we thought it is this day that we will leave a burden for the deadcart, but it was not so. There was mother sitting up in her bed and asking why is it so dark. She is brought to life! The toad upon her belly was sodden with the poisons and we cast it from the window – and there away it went, hopping down the street alive with its putrid waters. So the judgment passed over us, and truly we were in debt to that man. I resolved to find him, and contrive a way of giving him payment.

There were two things I knew of him. The first was that he lived in the house of Robert Jameson in Covent Garden. And the second was his name – John Taylor. Two more things I came to know about this were that Jameson was more fond of his ships than of his own life; he choosing to stay in the town and not flee as any people of worth were doing. And this John

Taylor was making out to be what he was not. I speak not of his profession but of his name. Such a good English name sat upon his head askew like a stolen hat. For he was no Englishman, see – he was a something else. And this something else – which is what I figured out in those days in the tomb when I had naught else to do but think – was almost certainly, almost beyond a doubt, a thing that was not a Frenchman or a Spaniard or a German. It was a Dutchman, sure as anything. A spy, a saboteur, an agent of the enemy – this is how I took it first, for we were at that time not friends with Holland but enemies, and those of us the Plague was not feeding to the worms were being sent to the fishes by De Ruiter and his mates on the high seas. And then I thought no, he has nothing to spy upon here, the King being fled and Parliament gone and all the Lords and their fancies gone away, there was nothing at all but to stay and bring comfort to those condemned. He had changed his name, that much was true, but it was only so as to live amongst his people's enemies and not find himself hanged as a spy and his head stuck on the bridge for an ornament of ridicule. That was the first secret I had of him, but it is not the one that matters to us here. There is another that comes later, much later when the Plague has run its course and the Fire has come and purged the city and I am gone out of it and have become a Traveller and a collector of strange tales.

Diary

Notes of an Ordinary Doctor in the Year of Plague 1665
(For his own use, personal, and not for printing,
even if this were to fall into unauthorised hands by theft,
misplacement, &c.)

June 4

Today exceeding hot and the worst I have known since coming here. I to the Red Dragon for ale, and there meet Dr S–who tells that all should leave who can for this weather is to the contagion as a flame to powder and we shall all soon regret our tardiness and know that he speaks the truth. I would argue with him there but know he is regarded highly and is a friend of Mr. Boyle, having published a Treatise on fevers, the which I have not read but resolve to do so at soonest. Already hereabouts are doors shut up and red marks upon them and I suspect soon I shall be pressed to give help, though there is likely to be no money had for it.

By which course of thought I am reminded of what I saw yesterday and did not record but will do so now, this being an observation of the MAKING OF PROFIT IN TIME OF DISTRESS: And this concerns those doctors rightly called Quacks which now are become a plague of themselves and do more harm than the *Pestis* (and not just myself of this opinion but others too). So I, walking by More-fields, see one upon a stage there and a crowd gathered about. This 'Worthy Doctor of Constantinople' as he so calls himself, and wears a Turk's hat to prove it, brings up a man onto the planks close to death, his eyes rolling, the black marks clear on his neck. Now the sick man cries out and begins to strike his head upon a post until there is a mess of

144

blood on it, and this a sight almost to weep for though I know it is a pretty trick. Then comes the Quack and pours an amount 'Equal to a Nutmeg' (so saying) in the man's mouth and lo, he does cease with his crying and turns placid and full of words praising this 'Miracle' of him being returned to health. I want to shout out Good Fellow, is that a chicken feather I spie in that blood upon the post? And these great orbs upon the fellow's neck, are they not rather too black and rather sooty, and have they not already smudged his shirt? But I have no chance for there is a great motion of the poor forwards like so many sheep clutching alms and crying out for their bottle of deliverance. It is a shame to witness it, but there is nothing can be done.

Herewith a true cure learned today but not for Plague, it is for the FALLING SICKNESSE: Take a hot iron or melted wax and make a burn upon the neck, so to create an Issue or Blister. Whatever is in the braine of a putrefied nature will gather in the Issue and be drained.

June 10
There are some who say the people fear in vain for this contagion will soon abate. But the old men remember the last plague and say this one is the same. And some do say it will be the worse, for the oppression of this heat. I say there is no reason for alarm as yet. This week as recorded in the Bills there are but 50 dead of plague in all of London. It will all be brought to an end if the Lord Mayor but takes action. Herewith sure measures by which it is reckoned this affliction might be contained:

Fires – these to be lit in every street and made to burn from sunset to sunrise. Fires also to be carried on the river up and down to dry the air.

Guns – to be discharged upon the hour to break the miasmas.

Dung heaps – these to be cleared. Rats and vermin to be killed for their unwholesomness which does attract putrid vapours.

Quacks (this a remedy of my own invention) – to be arrested and forced to take their own poisons.

June 13

This day have begun what could not be put off longer, viz. Treatment of the Poor, if they are Struck with Plague. It was no intended thing but came by accident where I walked from the Wapping docks back through the City, I wishing to save the fare of a boat. It were better I had endured the expense and carried myself safely by on the water than I had descended into that place which is a very Cooking Pot of the Plague. On Thames Street I cannot go twenty paces but that they call out 'Doctor, have mercy on my poor childe,' or some such thing, and I may not walk by but must go in there, even if it be a poor place and of little hope.

RESOLUTION: To find sure methods by which a person may be cured of this ill. And talk to Dr S– further on this subject of fevers, if he has not already left us and gone for safety.

June 14

AN EXPERIMENT: I go by water to the house of Dr T– to see the cutting of one dead by the Plague (he not revealing where the corpse was procured, or with whose permission; notwithstanding it is a good experiment and one with the conclusion presently given). This being: that the whole body of it is filled with an ichorous liquid, the veins o'erflowed and the tissue as if putrefied, though T– protests that the corpse was fresh dead the day before (it not yet causing a noisomness in the Aire, or a stench). Furthermore is the truth of what we have learned previously confirmed: viz. that cold and dry be the conditions for health, and that which is warm and moist being deleterious. Such good influences are North winds and Easterlies which are dry. The worst are Southerly winds, especially those from Arabie, from whence it is thought that this present affliction does come.

The experiment concluded I return on foot through the old City. In places there one cannot breathe for all the fires they light, and this is a good measure against the Plague (serving to dry the air) but I do fear that so much open flame

146

will bring down another type of judgement upon us and we might be cured of the pestilence in a manner we may regret. Through Black-Friars which as always exceeding noisome, but more so from the heat of this summer, and I having a mind to speak to R– about the custom here of throwing the offals and carcasses of oxen on the bank of the ditch. In other nations there is not such a slovenlyness, but perhaps he will be offended and so I shall not ask but only wonder, and consider a moment why I came here and dwell on the question of whether it were a good thing or no, or whether I had the choice or merely thought I did – Fate being a thing beyond our means to know. (But if I had refused, then perhaps my life would be saved and I not lose myself to this Plague, but also I would lose that which is dearer to me than life – and now I will not say more for I have promised silence on this).

A purchase

In Africa, it is said, there is a golden land with a golden king, and the king is a wise man and his riches were once the envy of Solomon. It is also said that the people there are tall and beautiful, and that once this was the home of Sheba, the one who came from the South with no warning and stole away the great king's heart. And furthermore, something that is spoken about this land is that there is a river, and this river has a name as beautiful as its people. It is called Camissa, but nobody can remember why.

Many are the people from the North who have heard of this place and written about it and marked it upon their maps, though nobody has seen it for themselves. On a map you will find it in letters spaced wide so that it covers as much of the paper as possible, it will say M o n o m o t a p a. Or maybe it will say, if the mapmaker has a large expanse of paper to cover, K i n g d o m   o f   M o n o m o t a p a.

The Commander of the settlement at the Cape is marching on that kingdom now. His official purpose is to find the mountains of copper that the Hottentots have spoken of, but somewhere beyond those mountains, somewhere perhaps not too far off, he knows there will be a river, and it will be the one. There are fifteen wagons and over a hundred men in this grand expedition. The wagons are laden with provisions for a long journey. There are barrels of water, casks of arrack, cases of biscuit and dried meat. There are also two light cannon to ward of attack by man and beast, and there is one boat. This is for the Camissa.

Behind him in the Cape the officials sleep peacefully. The

148

members of the Council of Policy meet with Secunde Andries de Man and together they look to the running of the settlement. There are no outbursts, there are no rages against incompetence. Civilization continues its quiet march undisturbed.

In the Tavern of the Green Door Isabella Meyer approaches the man sitting alone at his table. "It is time," she says to him. "We have waited long enough."

The man smiles in his mirthless way. He has indeed been waiting. It has been a while since he paid his Spanish silver in expectation of this moment. Not yet, the taverner's wife had always told him. There are too many eyes upon us. Wait until the Commander is gone. So now the time has come, and Isabella points to the ladder going up into the loft. "Up there," she says. "She is waiting for you."

Diary

June 16

Ventured not far abroad this day but stayed close about. To my apothecary B– on the matter of preparations and there a pleasant discourse on this thing which vexes us both – the composition of True remedies and False; and how a man may make a greater profit from a lie than from what he knows to be real. Whereby thus to a sure Test by which one may know the difference, and this being that one should ask of the one purveying the Cure what is the Method by which it cures, and if he has an answer that satisfies then is it a Real Cure, if not then make haste away from him for his Remedy will do harm to body and purse alike.

As for the Method, let it be any reply to the Causes of this Plague, which are several: The First being unseasonableness of the weather (for which there is no Cure and any that is is False); the Second being miasms of dung heaps, pits, and unsavoury places, for which take that which will break the setting of the aire, or its putrefaction, and for this meaning smokes of brimstone, amber, saltpeter, and smokes of herbs – rue, wormwood, tamarisk, and cloves, and for the mouth – myrrh and zeodary; Third is the reason of the susceptible body, meaning those whose Pores are open and thus more readily accepting of Infected aires, as also those whose veins are full of gross humours and infected qualities, especially those whose bodies are moist and Phlegmatic, and also those who are bent towards putrefaction by reason of grossness, sluttishness, poorness, lethargy, costiveness and bearing of children, for which the standard treatments do apply; and Fourth is those whose starres are pestilentially bent against them for which there is no cure but Prayer.

By contrast to above, here are those who are least apt to suffer this infection: Old people for their bodies being cold and dry; milch-nurses for the children sucking the evil juices from them; those with open sores, ulcers, hemorrhoids from which the humours are drained; and lastly those that keep themselves apart from others and are calm with little passions by which the humours may become inflamed.

A CURE:
Take a toad, skin it, make an amulet from the skin and while still wet tie it in the pit of the arm. It will raise a welt, from which the corrupted liquors of the blood will be expressed.

June 17
To Deptford to search the Navy places for sailor's remedies. This against the day R-'s ships come home. Little success, given the sea war and the great drain of the pestilence. I have not near enough of simples and suchlike to acquit myself well if R– were to call on me to earn my board. Perhaps the ships will not come till all here is well. It were better so.

Home again by foot, all the while thinking of my Employer and of my fortunes and how I would not fail. This until a happy distraction in Drury Ln. where I spy one standing in a doorway, very fetching and complimentary of myself and I would go in there, but then I recall my Fate again which has brought me far better, and I say to her I have nothing to spare and God keep her. In truth I have her price but will not pay it, for I am spoken for (not by Marriage but by Love).

June 19
Through St Giles and home to Covent Garden where I find the servants out and all exceeding quiet. And in the kitchen not even a fire going for this evening's meal. Perhaps they are sick or dead. Not so, I say (and I am speaking to myself more now than before and wonder where it will lead) they are merely out in the town, having to go far to procure meate or bread

with the shops closing now. I find there a bucket and fill it with water to wash my hands and also my head beneath the wig, which is itching from the heat. Here is a question I heard today: Would you buy a new periwig in these times if it cost but half the normal price? And I said no (being wise to this question), for who knows if the owner of the hair is not the half of his normal self, or less. I will not wear a dead man's head, even if it be odoured like a rose garden or offered gratis. And this reckoned a good joke, yet true.

Now, to the thing which makes all well, though it can only end in tears. (And it will do no good to protest as last that I will desist from writing on this subject – it is not possible!) Thus I alone in the house with her, Beth and Grace out and R– at his work. What a traitor I am and deserve every punishment that will come to me. But thinking not on my guilt I go upwards, making my shoes heavy on the staircase knowing she will hear it where she reclines in her Library. I open the door and see her face. She does not look at me but plays that I am a servant or that she has not heard. Forgive me, my Lady, but it is not that volume by Mr. Hooke that has made you blush. (Lord, when the Plague is gone I will burn these papers and all their Vanities.)

And now I will say no more on this subject but make note only of things Important and of an aid to Physic; or of notable things said that will come of use in future, God Willing (meaning – if we are spared).

ADDENDUM: (And following from above) herewith a note concerning children in time of contagion – Let them be protected against Worms. This evil arises from a putrefaction of excrementitious humours in the bowel, causing a heat which doth inflame the blood and cause openness to Infection. To remove Worms, a mixture as follows:

Wormseed two drachmes, Seamosse,
Harts horn burnt a drachme each, a scruple each of Piony
root, white Dittany and magister of Coral;
Make all into a powder and take in any liquor.

Cabo de Bona Esperança
1686–1687

Two letters

It is almost a year since the *Tulp* sailed into the bay. Summer is here again in all its restless brilliance, and Commander Van der Stel has this very day returned from his travels in the interior. Now Adam Wijk sits with a problem. He has not been looking forward to his superior's return, for while he has been away something has happened.

The gardener stands in his kitchen now, looking out through the back window. He spies his three chickens and one poor goat, and also he watches the back of the woman as she crouches there in the dust feeding the birds from her hand. The goat nuzzles at her hair. It has been two weeks that she has been living here with him again, two weeks since she absconded from the house on the strand and returned to her refuge in the garden. What now, thinks Wijk? What trouble now?

Trouble is a small, white envelope addressed to a certain Jacob Huismans in the town of Delft. In it is a letter, and the writer has begun it thus: *My Dear Papa.* The writer then goes on to relate the sad circumstances of her life since last she wrote. There are many things that have gone against her; many plans that have come to naught. Still she is without her fortune, and still her husband shows no sign of regaining it. She hopes her father is well, and she makes a request. She asks that inquiries be made regarding a certain doctor. There are too many things not known about this man, she explains. And where there are things not known, there is almost certainly a reason for them not being known, a reason that could change everything.

Of course, the writer knows that even if the inquiry thus instigated delivers something of sufficient darkness to sink the

155

meddlesome gardener, it will be a full year before she gets to hear of it. In the meantime her daughter (yes, she had begun to convince herself the relationship is real) languishes in the clutches of that sorcerer in his forest. And what is she to do? In the absence of the Commander she had gone to the Secunde and made her complaint, but he had merely told her to wait until his superior's return. He made it clear he was unwilling to get involved in the matter, which he regarded as petty and vaguely sordid. To him it was all a matter of women, of breeding, of husbandry. And in any case, a deaf girl was of as much value as a bag of meal in a place like this. Would she not produce dumb children, a tribe of halfwits who would only serve to dull the edge of this new colony? Let the gardener keep her, but let him keep her quietly and cause her to cease with those terrible sounds of hers. And besides, Secunde De Man was not without his suspicions. He did not trust this Isa Meyer. And he did not trust his superior in certain matters either. When the man was not employing himself about the place as a petty tyrant he spent his time engaged in flights of sentimental idealism. The Secunde knew that in truth this was not a world of mythic kingdoms and new civilizations. It was Africa, plain and simple – a cruel place and one that God was satisfied to leave forever in its own darkness. The Secunde predicted a certain coming down to earth for the Honourable Commander, and perhaps – he thought – it would be sooner rather than later. The expedition was still away and what would they have found? Nothing, plain and simple. A few pieces of copper, some benighted heathens, and that would be it – the lot.

Adam Wijk, of course, has a plan. He knows that when he receives the inevitable summons to appear at the Castle he will be ordered either to return the girl to her keepers, or to marry her. The gardener is not about to accede to either of those injunctions, and so he has prepared a third option. The third option goes by the name of Hendrick Claudius, a young man who even at this moment is seated in the gardener's cottage painting orchids for an appreciative feminine audience. Van der Stel will almost certainly agree, he finding the young Claudius highly to his liking and close to his heart on matters of botany and science. As for Wijk, well he will host and chaperone the young woman while this courtship is under way. In devising his plan, the gardener has conveniently forgotten that courtship is generally not a luxury that exported orphans are permitted to indulge in for longer than a week or so. For Adam Wijk, the courtship period has become quite open-ended. He foresees a wedding, but it is somewhere not quite in the real world where it can conveniently be attached to a date upon a calendar.

But no, it does not work out like this at all. When he finds the Commander he is sitting at his desk turning an ingot of copper over and over in his hand. He says nothing but listens to Wijk launch into the outline of his plan. The Commander remains seated, leaning back in his chair, tossing the lump of copper up and down. When Wijk comes to a hesitant silence Van der Stel looks up at him. He leans forward and puts the copper down on the desk with a resonant clink; then with his right hand he pulls a sheet of folded paper towards him. From the broken seal Wijk can see it is an official letter.

"Two reasons why we cannot entertain your plan, Mr Wijk. Firstly, our friend Claudius is merely on loan to us and will one day return to the East. Secondly, I have received a letter. It comes from the Lords in Amsterdam and it accuses me of being a fool, Mr Wijk, a fool for spending so much time on something that is no business of the Company. Do you understand what I am saying, Mr Wijk?"

Wijk nods his head uncertainly.

"Good, good – because from this moment, Mr Wijk, I want to hear no more concerning the *Tulp* or anything that came from it, not a thing. You will promise me now that you will return that girl to the tavern, and then you will wash your hands of her. She is no business of yours any more, Mr Wijk. She is spoken for by someone else now. And good luck to him."

So, it is true at last. She is no property of the Company, no concern of either of these two men. She and those others in her group were travelling privately, coming out to this wild place for reasons of their own. It seems Isa Meyer was not lying, then, when she explained that these were homeless girls, adopted by her brother-in-law and his wife. Upon the wife's death the family had decided to leave the Fatherland and come out here to start again. The Company was offering many incentives to such people as would venture out and settle, not least amongst them a plot of land and free passage to their destination. Once here they were to stay with Bart and Isa until they got on their feet.

It is a story that rings true. There is no reason to doubt it. And yet it prompts someone else to send a letter northwards as well. This one is addressed as follows: *My Esteemed Protector and Benefactor*. It thanks this unnamed man for his continued friendship and expresses pleasure that the artefacts he sends him from Africa are making such a grand contribution to his cabinet of curiosities. He hopes he will be pleased with the present shipment, and promises in the next one to send him more such items of interest. Perhaps this one will include that thing of which he last made request, an egg of the Rukh. Already he has put out the word that a prize is collectable on presentation of such an article. The letter concludes with a request. *If a trusted person can be found to perform a certain inquiry on my behalf I would be most grateful.*

Details on the *Tulp* and its unfortunate passengers are given, and the writer concludes by asking the recipient of the letter to pay the money owing on the shipment to the person undertaking the inquiry. Now the writer must wait, for it will be a year before he can expect any sort of a response. In the meantime, the girl of four names and none will have to accept the history that is spun for her by Mrs Isa Meyer. Perhaps the Lady of the strand is presenting the true history of the silent woman, in which case the letter writer will have wasted his money. But perhaps she is not. Whatever the case, the young woman will soon be married, and she will be expected to be happy. And why should she not be? Her husband is the best that can be found – a wealthy man, handsome, clean, refined.

Mrs Meyer is even a little jealous, though she has been recompensed for her loss. There he is now, sitting alone at a table in the Green Door, Mr Herman Bolck.

The wedding will be something that is remembered for years to come. There are many who are anxious to attend, but Isa Meyer has invited only those whose presence she wishes to countenance. Simon van der Stel has been invited but does not appear, sending instead his apologies and a deputy in the form of Lt Olof Bergh. Somebody else who is not in attendance, though one would have expected him to be, is the bride's former physician, Adam Wijk. He is not present for reasons of his not having been invited, though in truth he would probably not have gone anyway – too many people crowded together in a small place, all of them looking at him with questions in their eyes. He sits at home and celebrates with a glass of brandy.

When Dominee Mankadan pronounces the couple man and wife the crowd leaves the church and drifts towards the Tavern of the Green Door. Hester has swept out the place and rubbed down the tables. She has emptied the pot in the birdman's cage and she has given him fresh water. The birdman Voog is becoming thin and he lies curled up on the floor. Hester is scared for him, for Meyer will want him to perform today. He will have to sit on his perch and look responsive for the sake of the guests. When they bang on the cage he will have to cry out and look alarmed, and when they are nice to him and throw him scraps from their tables he will have to purr and coo. "Sad," she says to him, and she is sad for the both of them. Her sister is going to live far away and she may no longer go to the house in the garden to visit her. Now she will only have Mr Cardamom for a friend, and Voog.

Hester can hear the crowd approach and she goes outside to wait for them. Here they come now, Dronke Piet leading the way in his clean, white shirt; Krause and Matthaus following amongst a host of others. Hester darts back inside and fetches something from where she has hidden it behind Voog's cage. Then she goes outside again and stands with it behind her back. The guests are at the door now, but Bart Meyer checks them. "Have you no manners?" he scolds. "You must wait for the bride." So they stand outside in a growing throng, joking with one another and remarking aloud how thirsty they are and wondering what is keeping the bride and groom. Finally they arrive, Jan Klou driving the cart and the married couple sitting behind looking very fine. They come to a halt before the crowd and Bolck gets out of the cart, turning to offer a hand to his wife. She climbs down, keeping her eyes lowered. It is only when Hester steps forward that she takes note of anybody. The tavern girl offers her a gift – a bunch of wildflowers. "Happy," she smiles. The bride bends down and kisses her on the mouth.

Some time in the afternoon Bolck calls Jan Klou and he takes his wife and they drive off. They do not say goodbye but leave as if in secret. The revellers continue in their own stupid enjoyment. They have convinced themselves that the marriage is a happy occasion, that bride and groom will be good to each other. Those who know the truth of it, those who have been upstairs in the loft with her, keep their sentiments to themselves. It is not that they care for the woman; it is more that they wonder what they shall do for their pleasures now.

When evening falls the wedding cart is still some distance from home. Bolck orders Klou to stop and set up a tent. While he is working the husband takes his wife around to the far side of the cart and pushes her up against the wheel with her face away from him. Then he lifts up her skirts and he fucks her. Now the marriage is consummated.

It was not easy to accept what was found there. Copper, yes. A mountain of copper. And further north they came to a great river in a stark and arid place. Such were the rivers in the land of Judah; but this was not a land where Believers dwelt, and this river, although it was a great river, was not the one. The people along its banks were as ignorant of Monomotapa as

160

were all the others encountered on the journey. So he did not order the boat to be set down. Instead he drew a map and he marked the river and he wrote a legend on it where it emptied into the sea: *Here live people called the Camissans.* It was a joke, of course. It was all that remained of the fabled Camissa and the road to Monomotapa.

And now he is back in his domain, setting right what has gone wrong in his absence. The dumb girl has been taken care of; and that is one thing less for him to be concerned about. He had endured the petitions of the woman who came crying to him that the Company Gardener had stolen away her daughter. He pointed out that the girl was no relation to her but it did not impede her beseeching. What man understands the bonds of affection between women, what man understands the loneliness of a girl – and one so flawed in apprehension – in a dark and brutal place like this? What man at all, agreed Commander Van der Stel as he sent her away with a promise to make amends.

The Commander sits at his desk and watches the blue sky outside the window. He picks up an ingot of copper and turns it in his hands. What woman understands the contents of a man's heart, he thinks. The heart cannot eat a copper ingot, the soul cannot navigate by paper maps. But he knows he is being unkind; for they will know that better than he. If he had someone whom he could address as *My Dearest X*, he could say what is in his heart, which is that it is a shame that a dream should be sold for a few bars of copper. A whole kingdom is gone and all he has is a mountain of orange metal. It is not the same thing as the Queen of Sheba at all. She has escaped him; the missing thing is gone. Time to put away childish things, he chides himself. No more will I play the fool to hopeless dreams.

Now it is just the problems of the real world that engage him, and there are more than enough to provide a full-time distraction. For one, the slaves are growing bolder and more demanding of freedom. Every day now there are more of these wretches who run off into the country or escape to the

161

ships. So many have absconded they have been able to form a gang, a tribe unto themselves, to cause havoc along the borders of the colony. The farmers are complaining, and not only about the depredations of the slaves but about the Sonquas too. They are growing more obstreperous by the day and are causing losses to colonists and Hottentot allies alike. Captain Kees of the Chainouquas has abandoned his hunting grounds and fled towards Cape Agulhas to escape these mosquito men. Something will have to be done.

In the meantime, a new law: slaves who attempt escape will be brought in chains to the Castle; they will be thrashed and an ear will be cut off. No mercy shall be shown.

My sister is gone and I sleep in the roof with the brown man. We understand each other. When he sings I know what he is saying. My little man is singing about a crow. I can see by his body that he is thinking about a bird like this. He is a crow in a cage. At night I sleep in the arms of the crow man. He smells strange. In the dark I hear a sound and my hair is wet where he has been resting his head in it. I will free him. In the land of the crowman the people live in nests and do not own a single thing.

The gardener, in his humble cottage, has come to realise a sorry fact of his existence – that day by day he seems to own a little less of what little he owned before, that quite undeniably, and on several levels, there is a certain shrinkage going on. Observe him now in his kitchen, where he is engaged in a search for edibles. He finds a crust of bread; a last piece of ham. In the pot on the range is a broth of turnips and beans, now cold. Wijk dips the crust into the stolid matter and lifts it to his mouth. There is no salt in it. He was not aware there was no salt left when he set the pot going last night. Normally it is Trijntje who will tell him when he needs to buy supplies. But she is no longer in his service. Since the incident with the jam he is taking no chances. She has been told to stay away, and so also his fellow settlers. He will see nobody as a patient now, not even if they beg him. Go away, is all he says. Go away. The only person he welcomes is the artist Hendrick Claudius. Together they work at the *Hortus Africanus*, the gardener throwing himself into the labour as if his life depends on it. It is Claudius who takes over some of the necessary tasks from the slave girl and who keeps the older man connected with events of the outside world. He tells him of the things that happen in the town, what ships are in the bay, and he brings news and opinions from abroad. King Charles of England is dead, he says one day. Wijk's eyes grow distant. He gets up and fetches a flask of brandy and two glasses. "Let us drink to it," he says. Claudius assumes it is for pleasure in the misfortune of an Englishman that they drink. He cannot guess that it is for the gardener's secret past that he offers this toast. Perhaps it will be buried with the English king. Or not.

Diary

July 4

My Lady wears a pearl coloured silk robe with embroidered flowers of sky blue. On her feet are silken slippers. I have a mind to try a poem but I have no confidence in my power with the quill. Perhaps it would be an ugly thing and would cheapen what I first thought noble and good. So I come to consider how we are powerless in this world, even before such things as Words. I cannot make the smallest monument to one I love. How am I to save a life, or ten thousand lives, or even my own? I am reminded of a discourse by Dr S– on the subject of method in Physic and how therein lay our hope to gain a power over this contagion, and all others like it. Too much of our Art is founded on wisdoms never proven or examined, he said, and there was much dissent in this though I saw the wisdom in it. To consider that a plague such as this might be something not wrought by God but by forces of nature that perhaps could be controlled – what a comforting notion, though dangerous and many of us not willing to think more on it for fear of Retributions. What is the extent of our Power, and where must we Submit? These are the great questions now. If I could save ten thousand lives, or just one (if it were her) then I would gladly take whatever retribution came. But let me not think on that now; it is for another day.

July 10

How quiet the Strand is now and melancholy. In previous times a man could not walk safely in the road but that he would be run over by a carriage or drenched sodden by the wheels of them, they being driven exceeding fast and should be slowed by Law. Now all the better sort are leaving and I must share the street with the poor.

We hear today the King is gone to Hampton Court, for it being further from where the Plague is.

July 15

My Lady E– does love to play with words, in this she is master and better than I (even counting that I speak her language and she not mine). If I were ever in a duel with her I would choose the sword, for if it were a battle of words she would be the better and I would be ended. Here an example from today, I finding her in her lair where she reads on matters she should rather leave be: See here what it says of Paracelsus, she says indicating at the page. It says that he cured the Plague by wrapping the . . . and here she will not say the word but makes me say it, I leaning over her shoulder to see what is writ there. 'Excrement,' I must say. He wrapped this Excrement which came from pestiferous sources in balls of bread and fed them to the living.

I cannot tell if her joy is at this marvellous recipe (for disaster) or whether it is glee at my discomfort. I reply to her saying, Madam, you should not read so much. It is not good for women. Then she putting on hurt: And why is that, pray tell?

It causes them to become restless, says I. It agitates the choler. Too late, I think, now I am trapped: Oh, says she, and only men shall enjoy this agitation? She knows full well it is not what I am saying. I mean that it makes people want what they cannot have, says I. Ah, she says, but we are used to that, are we not, Doctor Taylor?

And to press home her Victory she will not let me touch her for one hour, not even to kisse her hand in surrender.

July 16

Further to above, of this matter of the chymical doctors. This place is now in danger of them and with all the good physicians going out to the Country. Every man with a little training and a new theory has acres of the poor and willing to lend him their ears and meagre purses. Now it is not to say they are all bad and possibly their methods do work, but in most cases not and they are murderers who feed the gullibles ground-up tin and iron and say 'It is a chymical preparation and stronger than your rustic Simples' – and of course it is true if one counts that it is a Strength that leads towards Death. This Paracelsus we know well and that he was mad and rude and sought a quarrel with all. Now it is quite obvious that the heart of any remedy is this one truth – 'quia contraria contrarius curantur'. Hence a surfeit of the Sanguine, as in certain Fevers, is countered by a stimulation of the Phlegmatic, which is a cold & moist quality and opposite to the fever. But these chymists do say that the heart of a remedie is that Like cures Like, which is madness clear enough. Hence my Lady's recipe for 'A Plague Bread' which will cure by administering a dose of the pestilence to those not yet infected! More need not be said.

July 19
This week are more than 500 dead. We are no longer hopeful that this will pass us by. And the weather continuing hot so that we are all in fear that much worse lies ahead.

For nosegays choose bitter herbs not sweet,
for sweetness doth attract that which is putrid,
and so will the pestilence be brought quicker to its host
than if no herbs were used at all.
And for like reason, avoid the smelling of roses, violets, &c.

(In a fragrant garden is much ill.)

July 20
My Employer has taken to sleeping some nights in a boarding house near his offices. He complains that now in this Plague time there are no watermen to be had to bring him to his office or home again, and if one can be found he is entirely capable of dropping senseless into the water midstream and leaving boat and passenger to shoot the bridge alone. And the

hackneys – who will dare travel in something that might last have carried a breathing corpse? As for walking, says he, it is a tedium to traipse all the way east of the City, and unsafe. I am witness to this when he reasons with her. I can see she bites her lip and I imagine what that mouth would say, were it not so constrained. I know it is a question with her why they had to move from their house on Tower Hill all the way to Westminster. I have heard her say how he will not admit it is for fashion, to be seen a success. Well if it is evidence of success he wants then why does he not buy a carriage of his own, I say, and am immediately ashamed for having spoken so against him. I know the ships are out still, and this house has cost enough. Lord hear me – if ever I am in a position to repay R– what I owe, then I will do it, and thrice over.

July 23
Met with Dr L– today and find him much troubled by the practice of shutting up of people in their houses if they are sick. It is a sure sentence of death on the whole family, and many abuses perpetrated by those who guard them, says he. But is it not better that the sick be made apart from those that are well, say I, but am now come to consider that perhaps there are more dead through this practice, or driven to madness or dying of hunger than by Plague.

To know when one has been taken by this pestilence, the first sign is as follows: A sinking of the Spirits. Also a sadnesse. To bring out that which is heavy, administer a vomitory of Bole-Armoniak. If the patient bring it up, wash out the mouth with wine and give it again. If he keep it down it is a good thing and promises well. If he bring it up a second time it is a sure sign of the Sicknesse and he will not recover.

July 26
QUESTION: Of what use is a ship full of spices and silks if you are dead? This is what I would ask of my Employer, but he is looking to his business down by the River. If he were attentive

and lived at home more – or if he took the both of them away to the Country – he would stop this thing. But I am ungrateful. Was it not he who brought me here from Amsterdam and gave me a life in this place? He calling it the 'Greatest City in the World', which I thought a conceit, though to be expected from an Englishman. It was he, but then let us remember it was I who bestowed the first favour and he owes his life to me. I could have walked past and left him to his fate with those vagabonds who would have robbed him or murdered him, but I did not. And thus it seems, through no artifice of my own, we are back at the subject of Fate, and I wonder now upon this question: Can a man refuse his Fate? By logic I would answer No, for then it would not be Fate at all. Now here is a second question that comes close upon the first, and it is this: If man does not choose, then can he be blamed for the consequences of his choice, which is never a choice but the following of Destiny? Are we then all innocent of what we do? A pretty conclusion that lightens my heart, though knowing somewhere in it must be a fault for it cannot be true. I will say one thing about this present state of affairs: If guilt be borne, then let him carry his share.

July 28
This week as noted by the parish Bills are 2000 dead of Plague.

The glass bead

He is eighteen years old. His chest is smooth and strong. His hair is not dull and lanky as others, it is golden. And like bronze are his forearms, the muscles beneath them firm and willing. The boy lifts a sack of meal onto his back. Another one, he says, and lets them load a second on top of the first. How strong are his hands and yet how fine; how almost delicate. If he could write, perhaps he would be a poet. Or perhaps he would use his voice only and not need to touch a quill. Ah, of such things are daydreams made. And the dreams of night as well. Such long nights, so far away, under a blanket of secrets.

And here a secret of the flagman up on his lonely pinnacle. It is this: that he has begun to see what others do not. It is no wonder, really, that a man who spends so much time looking outward into the distance should develop the second sight. His daughter will bring him news from the hamlet and he will say, Ah, that will end in tears. Or he will say, If only he had taken the farm next to that he would be happy. But now the wind in that corner will drive his wife mad and he will have to put her away.

This kind of vision might be regarded, for some, as a gift. But not for a lookout. A lookout must know what is real and what is not. Heaven forbid he should hoist a signal for something that is not there at all. But on this winter's day, at least, he has got it right. The gun below him fires to announce a thing that will soon be apprehended by everyone. A fleet approaches from the south. It is not the ships of the Company that return homeward, it is a foreign group. When they sail into the bay their colours become recognisable – white flags with golden fleur-de-lis. It is the French.

The fleet is again under command of Admiral de Vaudricourt. With him are some old friends of the Cape, the Ambassador de Chaumont, accompanied by Father Tachard and the Abbé de Choisy. They are returning to France bearing requests from the court of Siam that more priests be sent to them. They also, it seems, would welcome a detachment of French troops. Commander Van der Stel is ill at ease with such a large foreign fleet in the bay. This time he is more careful than last. When he receives a request from the Jesuits for accommodation on land he regretfully informs them he is not able to offer them his old tower in the garden. It is being repaired, he says. Instead he offers them the use of the Company farm at Rustenburg. It suits his purpose to have the Catholics out of town.

The distance puts off casual visitors, but it does not stop a few of the most faithful making a trip out to Rustenburg to confess their sins. And there is one visitor, at least, who goes there for reasons other than absolution. Father Tachard remembers him from before and welcomes him as a friend. He knows the man comes to talk not of God but of Science.

"Tell me of these hidden worlds that are discovered," says the visitor. "Tell me of these lands with their swarming atomites, their manifold tiny beasts."

The Jesuit tells him his country has a new and unlikely hero – a certain Van Leeuwenhoek. "He has indeed discovered new lands – amongst them, in fact, a whole new province for Holland, and this in the scum of his own teeth!"

The visitor frowns at the thought. He is not sure whether the priest intends an insult.

"And what is it that these little animals, these atomites, do? What are they good for?"

"They wriggle and squirm and are no good for anything at all. They arise by themselves from matter and return to matter when their short lives are done. It is a world incomprehensible to us; a world, perhaps, irrelevant. I think of these creatures merely as wondrous in themselves, as evidence of the great inventiveness of God. Nothing more."

The priest offers his visitor a gift. It is a flat piece of metal with a small hole made near the one end. In the hole is a bead of glass. It is no proper microscope, it is a toy used by leisured gentlemen and ladies to discover for themselves something of this new world of the miniscule. They use it to spy on fleas and lice, to marvel at the patterns in the wings of flies. The priest apologises for not having something better to give his visitor, but he promises to bring something with him when he returns. It will be a year, and then he will be back.

Now Adam Wijk sits in his old chair with his head in his hands. More specifically, he sits with his hands covering his ears. As a child he believed that putting a shell to your ear enabled you to hear the ocean, even if you were far away from the sea. Now he knows it is not so. It is not waves upon a beach one hears, it is the churning of the animalcules as they go about their secret lives in the caverns of one's brain.

The months pass, and the gardener drifts deeper into his private world. It is a world illumined now through the small, bright window of the Jesuit's glass bead. He sits at his table, clasping a moth between his fingers, peering at it through his magnifier. He scans the herbs upon the table, walking there through fields and mountains and valleys, falling into the secret life of the miniature.

When Hendrick Claudius comes to see him the gardener says he is in no mood for work. The artist says he has not come to work; he has come to bring his friend some food, to open the windows and get some air into the cottage. Leave them closed, says the gardener. It is how they come in; on the smokes of the air. What does? Adam Wijk is silent. It is the animalcules that come in thus, the seeds of the plagues. It is not a new idea this, it is one that gets dug up perennially by philosophers, only to sink back into the undergrowth of dreams and improvable notions. It is proposed by such that the causes of contagion are not some indefinable effluvia but rather material substances – substances that are able to be blown in the wind rather like the seeds of grasses and flowers. These pollens – these *seminaria* – arise from a stricken body like an evil cloud that drifts away seeking fertile soils in which to take root. It is an idea with poetic merits, but one that has never, itself, taken root. For how can such a thing be proven?

Claudius goes to the back door and opens it. The goat looks at him forlornly and bleats. He turns inside and walks over to the water barrel, emptying the contents into an earthen jug. Then he takes it outside and splashes some in the goat's water trough. The rest he sprinkles on the mute girl's herb garden. The young man feels angry now. Angry with the gardener for letting things go like this. He looks at the dull herbs and knows they will fail. They have been neglected, just as she too was neglected and betrayed. Claudius has no anger for Isa Meyer or Herman Bolck. They are only being true to their unlikable selves. It is Adam Wijk who is the guilty one; it is he who has turned away this dazzling creature, this nameless enigma. Claudius would have been happy to share her with Wijk. Not in that way, but to have her in his presence, to be able to come and watch her and sketch her and bring her gifts. Perhaps they could have worked on a language together, the three of them. It would not have been so difficult. What had the old man been waiting for? He had clearly fallen for her, though he had done his best to hide it. Claudius knew his friend well enough to see the signs. The gardener had gone soft; in her presence he had forgotten his scowl, his furrowed brow. Such were small signs, but they were enough. Now the artist smiles wryly to himself. Yes, they are the both of them bereft. How silly; how almost comical. When Claudius goes home he does not shut the door behind him but leaves it wide open. Let the madman close it himself. Animalcules be damned.

The gardener remains sitting, his eyes distant. He is back in the plague time, remembering a day on which his lover is fretful from being closed up in the house. She longs to go abroad in the streets, to visit her friends or to look at the shops. He says to her Close your eyes. And she says, Doctor – am I ill? He says Yes, quite severely so, and here is the treatment. So he tells her she is leaving the house now (her eyes still closed) and she is going with a friend to the river. Now they find a boat and they go out into the current. Where are we going? she wonders. He says Wait, the patient must be silent. Then he tells her of the things they pass and she cries, I know it – I know where you are carrying me! He says you will not know until we get there, I am a kidnapper and you are in my power. And so he carries her to the Chelsea gardens where he frees her, and they sit there on the grass a while eating apples and drinking wine. He has even brought pastries with him; how thoughtful he is.

The gardener smiles now. How thoughtful indeed. He is, after all, a gentleman, current failings notwithstanding. He picks up the glass bead and bends once more to his forests and valleys. Then he is back in that world of memory, watching her as she grows melancholy again after her brief reverie. When will this be over, she sighs, oh when? She stands and goes to the window looking out over the square. How dreary it is now, how oppressive. After a moment she turns from the window and asks him this: What does freedom mean to you? He is surprised and cannot think how such a question arose, but he tells her it is the liberty to go where he wants and do as he pleases. It is the ability to make of his life what he chooses, to call no man Master.

She dwells on this a while but will not let him be privy to her thoughts. What manner of freedom she is dreaming of he cannot say. It is only later that she comes out with it, in a sudden burst of passion. Wijk smiles now at those words of hers. Master, Servant, Man, Woman, Wife, she cries. What are these creatures beneath their burdensome labels? What would they look like if you freed them? Would they be beautiful or terrible? She knows what it is that she wants, she says, she

173

wants to be free of the definitions imposed by men. And by her sisters too. They do not know what to make of a woman who cares about questions of Philosophy and Science. Is air a thing that can be weighed or not? Of course not, they say. Air is air, for heavens sake! And what about the function of breath – does the breath serve to cool the blood, as many would argue, or does it perform some other function? They care nought for these questions but are happy with their superstitions. She would go and ask Mr Boyle himself, but she cannot. The doors of the Royal Society are closed to her, she being a woman.

A mockingbird

Hester feeds the birdman scraps from the tables. She knows he is going to die. He sits on his perch and looks ahead of him into a distance only he can see. First they took her sister, and now they will take her friend the birdman. She wishes she could talk to him and tell him that one day he will be free, but she herself is a bird within a cage. She is a prisoner of this house and of her own mind. Why can she not speak like other people? It is because of something that happened long ago, before she can remember. It must be so. The bird that is dreaming her has forgotten to give her a voice. What else can it be? She tries to remember as far back as she can, to before she came to this house, to before she went onto the ship that left her here. Who was she then? What was her name? The man who owns me bought me with a name, she thinks. Until I became Hester I was free. I cannot remember my first name, from before I was on the ship. They called me "girl" on the ship, but that is not a name. It is very strange not to remember, because it was not that long ago. Or maybe I was always on the ship. Maybe I was pulled on board in a net and almost eaten until I spoke. What word did I say that let them know I was not a fish? Maybe that is why they just called me "girl", because that is the word that I said. I don't know. Today the sea is green. I will sneak out and hide in the garden. I will hunt the peacock because it is beautiful.

Isa Meyer watches the girl slip out the door. Let her enjoy her freedom while she may. Tonight she will introduce this castaway to her new labours. The men have waited long enough.

Arent. Arent is his name. But I must desist. Oh Lord, if you can hear us in this place, let my eyes be cut out that I might no longer see. Let my hands be smitten that I no longer touch. There is no further place I can go on this earth to flee, unless it is that island that is called Hell. Oh Lord strike me down before I set my sails for that shore.

If men were birds, then would some be crows and some sparrows; some would be cockatoos and peacocks, and some, even, would be birds of fire and exist only in places remote and wild and, perhaps, not real at all. And some others would be birds that maimed or stole, as are the jolly hangman and the mockingbird. A mockingbird – such a one is this Anton Visser. There is nobody as good as he. All are ripe for scorn under his gaze. And especially such men as are less than men; men who are pale of face for their being indoors, who spend too much time with books, with children. So it is as the mockingbird that he climbs the ladder to the room above the granary. And what pale crane does he there find? It is the gentle teacher, this man who spends his nights in such fervent prayer, in such fear of hell. He does not know what to say when he sees this adult face emerge from the drop. Does he wish harm? Does he wish good? Perhaps tuition. And then it comes to him with horror this one thought: He knows. He knows the contents of my dreams. He knows how I defile the image of his brother. He can see it in me and has come for his revenge. Oh Lord, so be it. It is as I have prayed. Strike me down before I set my sails for the place of no return. But it is not for this that the mockingbird has come.

"Will you give me the letters?" he asks, still with only his torso showing in the doorway. "I want to read and write. What will it take? How much is to be paid?"

"It is not the money," explains the teacher. "It is the time, the dedication."

The young man repeats the word "dedication", twisting it

so that the teacher's earnestness is made small. "How much *dedication?*"

The teacher is loathe to answer. "It will take time," he says. "It is something learned more easily by children."

"More easily by children," repeats the mockingbird.

"Is this really why you have come, friend? If you want to learn it will take time and commitment. It will not be easy. Is this what you want?"

The torso with the yellow hair smiles its twisted smile. "Now what would I want that for, Meester? It is a thing for children, not for men."

"How right you are. So how may I be of service to you?"

"You may be of service to my sister, Meester. If you are able."

"Explain yourself, friend. If you have merely come to chat then I am grateful, but now perhaps we have exhausted our subject and must go our separate ways. I am a busy man."

"A busy man."

The teacher turns back to his class. "This Sunday after church," the visitor calls. "We will fetch you. Father wants to meet the teacher." And with that he is gone.

Oh is this possible? Is this true? Lord, how you have deserted me.

Diary

August 22

This week near 4000 dead.

My Lady again in melancholic mood. Today we shall require a stronger Physic. I go to her where she looks out of the window and kiss her upon her neck. Let us be brave, I whisper. Let us leave this house and go out into the aire. She does not look at me but says No, it will not help, I am in no humour for going a-dreaming today. I say But Madam, I speak not of dreams. My words are plain and have no meaning other than what I say: Let us go out into the aire. She turns to me surprised and hopeful. Then comes fear upon her brow. You can tell R– you went looking for a button and a thread, I say. Then she laughs: We will be in such dreadful trouble. I tell her Madam we are already in dreadful trouble. Let us get out before the curfew makes it too late.

So we take a hackney down to the river and find a boatman and go out into the stream. We row upriver to look at the empty palace and to admire the gardens of the well-to-do. How pleasant it is, how peaceful. How far away is any danger. From here in the water it is as if there is no Plague at all, as if there is nothing in the world that can keep us apart. The boatman must think us husband and wife, and it is pleasant to deceive him for a while. At Vauxhall gardens we turn around and drift downriver, watching the smoke above the City grow heavier with the sun going down. I am reminded of the dangers of this miasm but today do not care. Life is short; let us but live it while we may.

August 25

Stopped at a coffee house on Ludgate hill and there fell to conversation with one Mr Blaise, merchant and philosopher.

A dangerous neighbourhood, says he, and not only for the poor and desperate who so easily turn to thievery but also for that rotting heap of brick, by which he meant the Bridewell. What does a granary have in abundance that other places have less of? Food, say I. On top of that, says he, what a granary has is cats. One must look to cats as the bearers of this pestilence. It sits in their fur as an effluvium, which is released upon rubbing or stroking. A cat can go anywhere and no place is safe from a cat. Hence the Lord Mayor does good in ordering the culling of these sly beasts, so he says. And what of dogs? say I. Dogs are the same as for the effluvia, but not as similar in the question of mobility. A dog will not climb a house and will not rub itself against a person as a cat will, but rather waits until it is patted upon the head, where the infectious steams are less, the hair being short. Hence, the dogs are less guilty, but not innocent either and hence too must go. It is all a great pity, say I, and do mean that truly.

August 26
If you were to die how would it be? Of old age, I say, comfortable in a bed. More likely, says she, of youthful folly, poisoned by a jealous husband. Quite possible indeed. And now I must enquire of her the same, though I suspect she has some darker fate in mind for herself. We are not special, says she, we are weak. This thing outside will catch us soon enough, and I am no longer afraid. I am not pleased when she talks thus. I remind her there is no dignity in a death by the Pestis. It tells you that you are nothing, that you are no higher than a dog, that you can run mad in the streets and not care who sees you. Yes, says she, I will choose the death of the common man. The rich are interested only in themselves, in conflict, greed and politicking. What is this war between your country and mine? Nobody can tell me what it is for. It is for trade, say I, and thus prove her right. But I will not let her sentiment be the last on this, so I tell her that greed or not, the death of the common man is a low scrabbling in the dirt, a desperate clawing like a wounded animal. So be it, says she, it will be my own judg-

ment of God. Do not give dreams to people who may not live them.

RESOLUTION: I will speak to R– about her going away to the Country. We must take action now or lose all.

September 3
Today reason has prevailed, yet I am full of sorrow for it. R– has got a permit for her and she is gone away to Norwich. Now it will be just the two of us in the house, and things far safer that way.

Underworld

The possibility of death has come to haunt him. He goes at night and watches the hut of the woman Halsenbach. He follows her as she goes into the garden to steal his herbs and poisons. She will know who brought him that bitter gift, but she will not tell.

In the cottage the pot on the range boils without cease. Hemlock, datura, bitter almond, kganna. There are enough poisons in the locked cabinet now to give any army a night of horrors. And what is this all for? What does our gardener intend doing with his collection of ghastly dreams? It is perhaps not clear even to the gardener himself. One can merely observe his methods, which are remarkable enough in themselves. Consider, for instance, the case of the slave Scipio, a strong and healthy young man enticed to the garden cottage with promise of food and rest. What he gets there he will never forget. Food, yes, a tasty broth – and afterwards a growing numbness in the bowels, a shivering in the stomach. Save me, Master, I am ill, he cries, but the black-eyed master merely sits and watches. Poor Scipio, such dreams he has. Afterwards, when the miasms of the Underworld have released him, he is given money and told never to say a word of what has happened. There is a crack, a fissure, that has opened in the earth beneath the gardener's cottage, but that is a thing that cannot be said.

Such is the nature of our gardener's current work. The *Hortus* is no nearer completion, though the Commander enquires regularly after its progress. What are the names of these specimens he has brought from the North; what are their properties, and what are they good for? Always after a profit, our Commander. But the gardener has lost interest in that world. He is absorbed in smaller, darker things: the silken valleys of an orchid's sex; the eye of a moth, watching him impassively through the glass bead. In the space beyond that tiny sphere untold creatures live their teeming lives. Worlds dissolve into further worlds of the inscrutable. So where is he going with this journey? The gardener does not know, and does not care. It is not the Plague that he cares for now, or making a discovery, or finding the true cause of anything, and even less a cure. He knows his quarry hides behind the glass bead. Somewhere in that underworld lie the seeds of all the plagues. And let them stay there, for such a notion cannot be demonstrated with his meagre tools. What is he to say to prove his thesis? Come, take this cup and drink of this electuary, and you will see? There are many worlds in our Creation, and they are beyond our control. No, such a demonstration will not win any converts to his truth. We desire the light, they will say, not this creeping horror you offer us, not this dark ocean you would drown us in. Come, dear gardener, they will cry, come out into the light before you are carried away forever. But he does not go. He sits in his cottage. The dog of plagues lies at his feet. Well done it says, you have found me. And what now?

And now nothing. All the knowledge in the world cannot bring her back.

The man does something to me. He is searching inside me for the bird that dreams me. I want to help him but I am tired. He makes my body tired. Today the blood comes out of my body. It tastes of old spoons. What if it is not a bird that is dreaming but the whale. This is why I cannot say more than a word. I try to speak in a bucket of water but the words do the wrong thing and will not be words. To speak under water you must make a sound like crying or groaning. It is easier to sing under water than to speak. I think I am the only one who knows this and I am not as stupid as people say.

Diary

October 25

I will soon end this journal for it seems I have lost the cause of it. There are no new remedies and all that is a Doctor or Physician is silent and keeps his wisdom to himself, lest it be proven false. All things now are false, and I am loathe to say it here but it does seem this plague has reached up to the very heavens and overcome what dwells there, for there is no more comfort from that quarter. All is a great silence. I heard today at the water's edge a sound like the creaking of a gate that will not stop, and I asked a man there what it was and he says it is the gates of Hell, but I, not satisfied with such an answer, asked a boatman and he says it is the waterwheels beneath the bridge, which now we can hear for all else being so quiet. Another one said to me it is like a dream, this quiet and still-ness, and perhaps we are all dead but not yet wise to it. It cannot be, said I. And he replied that I must prove it that it cannot be, and so I walked away for I knew he was wrong yet had no words for saying why.

October 26

I lie abed this morning with a dream, which is a strange dream for I am awake in it, and thus have come to doubt my certainty of what is awake or not, or living or dead. It is as the man sayeth yesterday, that I must prove it that we are not dead or dreaming, and now I cannot for this dream so exceeding mar-vellous and strange. I am walking in a place in the country. The sun is warm and there are birds in the trees and butter-flies. I come to a river, a stream, and there is a pool of clear water in which I would bathe. But here come now some ladies to the water and I must stand back. I hide behind the trees and spy upon them, their pretty ankles, their laughter, their rubbing their arms as they step within the cold water. I come out from the trees and go to the ladies and they shy not away; I come to where they bathe and dally amidst the fountain and I do not find they are repulsed or that they cover themselves, but that they continue in their play with a splashing of the water against the backs and fronts of one another, and so there are so many small sleek pelts some dark and some like honey-biscuit and some more of ginger, so I hold out my hand and they do not cease with their playing. There is one there, her hair dark and her eyes likewise as night, and I am sure I know her but cannot say her name. I touch her upon her haire and she does not flinch; I say Will you look at me, and she does not hear but continues with a pouring of water on the breasts of her friends and laughing at the cold of it. And then I turn away and know I am dreaming and nothing is real, and I walk away forlorn yet also full of wonder for the marvel of being awake while I am not.

How I do long for my Lady E– and fear she is perhaps not as safe as first thought.

November 20, four o'clock
I shall not wait till evening to confide here in my journal what has happened. And thus I shall say it now – she is back! She rests within her room and I am told she will see me later when she is recovered. Truly now our dark days are behind us.

Hour of midnight
This the final entry in my journal. (O pen, be steady now – Dispassionate). Here is the record of events: I go to her in the library. I think beforehand that she will strike a pose, as before, but it is not so. When I come close I see her eyes have deep shadows beneath them, as if she carries a secret. She holds her hand to her stomach and draws in a deep breath. Then she smiles at me. I wonder at first if she is real, if she is

not some apparition. But it is her – no spirit would smell as sweet, would reach up to caress me as she does then. We sit together in her couch, I resting my head on her breast. You are crying, she says, and I tell her she is mistaken, I merely have the Hay-fever. (Henceforth shall never any more tears be shed by me. It is a Vow.) Then she says, are you not pleased that I am back alive? And has not the Plague abated, do not the people stream back into the city? It is a new world that begins. I tell her I am sad for what has gone before and that very nearly I have given up all hope.

Then she speaks kind words to me and tells me of her time in Norwich and of silly things she has done there, and of her friend called Quince, who is a tabby cat and very fierce. You should have kidnapped him, said I. We have need of such brave fellows here to entertain our rats and mice. She does not laugh but says only she needs to sleep now, being very tired. So I sit up, ashamed that I have been so weak before her and not more attentive. I have words of apology upon my lips but never speak them.

For now I see what it is, that secret she bore when first I saw her. Her face, it does not show gently in that evening light. Her eyes are black and her brow is glistening. I am cold, she says. So very cold.

December

A final entry for the closing of this Record.

Two days I am with her and then it is finished. I go down the stairs and Robert is standing there in the shadows. She is gone, I say. And you (though I do not say it) will soon follow. There is a glint in his eye, the forehead damp with the seeping poisons. The judgement of God has been made and there is naught to be said on it. Robert draws his sword and holds it against my throat. I know what you have done with her, he says. All this time in my own house. I brush away the sword and move to pass, but he will not let me go. He strikes a chair with the blade. Traitor! cries he. I have no weapon to defend myself. I pick up the broken chair and hold it before me like a shield. It is too late now, I say. There is no remedy for us.

But he will not be swayed. The madness is in his blood. He lunges for me, striking the chair from my hands. I feel a blow in my thigh, and when I look down I see the blood coming up where the blade has passed. Robert is grinning. He makes to strike again, but I turn and flee.

Now I know that it is true; we are none of us alive but merely dream we are. If we but woke we would see where it was we dwelt, it is in Hell, and no place else.

Fruits of the body

The Commander stands on the Nassau bastion, looking out over the hamlet. It is February, the month when this little valley turns into a cauldron, a devil's kitchen of heat and wind. Out on the flats the farmers stand helpless as their crops are stripped; in town there is a new gable that has crashed. How many of our beloved Holland things will take root, he wonders, and how many perish? Possibly we will end up living in round huts. I will wear a coat of skins, and around my head I will wind the innards of a sheep. The Commander blinks as a gust of heated air blasts dust into his eyes, then he retreats inside.

In the safety of his attic the teacher frets over the groaning wind. The scouring breath has dragged his soul away and left him raw and fragile. He lies naked on his bed, praying for winter and dreaming his hopeless dreams.

And then the dreaded Sunday arrives. People walk to church, coming in brisk family groups or on their own at a more leisurely pace. Joachim van Arckel arrives last, finding a place for himself at the back. There before him in a pew are the four brothers, lined up like organ pipes, then old Zacharias and his wife. And next to her the great beauty, the blonde wisps escaping from her cap, the pink sateen of her bodice aglow. Poor Joachim swallows. He is going to his death, he can see it plainly. There will be no escaping this fate. The family fills the pew from left to right, with one space left over. It is for him. In one intoxicating moment he considers rising to his feet and walking up to the pulpit and spilling out his dreadful secret. But, of course, he does not. God has brought him here to be cured, not to make a fool of himself.

He will submit. He will go meekly. He will not keep staring at a certain person's golden hair.

It is a noisy group that makes its way back to Allemanskloof. Anton, Barend, and Lukas are on horseback, talking loudly of expensive horses they have seen and of girls they have spoken to or stolen a kiss from. But Arent has a twisted ankle and rides in the horse cart. The teacher sits in the back of the cart and wonders what to say. He has already tried showing concern in the state of the young man's ankle, but the youth has been unresponsive. Perhaps it is because of the pain, or perhaps he is just shy. Van Arckel smiles at Anneke. She looks at him apologetically. "Tell us about Batavia," she says. "Are there many fine schools there?"

"Many schools, yes," says the teacher. "All the things there are . . . "

"Are what?" she asks, sweetly.

"Are . . . different."

"You mean they are better, don't you."

Van Arckel smiles. "I didn't want to say it. People get offended. I should be offended if somebody said it to me. I am the schoolteacher, after all – even if I have to teach in the roof."

"I am sure you do just grandly."

Van Arckel begins ever so slightly to blush. "Not so," he says. "We are only on the letter 'M' with the young ones, and the older ones forget their A B Cs by the time they get to their X Y Zs. We go round and round a lot; it makes us quite dizzy sometimes."

Anneke smiles. "You should ask Arent to spell something, Meester. He knows his alphabet. I taught him."

Van Arckel raises his brows in surprise. "I don't believe it."

"It's true. Ask him to spell something."

"S-O-M-E-T-H-I-N-G," spells Arent.

The teacher claps his hands together. "Brilliant!"

"B-R-I..."

"Stop Ari; you're being cheeky now."

188

No, let him speak, Van Arckel wants to say. It is a great pleasure for me.

Zacharias leans back in the seat and beckons to the teacher. "Come sit up here with us," he says, nodding to his wife, Antje, to move up. "I want us to get acquainted." So Van Arckel gets up and squeezes in between the two of them. "Don't be fooled by that one," says Zacharias, casting an eye back towards his son. "He has only learned the letters to impress women. In truth he has never read a book."

"He can be encouraged."

"That's exactly what I have been thinking," admits Zacharias with satisfaction. "Now come, tell us about yourself. What was it like in Batavia?"

So Van Arckel tells the couple about life in the East, and when there are questions he gives answers that please them. It is not long, however, before he finds himself merely listening as the old man embarks on a lecture in his favourite subject – the importance of learning. The teacher punctuates his lengthy silence with grave nods, finding himself at last amused by the notion that constant agreement is really quite an exhausting thing and not a pleasure at all. What a wicked joy it would be to spring from this cart and shout out loud, No, it is not like that at all, you are wrong! You have no idea what manner of criminal you are dragging off to your farm. But, of course, he cannot give in to the seduction of this thought. He nods, says, "Indeed" many times, and wonders how far they still have to go.

When the teacher looks behind him occasionally he sees the boy watching him disinterestedly. Their slow progress across the flats is making him drowsy, though he is awake enough to swear softly when the cart hits a bump and hurts his ankle. "Don't speak so," his sister chides him. "It's rude." The boy smiles wryly and swears again.

At Allemanskloof the sweating travellers are greeted by a pack of unruly dogs. Zacharias scatters them with his horsewhip. "Don't let them jump up, Meester. They have no manners."

189

Van Arckel climbs down stiffly from the cart and looks about him, allowing his hands to be slobbered on by the dogs. He had been dreading what he might find here: some mean hut, perhaps, or a bleak cottage propped uncomfortably on a flat and dry expanse. But he is encouraged by what he sees, for there is evidence of great industry, even if the surrounds are rather bare and unsheltered. The teacher steals a glance at the sun before he enters the house, realising forlornly that it will be impossible for him to return home today. He will have to sleep over in this dangerous place.

The slaves have prepared a feast appropriate to any number of returning prodigals. Antje marches through the house issuing commands. "Quick, get this onto the table. Our guest is hungry, he is looking pale."

Old Zacharias picks up the large family Bible and sits down in a chair to prepare a reading. "Anneke," commands the mother, "pour the Meester a bowl of water to refresh himself." The girl leads him to a room off the *voorkamer* where there is a washstand and a mirror. She picks up a jug and pours water into the bowl. "Thank you," says Van Arckel. He is grateful for the chance to clean the sweat from his face and hands, but he hesitates, aware of her presence. Anneke smiles reassuringly. "Wash, Meester. I won't look." She turns her head away and makes a show of squeezing her eyes closed. Van Arckel knows she is enjoying his discomfort, and in a strange way it makes him warm to her. She has a certain spirit. She will not be just a lump of pretty flesh. The teacher splashes water on his face, enjoying the coolness of it. When he looks up to reach for a towel he finds she has left the room. Then he hears her voice outside where her brothers are sitting on the stoep, sharing a pipe before being called inside.

"He is not very strong, my sister," says one of them.

"He is not very broad," sniggers another.

"But he has long feet. You know what they say about long feet, sister?"

"Stop it!"

Van Arckel blushes. He is not very strong or very broad, it

is true. The poor girl, surely there must be other men she would prefer. It is the father who is forcing her to settle for him, because he is apparently a learned man. Well, thinks Van Arckel, it must indeed be something of a trial for a man to be saddled with these boorish sons (barring one of them). The old man's sentiments are well placed. Why, indeed, should there not be some learning, some culture out here in these wilds? If it is strength and broadness of mind that the patriarch is looking for, well then he has found the right man.

Van Arckel is placed next to his intended at the table. She blushes as they sit down. The father opens the Bible and waits for silence. "Today I have chosen the prophet Isaiah," he announces.

The Lord shall establish thee an holy people unto himself, as he hath sworn unto thee, if thou shalt keep the Commandments of the Lord thy God and walk in his ways. And all the people of the earth shall see that thou art called by the name of the Lord and they shall be afraid of thee. And the Lord shall make thee plenteous in goods, in the fruit of thy body, and in the fruit of thy cattle, and in the fruit of thy ground, in the land which the Lord sware unto thy fathers to give thee.

When Zacharias has finished his slow and dignified reading he bows his head and invites the family to pray. The teacher prays that this thing about the fruits of the body will not apply to him, but he knows it is a vain hope. He has been brought here to increase the tribe, to add a strain to it that is tolerant of learning and of finer things. Perhaps there is some place else he can flee to, somewhere even further away and more remote than this Cape of Good Hope.

"Come, Meester. You can stop praying now. It's time to eat." And so the feast begins. Zacharias brings out a flagon of wine and splashes himself a glass full. "And you, Meester? Pass me that glass." Van Arckel obeys. Zacharias fills his glass and passes the flagon down to the boys.

"These glasses come from New England," explains Antje.

The teacher smiles appreciatively, though he doubts the veracity of her statement.

"It's true," confirms Anneke, softly. "There was a ship from there that ran aground."

"That's what they told you," interjects Barend. "But nothing gets made in New England. These glasses come from England England. They are English glasses."

"Never."

"Yes, Ma. It's true. Once there was an Englishman touching these glasses with his thin lips."

"Cheers!" calls Anton.

"Prosit!"

"You're all lying. Eat up or the food will get cold."

The teacher finds his mood lifting as his hosts lay into their fruits of the ground with practised gusto. It is indeed a good and generous meal, and the wine certainly helps to ease the way. When they have finished old Zacharias stands up and gestures to the men to follow him outside. They will sit on the stoep and smoke tobacco while the women supervise the cleaning up.

Zacharias sits on a wooden chair and fills a pipe. "You know, boys, and you, Meester, it is a fine thing to be married. A fine thing." The younger men all know there is an agenda behind the patriarch's casual comment.

"Pa, the girls in town are too common," says Anton.

"If you want to go home to find a wife then go. I won't stop you. Just don't come crying if your beloved leaves you when she gets here. It's not easy for them. Ask your mother."

"She was all right in the end. Now she likes it here. Lots of space."

"She used to live in a broom cupboard when she was young," says Lukas.

Zacharias smiles. "Almost a broom cupboard, yes. We all lived like that. Upstairs and downstairs like books on a shelf."

Lukas looks at him puzzled, then turns away. A yellow dog begins to bark as a slave approaches round the side of the house. "Yes, Booi, what do you want?"

"The cow, Master."

Zacharias frowns. "I forgot about the damn cow. Anton, will you do it?"

"It can wait for tomorrow, Pa."

"No, do it now. The volk has had no work today; they're getting idle."

Zacharias indicates to the slave that he should bring the cow. "You boys can help. Meester, go along and watch. You will teach us books and we will teach you farming. Go along now."

The boys stand up, except for Arent who remains seated on the ground with his ankle raised. "You can watch in my place, Meester." Van Arckel glances at him, trying to judge whether there is a note of irony in his voice. He is not sure what he is being called upon to watch, but he is sure it will be something unpleasant. He follows the boys to a holding pen near the side of the house. Booi reappears, leading a red and white cow by a twisted leather thong tied round its neck.

"So, Meester," says Lukas. "Have you ever seen a bull taking a cow?"

Van Arckel groans inwardly. "Of course yes," he answers, assuming this is what he has been called to witness.

"And have you ever, you know, done it?"

"Done what?"

"Like the bull."

"Of course not!" Van Arckel is horrified.

"Not with a cow, Meester. That's too easy. But with a woman." Barend overhears the exchange and laughs out loud. Van Arckel moves a short distance away. He wishes they would take him home. He is a fraud. He will not be able to mount that lovely girl and pound at her as a bull does. It is not for him. He, if he had a choice, would be the one to surrender – and most certainly he would not tolerate any of that blind rutting. His lovemaking would be soft, like running a cheek along a stomach, like caressing something precious.

"Are you ready, Meester?"

Van Arckel nods and comes closer. He must put on a brave

face. If this is going to be his new family, he had better do some work trying to fit in.

"Hold this." Barend takes the thong from Booi and gives it to Van Arckel. The teacher looks into the great, dark eyes of the cow and feels a rising nausea. "Keep its head still Meester." Anton comes up behind the cow and stands near the beast's shoulders, facing the teacher. He places a wooden bucket under the cow's neck. Booi stands on the other side, hiding a knife behind his back. Then Anton nods at the slave and in a sudden, practiced movement he raises his knife and sinks it into the back of the cow's neck. It bellows once, then drops to its knees. Booi kneels and makes a pass across its throat, sending blood gushing out into the bucket. The teacher steps back, appalled. He smells the blood and wants to gag. "You can let go now, Meester," giggles Lukas.

Van Arckel looks dumbly at his complicitous hand and drops the lead. The sound of the blood spurting into the bucket makes him want to throw up. He grows faint. Then he hears a clear, feminine voice calling from the stoep. "Does Meester not want to come inside for some coffee?" It is Anneke, God bless her. Yes, he nods, and flees towards the house. Arent watches him approach from his seated position on the stoep. It seems to Van Arckel the boy is wearing an expression of sadness, but he puts it out of his mind. He has been cured – at least for the present – of his desire for any association with the men of this family.

The gardener does not work outside but leaves the garden in the care of the slaves. Borders overflow, the beans and gourds advance upon roses, weeds disguise themselves amongst the jasmine. Inside the cottage, in the darkness, Adam Wijk sits with his eyes closed and listens to the millionfold whisperings and groanings in the waters of his brain. It is the copulation of the worms that he hears. They are preparing themselves in their multitudes for the event of his death. The moment he stops breathing the animalcules will come out and devour him. They know who will be the victor in this struggle. They are patient. They bide their time.

It is as Wijk sits thus, head in his hands, that he hears a knock at the door. It is not Claudius's knocking, it is shy, like a woman's or child's. Go away, he mutters. But the knocking comes again, and now he hears a voice outside, desperate. "Please," it calls. "Please."

"Go away!" he shouts. There is silence, and the gardener relaxes. But then it comes again, a simple, pleading voice. "What is it?" he cries, getting to his feet. The brandy he has been drinking has made him volatile. He is in a mood for a fight now, to yell at somebody, to pour out his choked rage upon them. He goes to the door and pulls it open violently. There is a girl standing there, trembling.

"Come," she begs, and points with her arm in the direction of the sea.

It had begun like any other night in the Tavern of the Green Door. Smoke filled the room, candles guttered and cast shadows against the walls. Coals burned in the range, where a pot of venison stew gently simmered. In one corner sat Franz Rijkhof, Krause and the others. Dronke Piet leant against the wall talking with a group of sailors. And near the front, near the cage, sat Herman Bolck. He was alone, as usual. Jan Klou was in attendance but kept himself apart. Bolck sat with a mug of wine and a plate of the venison. Some of the regulars had tried to engage him in conversation on matters other than business – on the state of his health, on whether his wife was expecting yet – but to all these he had said nothing. Herman Bolck was in town to do business, not chat about inconsequentials. Ahead of him in the cage the *bosjesman* crouched upon his perch. Bolck threw a bone through the latticework and laughed when it struck him in his face. "You're getting slow." Voog sat on his perch and watched the scene before him. His eyes were distant.

"I think we need a new attraction here," commented Bart Meyer. "This one's getting old."

"I'll see what I can do," said Bolck, throwing another bone at the cage.

In the corner Dronke Piet laughed out loud at a sailor's joke and began to tell one back. A man dropped coins into Meyer's hand and began climbing the ladder into the loft. Herman Bolck took a hunk of bread and wiped the gravy off the bottom of his plate. Nobody paid attention when Voog stood up in his cage. Nobody saw when he turned his loinskin aside and took out his tool. The stream of piss went quite unnoticed until it hit Bolck's plate, drenched his bread, and splashed his face. The room was instantly silent, the last drops of the *bosjesman*'s piss splattering loudly on the floor. Voog sat down on his perch and waited. With a cry of rage Bolck jumped to his feet. Drawing his sword he stormed the cage and began hacking blindly at the structure. "Stop! Stop!" cried Meyer, but the maddened Bolck would listen to nothing. Voog cowered on his perch as the cage gave in around him. Then the blade came through and split open his face. Another blow sliced off a chunk of his skull and ripped into his shoulder. Voog staggered blindly to his feet and Bolck cut him through the stomach, dropping him to the floor. The assailant stood there panting uncontrollably, his sword dripping. Nobody came close or said a word.

When Adam Wijk arrives at the tavern the patrons have left. There is a body lying in the dust outside the door. The girl begins to cry. Wijk stoops to look, but he knows it is too late. "It's finished," he says to the girl. Jan Klou appears and begins tying a rope around the victim's ankles. "No!" cries the girl and rushes to attack Klou. He laughs and brushes her aside with his hook. Adam Wijk looks down and turns to go. There is nothing he can do.

Joachim van Arckel climbs sweating and breathless to Lion's Head. It is not for recreation or exercise that he has made the journey; it is on a mission of concern. When he finds the flagman he is sitting on a rock with his back to him, staring out over the bay. Van Arckel clears his throat, is about to introduce himself, when the flagman speaks: "I know why you have come."

The teacher looks taken aback.

"Let me tell you what it is," he says, turning to face his visitor. "You have come to ask me what you are doing here. I can see it. You have come too far from home. Perhaps you should turn around now and go back."

"Actually," objects the teacher, "I have come to talk about someone else."

"You want to take my Greetje away from me, that is what you have come to ask. I see it now."

Van Arckel nods. "Not to take her away. Just to have her at school every day. Young people must learn; they must not grow up in ignorance."

The flagman turns away. He sits for a while in silence, occasionally rubbing his eyes. "Do you know, young man, that a lookout sometimes dreams he sees things. He sees galleons, whole fleets that crouch forever on the horizon and never approach. It is like a ghost fleet watching from the horizon. What do they want? Why do they not come forward? These are things I cannot answer."

"There are people in the town who say bad things about you and your daughter. Do you know that?"

"Let them talk, they know nothing."

"May I make a prophecy of my own, Mr Moolman?"

"Go ahead."

"That when the Commander discovers the truth he will scratch your name from the paybook. You will be poor and alone."

The flagman laughs bitterly. "And you are so sure of the truth."

Van Arckel knows he will lose any chance of helping them if he gets it wrong. "Yes," he says. "The truth is that you cannot do your work alone. You are going blind."

The flagman is silent a long time. "And now you are going to tell him."

197

"I cannot predict that."

"Then I think you should leave. We have nothing to say to each other."

"I am ready to help. We will get you an apprentice."

"Listen, Mr Teacher. You do not belong here. You come here with your new ideas and your fancy ways, but things don't work the same here. When Lord High and Mighty finds I cannot work my life will be over. There is nothing you can do. An apprentice will only spread the news quicker."

"You will be given a pension."

"I will be given a pittance and I will lose my house."

Van Arckel sits down on a rock and picks up a pebble. "You know that she will leave you soon enough. She will find a husband."

"When Greetje goes then so will I."

"You will live with them?"

"Meester, that is not what I am saying."

The teacher scratches the pebble against the rock. "You must have family back home, in Holland."

Moolman laughs. "Always looking for a happy ending, Mr Teacher. But you look in the wrong place." Van Arckel gets up to leave. "Don't looks so sad, Meester. Life is short anyway. Now, come stand over here I want to show you something." Van Arckel goes and stands with the flagman looking out over the bay. "Tell me what you see."

"I see the ocean, sky, the island."

"Meester, you say I am going blind, but I see more than you. Perhaps it is the sun that makes the water like a mirror, but when the clouds come over then you can see it moving down there, just beyond the island where it goes very deep. That's where it lives."

"What does?"

"The whale. Bigger than any you have ever seen. A monster."

"A shadow of the clouds."

"Listen, young man. You know nothing, you cannot see what these eyes can see. If the sailors knew what evil watched them from below they would not take to their ships. They would stay at home and raise cattle; they would not put themselves at the mercy of that thing."

Van Arckel grows sad. He will come away from here not having found a new student, having found only madness instead. The flagman winks at the teacher. "You, Mr Teacher, you don't have to look so superior. You have one of them swimming about inside of you. A whale. I see it."

"I'm sorry, Mr Moolman. But I must be going now. It's a long way down."

"Swim, swim," cackles the flagman. "There, inside your heart, a great lie. I can see its little black eyes."

Isa Meyer searches the house. She looks behind cupboards, under beds. She has been up into the loft and found it empty. It is not the first time that she searches thus; she has done it every day for the past three days, since Hester disappeared. Men arrive with coins in their palms, and she has to turn them away. It is such a waste.

For a while the disappearance is the subject of conversation in the tavern, but not for long. What could have happened, anyway, to such a girl? The choices are few. Abduction, desertion, misplacement. One of such a flawed intellect could easily get lost on the way back from the market. Perhaps she has gone off to join the gangs of escaped slaves, or she has become a Hottentot's wife. Let her go, then. We never believed such a one had much of a chance of living to a great age. She was doomed from the start; she never quite belonged. Isa Meyer knows this as well as anybody. And yet, quite by surprise, she discovers one morning while busy before her mirror, a tear upon her cheek. How did that get there?

It is some time before anybody notices another disappearance. Mr Cardamom has not joined his cronies in the tavern for some time now, and when enquiries are made it is established that he has not been seen anywhere in the hamlet for at least a week. He has gone home to England, say some. He has gone off to the Island of Mu to find his pot of gold, joke others. Either way they are slightly aggrieved that he did not have the courtesy to say goodbye. They will miss his lies and exaggerations. But perhaps he will come back. He will appear one day, like a rabbit plucked from a hat, bearing an armful of improbable stories. Not to worry, the rascal will return.

Moonlight

In the heavens the shy moons of Jupiter blink their message of passing time. Summer grows old; the weary south prepares for rest. In the cottage the pages of the gardener's notebook fill with unholy shapes. Pollen grains like thorn-studded eggs, creatures made of brass with terrible, improbable mouths. Eyes watch back in gleaming clusters, fruits of some alien flower. And here – this crystal mountain – it is a grain of sand. Such a thing is a planet to the animalcules. One wonders if they know, these creatures, of the being who watches them – or is he merely one more fertile universe for them to colonise with their blindly teeming lives? The worlds of the atomites are not worlds ruled by God, they are realms apart, following their own logic with a purpose inscrutable to man. Their denizens live outside of time, they neither grow old nor die; they toil not, nor do they spin. There is no labour in these worlds beyond an eternal swarming, a never ending burrowing, a copulating and a festering.

Adam Wijk stands naked in his house. The moon shines in through the window. In this hidden light he will observe the secret life that feasts upon him. But he sees only shadows, and he sees that he is leaving the familiar world, that he is going mad. So it is that when she comes he imagines she is not real. The door is open and there she stands, a shadow cast in silver light. It is true, he thinks, I am done for now. But when she falls to the floor he knows she is no ghost. He forgets that he is naked but for his cloak of silver atomites. He goes to her, kneels down and touches her. She is hot, her clothing torn. Her shoes are bloody rags. "What has he done to you," he whispers? "What crime is this?"

And thus comes the news that Herman Bolck is dead. It is a band of Hottentots that brings the word. They tried to carry the man's widow with them but she escaped and is alone somewhere on the flats. So the search parties go out and scour the bush and find nothing. The woman hides in Adam Wijk's house. .

V*enus*

The gardener writes his alphabet. It is not an alphabet as children would learn it but one of his own invention, one that is designed for a single student. He has heard it said that the deaf can be taught to speak and that a system of signs has been devised that stand for sounds. He has thought to ask his benefactor to find this tract for him, but it will take too long. The woman watches him with his contortioning of the hands and is amused. She copies him and he looks up, perceiving her actions, and smiles uncertainly. It is not clear whether she is mocking him at his efforts or whether she is truly intrigued. He makes an incomplete pinching movement of thumb and middle finger. "C" he spells. Then he makes an "A" and a "T". "Cat," he says. She looks at him with raised brow. Adam Wijk casts about him for help, but there is no cat that he can point to and repeat his gestures. He picks up his quill again and bends to the paper. "A cat," he says, lifting the sheet and pointing at the figure he has drawn. The woman leans forward and examines the likeness. She looks at her tutor and nods her head, C-A-T, she spells with her fingers. Adam Wijk claps his hands and laughs out loud.

The woman of four names and none will try her best to please her tutor. She will lie awake at night and practice those twists of the hands in the dark, making cats and dogs march across the darkened rafters, every day adding new animals and objects to the parade. After a while she is able to inform her tutor that tonight she will cook a C-H-I-C-K-E-N in a P-O-T. She can, finally – and with much insistence from the fiscal – explain how her husband died. It was his S-T-O-M-A-C-H, a great swelling of his belly that made him writhe in pain for days. In this explanation she demonstrates her own weeping, and her fearful escape. Poor girl, thinks Adam Wijk, she must have been so frightened by the sight of death she could not imagine where to summon help. She could only think to flee to her refuge here in the garden. Her protector allows himself a brief moment of self-congratulation, then sternly cuts off any elaboration on that heroic theme.

She is permitted to stay on sufferance, of course. It is because the Commander has relinquished his reservations about her marrying Claudius. If the young man takes her away eventually, to Batavia or wherever, well then perhaps the colony will be the better off for it. So now the gardener plays the chaperone to these lovers, having to escape often from the house and finding himself thus drawn back into the work he has so neglected these past months. There is much to be done in the garden now that winter is approaching, and the slaves have grown lazy.

It will be something of a double wedding. Claudius and the deaf woman; Joachim Van Arckel and Anneke Visser. The ceremonies will happen one after the other, on a Saturday afternoon a mere three weeks away. The teacher has decided it will not be such a bad thing to be married after all. He likes Anneke. She is indeed gracious and beautiful. She has a gentle soul, a quick mind. Perhaps they will be able to have discussions about interesting things; about the world and places in it and how it all works. Deep inside a part of him is glad. He has the good fortune of finding such a wife and not being saddled with some bovine lump who will demand from him money and children. They will have to have a child or two, but not too many. Van Arckel's eyes go soft and distant at the idea of children. Yes, this marriage will not be a bad thing at all. He is a very lucky man. Perhaps, at last, he will be coming home, in a manner of speaking. He will not have to be such a fugitive. An unmarried man of a certain age is always under some suspicion, rightly or wrongly.

Only three weeks now. The time will pass quickly.

Bart Meyer walks alone on the shore. He has begun coming here often now just to walk, and sometimes to sit and to look out over the sea. How strange it is to meet one's fate, he will think. He never planned for his life to be like this; it is not a bad life at all, but he has become aware of some inexplicable hollow in the centre of it. It is a hollow that appears to be growing. One day – he is sure – it will overwhelm him, a great, obliterating darkness. He looks out over the sea. The girl has gone away. She was not long for this world. Poor scrap.

People call her Maria now, but Adam Wijk never refers to her by that name. It is an invention of the lady of the tavern, and as such he wants nothing to do with it. He tries each of the names he knows are possible for her, but cannot settle on any one. Elsje, Katryn, Magriet, or Klara. In the end he refers to her simply by the feminine pronoun, or – when addressing her directly – "my dear". It strikes him the term is rather more fatherly than he would like, but it is certainly better than Maria.

Adam Wijk looks at Hendrick Claudius across the kitchen table. He is drawing a plant with a long, turnip-like root that is known to be edible. It is called "thumma" by the Hotten-tots. The woman sits on a stool at the range and stirs a pot. It is not food that she cooks but another of those experiments in pharmacopoeia. She lifts the spoon to her nose and sniffs at the sample. She is about to taste of it, and Wijk waves his hand to gain her attention. No, no, he gestures. Do not touch that just yet. It may be a poison, we do not know. She looks at him and perceives his gesturing. It is quite clear what he means, but she looks him calmly in the eye and brings the spoon to her lips. Adam Wijk sits with both hands holding the edge of the table, observing with raised eyebrows. She has defied him. Well, on her own head be it then, if what she is tasting should turn out to be other than medicinal.

Still, perhaps she knows what she is doing. He has noticed this about his guest, that she falls naturally into this work with the herbs. She seems to have some talent for distinguishing the useful from the merely interesting or decorative. Perhaps she worked at some time with plants and their essences back home. Perhaps her father had been an apothecar or physician. The gardener finds himself again meditating on the girl's history. It is no good at all that somebody should be so lacking in a personal narrative, at least one that is known to others. Almost anything one imagines about her is likely to be an untruth, an imposition. Perhaps one day when she has learned enough of an alphabet she will be able to tell them all of her life, but until then his only hope in discovering more is the letter he has sent to his benefactor asking that enquiries be made regarding the passengers of the *Tulp*. Our gardener has not forgotten that small mystery merely because he has not been able to solve it. There is something about the whole affair that bothers him still, yet he cannot say what it is. He has the impression that a large piece of evidence is standing right before him and that he cannot see it. How frustrating. He awaits a reply from abroad with interest.

In the meantime, the young couple pursue their earnest, hesitating courtship. Claudius glows with happiness. He has never met a woman as beautiful. He knows that behind her silence there is a fierce intelligence, one that unnerves him and captivates him at the same time. And she, well she seems to enjoy his attentions. She touches his shoulder when she walks past, she smiles at him when he makes sketches of her. One day she catches his attention while he is drawing a flower and she spells a word with her hands. Claudius laughs and dashes off a comical picture of a cat. She claps her hands in delight. H-O-R-S-E, she spells, and the young man draws a cavalier upon a charger. But how is she to spell a word like Love, the artist wonders. It is not a thing that can be touched. And it will not do to use that new word the gardener has taught her, the one that spells H-E-A-R-T. Those gestures of the hand will signify nothing more to her than a small red organ in the breast of a dead chicken. It is not the same as love at all. He will have to think of some other method to spell such a word if he wants her to be able to use it.

The happy suitor is at this moment unaware that he has become the subject of deep and uncharitable thoughts on the part of certain authorities within the Castle. The Commander has received a package from abroad. In it is a book with a slip of paper giving a page reference. The work is titled *A Voyage to Siam*, and its author is none other than Father Guy de Tachard. The page in question occurs in a chapter relating the author's recent experiences at the Cape. It mentions the hospitality he and his party enjoyed, it mentions something of the fauna and flora of this intriguing corner of the world, and it mentions by name a young man who proved invaluable in providing the mission with information on all aspects of the colony. The young man is none other than our own Hendrick Claudius.

So, broods Van der Stel, the French have been taking an interest in more than the southern skies during their visits. So much for the brotherhood of Science. Van der Stel calculates the damage this chapter will do his fortunes and emerges from the exercise with no cause for cheer. He will simply have to make sure that nothing like this happens again. And he will have to keep an eye on possible traitors: Claudius being top of the list.

Of course, the young man was innocent of malice when he spoke to the French; he was merely being his enthusiastic self. He is not one for politics, but – unfortunately – he has found his way into this game and he will have to tread carefully. The fact that he is on the point of marrying a person who has given the Commander more than his fair share of headaches is hardly a point that counts in his favour. Nonetheless, all is not lost. Not yet. It will all depend on how peacefully things turn out, on there being no further drama.

The Jesuit is true to his promise. It is a year since last he saw the Cape, and now he stands on the decks of the warship *La*

Normande and watches as the great slab of Table Mount rises from the waters. He looks about him at the mass of sail and rigging. This time they come not as some small, exploratory mission but as an army. Six ships, row upon row of guns, six hundred soldiers or more. The glory of the Sun King sails the waters of the southern seas. Very faintly upon the land he spies a gout of smoke, and then another. It is the signal gun on the Lion Mount, welcoming them.

But Father Tachard is wrong. The gun fires not in welcome but in alarm. He does not see an answering report from the gun on the Tijgerberg, then the one in Stellenbosch. The whole colony is alerted now to this great fleet of war that has entered the roadstead. At the Castle Commander Van der Stel watches from the bastions. Then he goes inside to await news of the fleet's intentions.

When the request for provisions and medical assistance arrives it is expressed less diplomatically than might have been the case had the fleet consisted of a handful of mere merchant ships. The phrasing is something one might expect from a General of the Sun King, and one with more troops under arms than there are able-bodied men in the whole of the colony. Understandably, Commander Van der Stel is piqued. He would like to reply by saying there is nothing here for them, that they should sail onward and find other places more inclined to entertain their arrogant demands. But, of course, he cannot. It would not do for the fragile peace between his country and France to be shifted to a more martial footing because of some unfriendly incident in the distant south. Given Louis' recent excesses against his own Protestants it is not inconceivable that he should turn against those others who fail to share his prejudices. And besides, would the King not love an excuse to capture this Cape for himself, given his growing interest in the East?

It is all too precarious, and thus when the Commander calls his council together they decide on a guarded compromise. They will allow the sick to come ashore in groups of sixty at a time. At night, all who are not ill must return to their ships.

The council members know they have not the manpower at the Castle to enforce their decisions; they will require reinforcement. The signal guns carry the message north and east – Send all the men you can; leave the crops and ride. And so the Castle fills with armed burghers and great preparations are made for the outpost's defence. The Commander spends much time up on the bastions with the gunners, watching the French and measuring the distance of their vessels from the shore. Any approach will be seen as an act of aggression.

On board the flagship the Jesuit watches the land. He sees the guns of the Castle pointed at him, and he is saddened that it has come to this. He holds Commander Van der Stel and this whole outpost in genuine affection. And yet perhaps caution on their part is not unjustified. The Cape is indeed a jewel on the route to the East; and he has become wise to his government's intent with regard to expansion in this part of the world. The poor King of Siam; how trusting he is. He does not know the ways of the Christian West. He has glimpsed barely a fraction of its great dream of domination. But soon he will learn. It cannot be helped. In the end, though, his countrymen will be the better for it. They will receive the sacraments and be saved from the hell their birth has consigned them to. All things will come to the light, in time.

Adam Wijk has paid the drama scant attention. If they are suddenly to become a possession of the Sun King, then he will just have to dust off his French. *Le Chat, Le Cheval*, he thinks, wondering how on earth he will explain this to his ward. They sit together in the kitchen, he with paper and quill, she with a peeled fruit of the kanobe tree and a knife. They have an idea an extract of this might be a good a potion against diarrhoea. Wijk starts slightly at a loud knocking on the door. He knows immediately it is someone from the Castle – they have a particular kind of disrespect for quietness and privacy. When he opens the door he finds a soldier bearing a package. "Delivery, Sir. From the poxy French." Wijk takes the package and carries it inside. He lays it on the table and removes the paper covering, revealing an attractive wooden box with a hinged lid. The woman cranes forward to see. Wijk slips the brass catch on the lid and opens it. At first he cannot make out what he is looking at, but then it comes to him. It is a microscope. Wijk carefully lifts the gleaming brass instrument from its resting place and stands it on the table. "Now," he wonders aloud, "how do you suppose this thing works?"

The two of them, while figuring out how to work the Jesuit's gift, are innocent of one aspect of this crisis that affects them directly. It is the following: that the garrison troops have this morning gone about the hamlet interrogating Catholics and arresting anybody they deem a possible threat. One of those now held in the Castle awaiting deportation is Hendrick Claudius. He has protested his innocence but his fate is sealed – the Commander has singled him out by name.

And how does the bereft bride feel about this? It takes the gardener some time to explain to her that her man is gone. The message dawns upon her and she accepts with no sign of emotion. Yet who is to say what she thinks? Possibly she is relieved that this constant shuffling of her from one situation to another is over. But, of course, it will not be over. If the past is to be taken as a guide, then what will soon happen is that Mrs Isa Meyer will pay a visit to the weary Commander and demand the return of her daughter. Soon the soldiers will come and bear her away to her life of slavery. Nothing will have been gained at all.

Adam Wijk knows better than to appeal to Van der Stel. It is not the right time to step in there and talk of mercy. They will have to accept the dictates of the god of war, a being now holding firm sway at the Castle. In the meantime he does his best to offer the woman comfort. He makes her cups of tea; he brings her trinkets from the market. Sometimes he will sit in his chair and watch her as she busies herself about the cottage. How audacious is this fate that has brought her here, once again living unchaperoned in his house. The gardener will not admit it in as many words, but if Mars is the god that has taken up residence down on the shore, then is it Venus who has claimed this humble cottage as her own. Perhaps something will be gained, after all.

So now there will be only one wedding. Notwithstanding some act of God or an invasion by the forces of King Louis it is due to go ahead this very Saturday. The teacher lies in his attic and dreams of a military disaster. Will it come before the wedding, or afterwards? Which is better? He chides himself for being such a coward – there will be no getting out of this union, none at all. He could have himself arrested as a spy and be deported, along with his erstwhile brother in matrimony, but no – it will not do. He cannot go back to Batavia. The only alternative would be Mauritius, but there is no call for schoolteachers there. He will have to stay. He will accept his fate; he will rise to the occasion. Van Arckel makes a vow that he will give his betrothed a happy life. She will have to overlook some of his bookishness, his inability to do manly things like chop down trees and slaughter cattle and chastise slaves with a whip. But it should be only a small loss to her; he will make up for it in other ways.

Time flies faster than Cupid's arrow. The big day is upon us at last! A festive spirit reigns outside the church as the guests arrive, the warships out in the bay proving no distraction but adding, rather, a touch of colour and pageantry to the scene. The bride's family arrive on foot, having taken lodgings the previous night in a guesthouse in the hamlet. The eyes of the boys dart amongst the waiting guests to solicit glances of appreciation from susceptible women. The groom waits inside the church, sitting nervous and uncomfortable in a dark coat, nodding shyly to the guests as they slowly filter in. Eventually all are gathered inside and they await the arrival of the bride. Van Arckel closes his eyes. He is thinking of his mother. How proud she would be now.

And yes, the mother of Joachim van Arckel would indeed have been proud; in fact, the mother of any son in the colony would have been in the highest heaven over this daughter. When she eventually arrives she causes such a gasp of awe from the guests that it causes Van Arckel to jump in surprise. He turns to see her coming down the aisle, a light-drenched being of glowing silk and shining pearls and glittering golden filigree. What have I done, oh Lord, to deserve this? Surely it is a mistake. Surely, oh Lord, you will call out now and say it is not to be. But there is no voice from the heavens, unless it is Dominee Mankadan calling him to awaken from his reverie and to play his part.

And so it is done, and there is – at last – no more chance at all for God to call out and undo what has been brought together. The guests rise and file out of the church beaming and happy. They slap the teacher on the back and remark what a good and lucky fellow he is, and fathers promise in great numbers to send their children to him for instruction. "You will have to wait at least a week," the groom stammers. "I expect to be busy for a while." It is a jest that earns him more slaps on the back and red-faced winks. Now they all proceed up the street to the house of a friend of the Vissers where the reception will be held. Already there is an ox turning on a spit, and barrels of wine and homemade beer stand lined up on makeshift tables. What festivities are about to commence!

At last, when the speeches have been made and the couple have danced and the musicians have traded their waltzes for bawdyhouse ballads, the youngsters are able to slip away. They are now alone in the cottage that the new husband has rented. His head swims a little from the gin he has been compelled to drink. His wife waits for him in the bedroom. She has undone her hair. "Will you help me with the laces?" she calls, holding her tresses aside so that her husband can loosen her from the strictures of her corset.

She smells warm and fragrant – a scent of jasmine or some other sweet flower. The husband's fingers tremble as he disrobes his wife. Will his lie be merciful to him tonight, or will it betray them both? The young man prays, and then the scent of her overwhelms him so he finds himself burying his face in her hair, kissing her neck, letting his hand push the sleeve down off her shoulder. She turns to him and kisses him. "Take me," she says, and the new husband discovers he is capable of doing just that. Never was a man more relieved on his wedding night than this Joachim van Arckel.

So what is one to make of this? For we know that our gentle teacher is a man with certain preferences – ones indeed that should not suit him to marriage at all. And yet who of us – in the end – should presume to say whence love should come, or to lay down rules for love to follow. In truth it is not possible. No, more than that – it is a blasphemy! The philosopher of doubt was wrong in the end. Let all be doubted, yes, but let things stay that way always. Let nothing be made certain, even though it be numbered and labelled and have all the appearance of an eternal Truth. This teacher is a man who has been tagged and labelled. And look at him now. He has a beautiful wife and there is desire for her flowing through him like an intoxicating potion. Who is he really? The teacher himself cannot say.

And the bride? She knows exactly who she is marrying. She knows he is a man divided and that she will never be the only beauty in his eye. But that is not so great a thing. It is not worship and exclusivity she requires from a man, it is kindness and respect. Love, too, is what she requires – and one thing more: the leave to be herself and to make of her life what she will. It is freedom, and she knows her husband will offer this completely.

With attention taken up so much by the French and by the schoolmaster's wedding, the arrival of two vessels from the North arouses little comment. And indeed, there is nothing much significant about them, except that they carry with them letters from home. There are the customary orders for the

Commander, sealed imposingly with the stamp of the Lords XVII, and there are letters of more humble origin. One of these finds its way quickly to its addressee. She has paid an urchin to enquire from every passing ship whether there is mail for her, and today her investment has borne fruit. The other letters find their way into the bureaucracy of the Castle, where they will tarry several days before finding their way into the hands of their intended readers.

Secrets

It is dusk; Venus blinks above Lion's Head, a veil of amber damask drapes fleetingly over the wall of mountain, and then is gone. The gardener stands near the kraal at the back of his cottage, prodding a bonfire with a long stick. It's a roundybout world, said Mr Cardamom once, and though Adam Wijk was not there to hear him say it he might at this time find himself agreeing. Now that he has stopped looking for what has been lost, here it comes and appears before him. The fire crackles, sending sparks shooting up into the sky. Sometimes things are finished, and it is well to accept it. The gardener's face glows sternly, impassively, in the heated light. Enough, he thinks. Then he bends to pick something off the ground. To the woman standing at the window it appears as a nest of wires that he holds. She knows what it is, though she cannot guess its significance. Adam Wijk holds the wires up, revealing a cluster of dark shapes gathered at the end, like a catch of small fish. He swings them like a pendulum, once, twice, and then throws them onto the fire.

The garden of the plagues resists the flames, the bottles lying black and sullen, filling slowly with a noxious, oily smoke. Then the glass glows red and begins to melt, releasing the dark breath of suffering to swarm upward in a tunnel of sparks and shimmering air. The atomites return to their elements; the gardener is set free.

Adam Wijk stands back from the fire. It is done. In the morning he will go to the Commander and speak to him about a certain proposition he has.

As chance would have it there arrives for the gardener early the next day a message that his presence is requested at the Castle. He tells the bearer that he is on his way of his own accord and will be there shortly. What is it the Commander wants? wonders Wijk as he makes his way through the leaf-strewn winter garden. He walks with a light stride, the pain in his leg almost forgotten. He is sure the Commander will react favourably to his request. It will solve a problem for him. Everybody will be happy.

So now, would you hazard a guess at what this proposition is that our gardener carries so lightly to the Castle? And yes, you would be right – it is marriage! Now the question that remains is this – what did it take for him to arrive at this point where he could relinquish his churlish reservations and accept another into his life? Is he doing it merely out of charity, a sense of chivalry to a helpless woman? We know that Adam Wijk has considered himself too old for the foolishness of marriage (he is not), and we know he has been haunted half a lifetime by a love that was cruelly taken from him. He has tried to bring that love back by conquering that which took her, by unmasking the nameless agent that causes destruction of the body through contagion. He has been certain that the old knowledge on this is unequal to the task, that if he looked hard enough and pursued a logical course he would have found the truth regarding contagia and thus gained power over them. In this, we know, his task was noble and well aimed. But fate is against him, or rather, it is time and circumstance that will not support his endeavour. He accepts now that he has not the tools or the wherewithal to launch a successful campaign against this foe. The microscope stands unused upon the table in his cottage. It will not do; the task is too great. He will live with what he suspects, and leave the proving of it to other men.

So one can say, then, that our gardener has merely faced the truth, that he has let go of his past. But that is an incomplete assessment, for it ignores the agent of this enlightenment, that nameless, quite enigmatic presence that has entered his life, arriving uninvited from a troubled sea.

The gardener has pictured a happy reaction on the part of Commander Van der Stel. At last, he will say, you have come to your senses. But it does not happen like this at all. When he arrives at the Commander's office he finds he has a visitor with him. She sits before his desk, greeting the gardener with a cold, knowing smile. Van der Stel does not invite the gardener to sit. Instead, he watches him with his small, penetrating eyes. To Wijk it seems there is some deep regret behind the hardness of that look. But whatever it is, it will not help him now, he can see plainly he is in trouble.

The Commander turns a letter over and over in his hands. Eventually, he ceases with his examination of Wijk's soul and unfolds the paper. "I have something here, brought to me by Mrs Meyer. I assume you have already met."

Wijk glances at the smirking woman and nods.

"It is something quite troubling, Mr Wijk. I am not sure, at all what we should make of it."

What the gardener hears in the next few minutes is something that makes his scalp turn to ice. They know. The letter – this reply to the query sent by Isa Meyer a year ago – tells of a certain incident in which a doctor, named quite undeniably in court papers as Adam Albertus Wijk, was sued by a wealthy family for improper practices. And his crime was this: that he had been called to treat a case of smallpox within the family, but had sought instead to spread the disease for his own gain. He had foregone the established practice – blood-letting and heated baths – choosing rather, as the defendant put it – to protect those still healthy against its further ravages. To this end he had prepared an evil remedy of his own, namely that he did collect from the patient – who subsequently expired – a small quantity of pus and then did mix this in with a piece of fruitcake and did feed it to the brothers and sisters of the patient, one of whom became infected and was only spared by the grace of God. When asked to explain his treatment the doctor could not. He was merely trying to save lives, said he, and the accepted practice seemed guaranteed to do nothing more than end them. This was not enough of an explanation, of course, and he was stripped of his licence, forced to pay a large amount in compensation, and advised – though this was not part of the sentence – to leave the country. In this way the exile of Adam Wijk began, and so also his quest to redeem himself by proving his cause. Now, alas, it has all come to naught.

Still, he reminds himself, he has the woman. He has love. When he tells Commander Van der Stel that notwithstanding his previous errors – which he has now forsworn – he has agreed to marry the woman of the *Tulp*, the cold observer cannot restrain a brittle and triumphant laugh. Van der Stel silences her with a look of dark distaste. "It is too late," he says, flipping the letter back to its owner. "She has promised to bring this to the attention of the Directors if you have anything more to do with her daughter."

"The girl is no daughter of this woman, Honourable Commander."

"Dear Mr Wijk, she is now whoever Mrs Meyer says she is. You will hand her over this evening. I will send some men to fetch her."

The gardener walks home through his winter garden. How grey it seems to him now, how lacking in any qualities of abundance and fertility, those things that had once given him such pleasure, such delight. Even the sun-coloured fruits in the citrus groves are not equal to the task of bringing back life to this place.

Wijk stops to test the ripeness of a lemon. How foolish was he to imagine he could merely walk away from his past, that it would let him go so easily. Had he imagined – when he burned his garden of horrors – that somehow he would be reborn, phoenix-like, from its ashes? How innocent. If one believes in impossibilities of this nature, well then one might as well believe that rabbits are created within hats, that love transforms all, that girls can fly like birds. All these things are lies. Time to put away childish dreams, dear gardener. Time to accept the will of matter, the grey inexorable will to inertia, decay, and disease.

The gardener plucks an orange. How sweet is its scent, and

sharp. He will take it and offer it as a gift to the woman. Such a small, pathetic gesture.

She can see from his face that he brings no good news. The orange – thank you, she mouths, holding it to her lips. He doesn't have to try too hard to explain what will happen. She has guessed it already. Adam Wijk sits in his chair. The woman goes behind the curtain to put away her belongings. In a moment there is a knock at the door. "It is not evening," he pleads. And the answer comes back, hesitating: "Letter, Sir." Wijk gets up and opens the door. The messenger hands him the letter and goes. Wijk examines the address, noting the distinctive handwriting of the benefactor. He steps outside, closing the door behind him, and walks into the garden. It is too late now, for any news. What is left to be said?

When he returns he finds the woman sitting on her bed, dressed in her satin gown. He smiles hopelessly. The low sun casts its watery light upon her. How beautiful she is, what a creature of cold fire. Come closer, she beckons. Adam Wijk comes to stand before her. He reaches out to touch her hair. "I am sorry," he says, knowing it is all too late. He turns and is about to go when she takes his hand. She gets to her feet and stands before him. There is something in those eyes he has never seen before, something feline and dangerous. Then she pulls him closer and kisses him on the mouth. She takes his hand and places it on her breast. When he hesitates, unsure as a boy, she pushes him down onto the bed, she unbuttons his clothes, she lifts herself up, swirling the silken waves of her skirt over his body to drown him.

They lie and watch the light fade upon their bodies. He would pull the blanket up, but it would cover her from his sight. In a moment the soldiers will be at the door. Every minute is an eternity.

~

And now she is gone. The gardener sits in his chair. He takes the letter out of his pocket and reads it again. The writer wishes him well and enquires after any progress in the search for the Rukh. When Wijk had first read this outside he had experienced a moment's irritation. Will the man not let this vain fantasy go? Now he skips through these paragraphs and comes again to the last few lines, the ones he had been waiting for this past year. The news comes as no surprise to him. He had expected something like this all along. And no, it does not change a thing; it will not alter his feelings for her. In fact, he is perhaps a little more awed. For what the benefactor has discovered is this: that the girls were indeed orphans, though their place of lodging before departing for the South was not an establishment run by the Orphan Chamber but one maintained by a certain Albert Karels, a well-known purveyor of quality whores. The girls were not coming out to find husbands, they were being imported by a shrewd investor with an eye to a profit. Adam Wijk cannot suppress a tinge of admiration for Isa Meyer's audacity. Her plan could have worked quite handsomely, if not for the hand of fate.

The gardener's leg begins to ache. It is winter, after all, and he gets no younger. What he needs is a pipe, a little of that Malay tobacco to help with this long night. He reaches into his vest pocket for the cabinet key but cannot find it. Strange – he is never without that key on his person. When he finds the key on the kitchen windowsill he is even more puzzled. He cannot remember leaving it there. Perhaps his mind is truly going. But when he opens the cabinet of poisons he knows it is not so. There is a bottle missing. He brushes the others aside to make sure it has not merely fallen over and thus become obscured, but no – it has vanished. Adam Wijk feels a chill down his spine. It is no medicine or bringer of dreams, this one that has gone. It is death, pure and simple.

Wijk goes over to his chair and sinks into it once more. He

spends a long time sitting thus, not moving. Inside, however, his mind is racing – for now he sees it, that piece of evidence that had so eluded him. It is suddenly so clear. The death of Bolck. The death of the four aboard the *Tulp*. No plague or twist of fate is necessary to account for any of these. And no old woman with a collar of potions is needed to explain his own poisoning – that small revenge for a betrayal.

So whom should he tell? He thinks of the Commander, of the fiscal, of the captain of the guards. And he thinks of those in greatest danger, the Lord and Lady of the strand. A slight smile edges his face. Little do they know what they have invited into their den, what black ship they have piloted into their harbour. Yes, there has come something for them from beyond the edge; there it lies within their sanctuary, nameless, terrible in its purity, utterly incapable of accepting anything less than freedom. So let them try to get the measure of this creature, let them decide what are the sum of its parts and what its name should be. Let them savour their short victory. The gardener, for his part, will remain silent.

Firebird

Down at the jetty the soldiers form an armed corridor leading upwards towards the parade. A slave ship has arrived from Madagascar, and its poor cargo must be brought to their holding pens without incident. When the unfortunates have all come ashore, blinking pathetically in the wintry sun, there is a small boat that leaves the ship and makes its way to land. This vessel carries – in addition to the sailors rowing it – a ship's officer and two others who were clearly passengers on board the slaver.

When the boat runs onto the sand the sailors jump out and pull it out of the surf. Then the officer disembarks, followed by the two passengers. They have some small possessions, the man a canvas bag of no great size, the girl a mere cloth-wrapped bundle. The man looks about him on the beach and eventually beckons to three youngsters idly watching the proceedings. "Come you," he calls. "A chance to earn some pennies." The youths sidle down to the new arrivals. "There in the boat," he points. "If you fellows think you're man enough for it." The three drafted bearers peer into the boat to see what it is they are being asked to carry. Lying on the bottom of the vessel is a long wooden case, like something muskets might be transported in.

"Guns, Sir?" asks one of them.

"No," answers their employer. "Not guns at all. And I shall not tell you, for if I did you would not believe me."

The girl watches the proceedings and giggles. She knows what is in the box and has pictured in her mind the reaction these youths would have upon seeing that absurdity. Nestled in a bed of straw, a giant egg made of stone! They would con-

222

sider it evil, perhaps, or wonder if a joke were being played upon them, and quite possibly they would refuse to carry it at all. But now they are ignorant of the contents of the box, and are this moment slipping ropes beneath it so they may lift it from the vessel. "It is very heavy, Sir," they complain, and the man takes money from his pocket and – with a theatrical flourish – begins counting it. The youths are persuaded. They lift the box uncomfortably onto their shoulders. "Where to?" calls the one at the front.

"To the Garden," cries the man. "Make haste onwards to our Paradise, to our Temple of Delights!"